NUV 1983

SAVE

THE

WHALE

*For David Willson,
all my best
Michael Koepf*

SAVE

A NOVEL BY

THE

MICHAEL KOEPF

WHALE

∽∾∾

McGRAW-HILL BOOK COMPANY

New York • St. Louis • Mexico • Toronto
San Francisco • Düsseldorf

Book design by Nora Sheehan.

1234567890BPBP78321098

Library of Congress Cataloging in Publication Data

Koepf, Michael.
Save the whale.
I. Title.
PZ4.K785Sav   [PS3561.0338]   813'.5'4   77-26677
ISBN 0-07-035280-1

For

MARY MORRIS

---

who taught her whale
to love and laugh

There's a whale, there's a whale, there's a whale,
brave boys, and she blows out every fence...

—from an old sea chanty

1

FLOTSAM AND JETSAM

I saw my first whale the day after I fled the city. I was a failure and—worse—I was broke. In contrast, the huge mammal that broke the water seventy yards off the rocky headland upon which I stood was a huge naturalistic success. Freedom and power in motion, as his glistening blue-black head and back cut through the water with a burst of vapor and violent small waves. It was the whales' annual migration back along the California coast to the cold yet abundant seas of the Arctic Circle after having spent the winter in the Acapulco of whaleland, Scammon's Lagoon in isolated Baja, where they mated and let the warm waters steal the polar chill from their massive bodies.

Almost as quickly as the first whale broke the water, several more followed outside and just ahead of him:

cows, calves, a whole flotilla of fun-loving leviathans frolicking back to their place of business totally oblivious to the problems of their land-locked cousins standing hapless on the continents they passed. From that day forward whales were an inspiration for me, although the inspiration itself seemed reasonless. Like a pubescent teenager I was caught up in a chemical passion, a mindless romantic admiration, a love of love. I was turning my back on life as I knew it and seeking in the whales—in fact in *the whale*—a release from the cares that beset me. I yearned for a life of constant and meaningful migration to some pleasant destination where time would become like the sea, an all-encompassing phenomenon, suspending me in an eternal weightlessness of now rather than dragging me down. I was also a man living in times of universal shipwreck. Without religion or politics, I was often driven to flights of pantheistic poppycock. I was part of the flotsam of our age. Sensing everything to be worth nothing, I was equally ready for anything but content to do very little. The tides of time carried me on. The whales, however, splashed their broad tails upon the sea and moved steadily and purposely toward their distant and meaningful goal.

It was also on that first day that I met Lorraine. Big Lorraine, that is. For a while she became a minor yet necessary love in my life. She helped me establish a shelter in the woods as I fled an existence I knew I never could return to. Until my best friend and I found our own whale with which to challenge the world, Lorraine gave me therapeutic labor, using my body for physical and psychological chores.

I saw her for the first time as the whales went

spouting off toward a blue horizon of sea and sky. She was standing alone like me. The only other people around were a family of moneyed whale-watchers standing next to a smart foreign car farther down the cliff and headlands from us. A man, woman, and small boy, each with a pair of binoculars following the disappearing creatures. Contented Homo sapiens, with their backs to the cares of the continent, introducing their offspring to their cheerful cetacean cousins. Tourists up from the Bay Area; I remember thinking enviously at the time that in a manner of minutes they would be driving to the nearby picturesque town of Mendocino, where they would dine at one of the quaint restaurants converted from long-dead lumber barons' homes. But my thoughts turned completely to Lorraine. She was picking wild flowers and throwing them into the sea after the whales. Whether the gesture was one of attention-getting for my benefit or genuinely "to decorate with beauty the way of the great monsters," as she told me when I approached and asked, I'll never know.

Lorraine was fat, a whale in her own right. Well, not truly fat, but stout—the kind of woman given to the wearing of mumus and overalls, draping her nonglamorous body in the necessity of constant casualness.

"They make you want to leap after them and cruise the depths of the world," she said.

"Not really; that water's fifty-two degrees and colder," I answered, but I hated myself for breaking her romantic train of thought almost as I said it, for she was merely verbalizing the same sort of gibberish I had been pumping my own brain up with only moments before. Her face was oval and her hair long, straight, and brown—its ends stopped below her neck in a veritable obstacle course of necklaces and baubles jangling and entangled above her ample bosom. The sound of bells on anklets floated up from beneath her long, flower-print mumu. She was barefoot and the crisp afternoon wind wafted the faint scent of patchouli oil off her body. Lorraine was a flower child grown older.

She gazed intently into my face in mock wonderment at my antiromantic comment. In that instant I knew she had something on me. Lorraine understood my mach-macho glibness and sensed the romantic in me covered up by the functionally foolish. She turned quickly back to gazing at the sea, making her head spin her hair out slightly from her body in a conscious gesture that would have worked better had her smallish head been anchored to a lesser body. Instead of ending in a fluidity of motion, her hair merely wrapped around her face and made her half-stumble as she stepped away. But she knew she had me and I followed willingly, feeling clever myself, giving in totally to her invitation to sit with her and watch the sunset with the whales.

Several more great gray whales passed before darkness overtook us. The spray from the oncoming tide forced us to move several times to different vantage points on the rocks.

"You learn more about a person during your first few hours with them than you do in a lifetime of continued acquaintance," Lorraine said. Our several moves and the increasingly cold ocean air had forced us next to one another. We let our shoulders press, seeking warmth. Lorraine wanted to do three things right off: build a fire, tell each other our life stories, and be the first people to watch the whales at night. I had a fourth idea in store for both of us, excited by our warm touch, but had to put up with hers first.

"Like a lighthouse guides a ship, our fire will guide the whales as they slip close to the rocks in the dark." With that Lorraine had me stumbling around in the twilight looking for bits and pieces of driftwood to kindle the fire of our fantasies.

The fire blazed away after Lorraine had me walk back up to her truck and get a can of kerosene. The whales continued to pass in the dark with or without the aid of our light. Every now and then above the crackle of the flames and Lorraine's tale of lost love and loneliness, a sea sound much like the sudden puncturing of an air mattress or air rapidly escaping from a tire reached my ears as the huge beasts cruised on, unaware of our fire and desires. Lorraine told me about the current disappointment and frustration in her life. Her old man, an aging rock musician, had jetisoned her and their idyllic home in the woods, which the two of them had lovingly constructed out of an old chicken coop. "'There's no music in goats and no bread in organic cucumbers.' That's the last thing he said," Lorraine confided with a sorrowful yet accepting note in her voice. I put my arm around her shoulders and pulled her tightly toward me as she went on with all the details preceding the already-known ending of her story. I listened intently but heard nothing, for my thoughts were my own as we sat upon that rocky western shore.

Misery does love company—but not each other's. My mind flashed back over my own short confusing life.

The last month had been a nightmare, a virtual horror film. A scratching search for true existence. I had had to make some money and failed. I was a veteran making my way as a sometime, aging student in one of those hip yet provincial university communities dedicated to the illusion that time and life stand still for those seeking an expansion of their awareness of the universe. I awoke late one morning to a letter from the Veterans Administration telling me they were cutting me off. The war seemed so long ago that I had forgotten or repressed it. The checks were the only link with that dismal part of my past. I felt nauseous and weak. I attempted to conjure up all sorts of reasons for their continuing my assistance and disability while the letter was still fresh in my hands. I was to report the next day for Termination Counseling.

I took the bus to the city in the morning with my notice of termination and alighted on Montgomery Street. A cool spring fog was swirling through the canyons of buildings. I walked up Montgomery Street checking out the secretaries in their short dresses scurrying along the gray streets, their legs moving against the cold rapidly like sandpipers on the edge of the sea. Businessmen alighted from and departed in cabs and limousines. Young men intently moved forward, their shoulders and heads rakishly set, into the crowds. But neither the beauty of the young girls nor the sense of determination on the faces of the men my own age had much effect on me; my heart was bankrupt of hope and fearful of what lay ahead.

In front of one of the huge new high-rise towers of glass, its top lost in the fog, there was a sunless plaza devoid of all life except a few business people hurriedly in transit. The plaza surface was of a polished black-gray stone, and central in the square was a large stone sculpture the size of a pickup truck. It was also black, but of highly polished marble and assumed the shape at first of nothing more than a blob, but on closer inspection it resembled the form of a gigantic frozen heart, limp, lifeless, yet nevertheless a heart with a depression running up and over the top separating it into a left and right ventricle. It was positively Aztec in intent and dimensions. Nearby and on the other side of the plaza there was a fountain circulating foamy water, and in it the stone figure of an abstract whale which for the life of me seemed to have absolutely nothing to do with its counterpart in plaza art fifty feet away.

I hurried on to my appointment to escape the bleak, bizarre reality of the place.

My Veterans' Assistance Counselor was obviously displeased with me. His manner and voice were perfunctory. His face was long and a stubbly beard darkened it along his jaws to his chin. He wore plain flesh-colored plastic-rimmed glasses that reflected the glare of the overhead lighting—as did his head, which was bald except for some glossy strands that swept by the tops of his ears. His collar was loose and unbuttoned above a dangling thin blue tie. He looked New-Dealish. Some distant historical appointment or promotion had stranded him at the desk across from me. But as he went on speaking, citing all the monthly payments of rehabilitation the government had expended for my well-being, I detected a hint of the inner man. His tieclasp was a long thin speedboat complete with a miniature American flag on its stern. Undoubtedly he was a man who started his life's task dedicated to "helping people" only to become lost in the function of bureaucracy until he found himself the turnkey to others' misery.

"Three years of the GI Bill, Mr. Curtis," he said with a scowl. "Two more years on a mental disability claim but little contact with government counseling, a complete disregard of all the correspondence we have sent you in the last six months except cashing your monthly allotment. Rehabilitation, Mr. Curtis. I'm here to help bring you back, not finance you on your way out of society indefinitely. Your record of feigned mental disorientation should have by now, according to our policies, run its course."

"I've tried to work part-time, but it interferes with my studies," I answered. My brain computed desperately for excuses.

His face took on a sarcastic and disdainful look. He snapped back with hard, cold bureaucratic fact.

"Your GI benefits ran out eighteen months ago, according to my files, while you were getting your second degree in something it says here is called Modern American Mythology," he said, glaring directly into my face, expecting an explanation and justification for my chosen course of study. But there was nothing I could say—especially since I had been around the department so long that the university had given up on me and allowed me to make up my own independent course of study, a course I was still uncertain about myself. I stared back in as undefiant a manner as possible, hoping for sympathy, but none was forthcoming. It was useless; he was already shuffling papers on his desk, conveying the fact that he was no longer listening. He told me he was taking my file into the board and promised a decision in a few minutes. He left carrying my file and all further hope of prolonged payments through a brown door to his rear.

He wasn't lying about the quick decision. The bare clock on the wall was nearing twelve and the counselors and clerks in the vast office were all putting on a display of last-minute busyness, rearranging stacks of paper on their desks. There was hardly time to fidget before my counselor returned.

"Mr. Curtis, we are going to offer you a full-time job opportunity here in the city with a proper relocation and clothing allowance as our final effort to help you with yourself."

I had to accept. I hardly had bus money back to Berkeley. My fate was sealed. I took their last chance and my punishment and two days later found myself a probationary junior executive in a finance company just six blocks away from the Federal Building. I was trapped behind a desk. It was as if a lid was being nailed down on my existence. A brown flannel Sears, Roebuck suit hung loosely on my body. Furnished at government expense as their last act toward my rehabilitation, it felt like prison garb. All about me in the office normal-looking people went about their work, participating in a ghoulish process.

My desk was right next to Clyde Walker, a stout young man who spoke rapidly and never to my face, for he was forever turning away to something more important. Clyde emanated professional confidence à la Dale Carnegie—the true sign of a coward. He hid a bottle of mouthwash in his desk drawer and hit off it before confronting any of the secretaries, discharging his spit into a paper cup also secreted in a drawer. Mr. Walker was my immediate superior; his title was Executive Credit Manager. I was Junior Executive Credit Manager, Trainee. There was one other man in the office—the boss, Mr. Hobart, who was the Executive Loan Manager, a frumpish-looking fellow who wore much more conservative clothing, as befitted his position and forty-plus years.

The rest of the office was staffed with a platoon of young girls, all of whom seemed to be fresh from Kansas or Fresno breaking into exciting secretary city life and spending the pittance of a wage they made with our Friendly Finance on clothes and Cost Plus imports to decorate their apartments.

I moved to the city into a five-fifty-a-day room at the Rex Hotel. My room was an island of youth amid a clientele of elderly on Social Security pensions who kept up a continual chatter about muggers, bowel movements, and the Great Depression. The basement of the Rex was a laundry, and I slept with tortured dreams to the tune of a steam press. Each morning I passed the sprawled bodies of winos cluttering doorways as I scurried on to Friendly Finance. I was at the abysmal bottom of the business world, devoid of any optimistic buoyancy. I quickened my pace lest my feet stick in the ooze of despair all about me.

The first week I read the company manuals, which depicted plain grownup Dick-and-Jane people with frowns on their faces in front of a breakfast table of bills. The next picture showed them smiling in front of a rainbow of new cars, TV sets, toasters, vacuum cleaners, and refrigerators after they have made The Reconsolidation Loan. None of the people who came to Friendly Finance looked like the people in the company manuals. Most were black, Spanish-American, or old people trying to keep from bottoming out. Young people made loans through Friendly Finance, but most of those were through stereo stores and car lots for whom we held the paper and interest.

"We're in the business of dispensing the ultimate medicine, and that's money," Mr. Hobart told me the first day I was there. And it did seem to help a lot. He had me closing a few loans, taking the people into little partitioned booths that assured the privacy of a confessional and making sure that the customer understood the small print. "Do you understand the small print and interest rate in the fourth paragraph of the second subsection?" I'd ask them. They quickly nodded and signed the loan note in agreement because their eyes were already on the check in front of them on the little plastic table we shared in the cubicle.

By the second week I felt like a dope-pusher. I was moved from closing loans to trying to collect them.

"Nobody cashes out on me," Clyde Walker told me when he introduced me to his deadbeat files. "They've got to take their medicine."

For three solid days I called homes where people would change their voices in midsentence, trailing off into gibberish. Children hadn't seen their parents in weeks, whole families were stricken with whiplash; everybody had moved or was out of town, in jail, or threatening to kill me if I called again. Old women wept, young ones connived. The happy faces I had confronted in the closing rooms had now turned to venom-spewing monsters by the middle of the second week. I was depressed.

The next day I was fifteen minutes late for work and Clyde Walker took me out on collections. We drove about the city all morning running Clyde's household errands on company mileage with his blanket philosophy of "screw 'em" justifying the jaunt, but in the afternoon he showed me how to get down to nickles and dimes. We cruised several shabby tenement addresses in search of skipouts, but by three Clyde was zeroing in on his quarry, some "dumb son of a bitch" with a color TV set that Clyde wanted for a new "bar-ette" he was installing in his apartment. The set had been purchased by an older couple several years before, but a shipyard accident to the husband and subsequent layoff had caused them to refinance the appliance four different times. Clyde could hardly contain himself as he explained how the original cost was $450, but due to the refinancing they had already paid back $726, with a remaining $150 outstanding and unpaid for six months. If he picked the set up he could bid twenty on it to cover paperwork and it would be his. He confided conspiratorially that he and his wife, a German girl he had met in the Army, had furnished their entire apartment in such a manner: "Nouveau Repo." He was angry with me when I refused to go into the dilapidated building to help carry the set down and even more angry when he came struggling out with the bulky box of tubes to find the back window of his car had been smashed in by a rock. I told him some Mexican kids had thrown it at me.

The next morning Hobart called me into one of the loan confessionals to have a heart-to-heart talk, but by then the Doctor Jekyll side of my nature effaced the Mr. Hyde that had overcome me the day before when I smashed Clyde's car window. I politely kowtowed to his tongue lashing about my being forty-five minutes late. We got our paychecks in plain white envelopes at ten that morning. After deductions I had made $149 for the two weeks. My room and meals and movies were costing me over $65, so that left me with some $10 a week for everything else. A suspicion like a spider crawled up my body and tickled my brain. I was not being rehabilitated but rather set up, written off, and driven by the reality of Friendly Finance into becoming part of the jetsam of the business world that littered the doorways and stoops of the financial district at night.

Clyde had me harassing deadbeats on the phone all morning. At eleven o'clock, drowned by the tears and pleas of a housewife who was in despair, believing that we were going to pick up the chattel mortgage on her furniture, I cracked. Not with a snap or in rage; there was neither scream nor scene. I quietly told the woman when her sobs had receded that she need not worry. In fact, she had just won our "close-out of the month contest" and her debt was canceled. With that I hung up, took her fat file of debt and despair over to the closed-out accounts and checked in all the monthly squares on her loan. After that I cautiously worked my way around Clyde (who was threatening some kid on the phone) and got into the heart of his deadbeat files, helping myself at random to as many folders as I could hide between the pages of the morning paper on my desk. At lunch I quietly walked out of the office with the bulging packet under my arm and took the elevator to the street, where I dumped the records in the first trashcan I passed and forever, I hoped, left the world of finance.

The warmth of Lorraine's body next to me protected me from the darkness and my own self-pity. A leviathan breathed a good night as he passed in the dark. Lorraine was silent for a few moments, for her life and love story had wound down to a recent suicide attempt.

"It was his gun," she said. "He had it to protect us from rednecks. I was hysterical. He was running out of the cabin with my best batik pillow and ivory hash pipe.

I really wanted to end it and grabbed the gun from behind the woodbox, but he got to me just as I was going to pull the trigger to oblivion. I had loved him so much. But when it was over all that was left were two holes in the stovepipe and one through his left ear."

The end of her story had strangely excited me. Lorraine was definitely a strong, passionate woman. As the sea churned below us in the dark upon the hard rocks of the continent's edge, I tried to pull her closer to me in a gesture of sympathy for her plight and lost love. I was also pleading for consolation for my own sad situation. But my arm was cramped from its continued rigidity around her broad shoulders and I misjudged the amount of force necessary to press her heavy body toward me. We both tipped clumsily off our rock, rolling toward the fire, and Lorraine was forced to disengage herself abruptly and slap out the smoldering bottom of her mumu. Seconds later she was back upon me with a speed I would have thought impossible in a girl with such a large frame. We embraced solidly on the ground and rolled away from the fire. Soon my ass felt glazed by the icy wind, but our breaths were synchronized in passion. At one point, as Lorraine nibbled away at my ear, our breath seemed to coincide with the explosion of breath from several passing whales. The sounds drove Lorraine into a state of ecstasy and I lost total control, spiraling primitively downward. The whales swam on as we embraced in the dark. I was beginning to dig country life.

2

THE CHICKEN PARTS
DONATED REVOLUTION

Lorraine set me up in the woods. Through the spring and summer I sponged off her. After our first night of cold passion on the cliff she insisted that I share her small piece of property.

"Stanley," she said, "you can get close to my body but not my head." She wanted me near her but not exactly with her, so what I did was build my own cabin in the woods nearby. Well, not exactly a cabin. There was an old abandoned water tank several hundred feet from Lorraine's small house, which sat on top of a low coastal peak looking out over the deep green woods. Woods that each morning were washed with a soft white fog that crept in from the ocean at night, stranding the peaks of hills and mountains in little islands of trees. The view from the water tank wasn't quite as good, but it was a far cry from the Rex Hotel.

A strange new ambition surged through my body

during those first few weeks and months: The ambition of natural survival. Lorraine had an old Dodge pickup truck which she let me use, and with it I scoured the countryside and abandoned farms for rundown chicken coops and woodsheds. I begged and stole boards with which to turn the old water tank into my home. The tank itself had been dry for twenty years, since the last of the alcoholic kin of the original pioneers who homesteaded the area left to seek their fortunes in Fresno or Bakersfield or wherever home-grown Okies go when they leave the land. Only a few bullet holes showed through the tank and were easily plugged with carved redwood dowels. On one side I carefully cut out several pieces of vertical planks and framed a door. On the other side I did the same thing in smaller proportions and framed a window. Lorraine and her ex-old man had torn down an old house and had a stash of several used doors and windows that went unused in their cabin. She let me take whatever I wanted. I laid four four-by-six beams across the open top of the tank and on it framed out a pitched roof, boarded the framing, and then set about cutting shakes with Lorraine's chain saw out of bolts of redwood from a nearby fallen log. A delicious energy surged through my body as I pounded away at the boards. My wayward and uncertain ambitions had been reduced to the barest necessities. One hot summer afternoon I laid the final course of shakes along the ridge of the roof and peered out over the surrounding woods below. Turkey vultures soared through the tall, pointed redwood tops on heated updrafts. The sky was light blue and without airplanes. If a crowd of a hundred had stood below me and cheered me on I couldn't have been more content. At thirty

16

years old I had completed one of the first real tasks of my life.

The summer wore on. Lorraine's and my relationship took on a functional aspect. At first I was free to pound away at my tank but soon, after it was completed, Lorraine was after me to get little jobs done, mend her goat fence, shovel manure on her garden, chop firewood, repair spring boxes—and once one job was finished another needed tending. Especially Lorraine's sacred dope plants. Several hundred yards down a southern slope from her coop, she had a small garden packed full of luscious marijuana which needed constant pruning and watering. She was religious about their attention. "Organic, altered consciousness, Stanley," she told me over and over again as I picked beetles with an attack of the munchies off the leaves. I was forever shoring up the seven-foot-high chicken-wire fence around her little green temple, for the deer were laying siege to the place, attempting to hurl their bodies over the top each night.

I was beginning to feel like a serf but feared direct rebellion would cost me my beloved little water tank. After all, it was her property. I made myself scarce not only to escape work but also, I knew, to find it. There had to be some task in the vast woods that surrounded me that would allow me to be self-sufficient. I knew it wasn't chopping down trees because I had seen the one-armed gas-station attendant down at Philo, and one look from the outside at a lumber mill with smoke and whirling chains, high-pitched saws, and the choke of tractor exhaust convinced me that it was no place for me. Besides, all the jobs in the lumber industry seemed to be held by violent young men who nightly cruised along the country ridge road nearby, parking in turnoffs littered with piles of beer cans before they cruised home again shooting mailboxes and roadsigns from their car windows. Lorraine had her thing, and when I asked for a small percentage of her dope harvest and sales her emphatic "No, haven't I done enough for you?" sent me directly into the welfare line.

The Commodities Distribution Center was on the outskirts of Fort Bragg, one of the larger towns in our county preoccupied with the industry of killing trees. Commodities Distribution was the county-seat politicians' answer to the fear of "creeping socialism" as they saw it embodied in the government food stamp program. As a substitute for its implementation they instead let the faithless and unfortunate in our country's great economic system stand up and be counted in a food line.

It was a dusty summer morning the first time I showed up at the Distribution Center. I felt strange, slightly ashamed to be in a breadline at such a healthful young age, but my years in the Army and connection with the government had somehow prepared me for it. Dependency had become ingrained into my character. The line was long and filled with the usual midsummer transients who queued up with forged rent receipts and thirty-five-cent post-office-box slips in order to receive the once-a-month distribution of Surplus Commodities trained and trucked to our neck of the woods in Mendocino, California. I used Lorraine's rural box number and put myself and one dependent down on the application form. Lorraine, I was sure, wouldn't mind me claiming her as a wife for an extra portion. She could feed it to her goats if she didn't like it.

Mendocino County is rural California containing woods logged over so many times in the past hundred years that land values have consequently stayed low, allowing hip and young pioneers to settle on the earth's now almost-permanent scar tissue. Still, the hulks of junked redwoods make much more pleasant viewing than junked cars and cities. In the summer the friends of residents flock north from the urban areas to crash in the tall trees. This lasts until the first big rain or, as those passing themselves off as old-timers put it, until the "scorpions crawl to heaven," a strange phenomenon I observed in my water tank in the early fall. Just before the first rains of the year, anywhere from early September to mid-October, scorpions for some unknown reason crawl up and out of the twisted roots of madrone and oak. Up they go. Any surface will do that takes them closer to whatever force pulls them out of their dark places like a magnet ever higher and higher. Walls of tents and cabins become freeways and streets, scaring the hell out of tourists and transients alike. It's just as well, for even if they could take the scorpions, the rains are soon sure to get them when the first big storm sweeps down from the Gulf of Alaska, cracking tops and branches off the highest redwoods and flooding the hills and earth so that the new growth can start to push through the loggers' bulldozer tracks of summer.

The day I first met Jorgi and Janett the lines in the Commodities Distribution Center had swelled to a high tide of humanity and hips. The reason for this was that two big encampments were taking place that summer in the Mendocino woods—the Three-H'ers and the People's Church.

The HHH was the "Healthy, Holy, and Happy"

bunch who wore elaborate bedsheets swirled on top of their heads into high turbans, which gave the participants what they thought was an exotic costume. They stood in line, stepping slowly and sure-footedly forward. No horsing around, or the turbans would fall off into the powder dust to be trampled by the milling crowd and darting barefoot children.

The People's Church was in the northern part of the county and my only contact with them was at the center. In line they were a relatively quiet bunch, much like the Three-H'ers, but they were somewhat on the creepy side. Their guru was a man named William Smith, a seemingly straight fellow who, it was claimed, had, believe it or not, raised forty-four people from the dead. As a result of a major newspaper doing an article on him in the Sunday supplement, he had taken lately to remaining holed up in his religious Utopia with several armed guards, two of whom were deputy sheriffs from the county seat of Ukiah. His church had a strange attraction to hip and straight community alike—including, it was rumored, a member of the county board of supervisors. The younger element was of course the only ones I got to see as they waited in line with the rest of us for our five pounds of flour, a small sack or two of pinto beans, Corn Meal Donated, two cans of Chicken Parts Salt Added, a pound of butter, and the various other items that could be had on the basis of America's vast surplus of foods pouring forth from the heartland to anybody, regardless of creed or color, who made less than ninety dollars a month. It was like Christmas with no thank-yous.

The line was moving very slowly that morning. The volunteer ladies up ahead in the center were doing their best as they disgorged the contents of boxes stacked high on pallets and placed them quickly into arms or boxes that the recipients moved along on rollers, but there weren't enough boxes. Most of the newcomers, thinking that all was provided for in our bucolic welfare state, had neglected to bring their own containers to receive their just deserts. Recipients' arms became overloaded with canned goods and the whole load would go crashing all over the floor of the center. This led to several mad scrambles as those dropping the food hurried to pick it up again lest someone impatient with waiting in line do it for them. Two people from the People's Church in line in front of me took the name of their Lord in vain several times while bearing witness to these delays. Their heads were shaved as clean as eggs, and crosses carved from abalone shell dangled from their necks by parcel-post string. I was sure their patron saint was Charlie Manson. Several nasty arguments broke out at the rear of the center near the garbage pile. As the ladies dispensed the food the empty boxes were thrown outside. The needy gathered around and fought for them in order that they might take them back in and fill them up again. None of this looked like it was prompted by hunger or impending starvation. The fact that they were getting something free drove these recipients to these minor encounters. I watched these hassles passively, content that I had had enough foresight to bring my rucksack, which was slung on my back, to carry the goods that would line the belly of my cabin against the onslaught of physical hunger.

The real reason the line was moving so slowly that day was the fact that two county officials were making a person-by-person check on the crowd. A right-winger had succeeded in registering his dog the month before for the surplus food. The officials were checking application papers for the commodities against driver's licenses or some such bureaucratic nonsense. From the looks of the piles up ahead in the center no one had to worry that it would ever run out whether the recipients were real residents of the county or not. Everyone bitched and moaned about the delays, but like me they seemed satisfied with their plight, content to wait their turn in line, moving slowly forward with subdued complaint.

I wondered why I had picked California after the war. My uncertain brain provided no answer to my body standing in line in this happy but dangerous land. That very summer, along with the migration of the cults to our county, several shallow graves of carefree bikers were found near Ukiah. The legendary Big Foot still stalks the woods, a Ubermensch breaking forth from the disturbed consciousness of an uncertain population.

There's a way small-time government men eye you. This one wore loose gray-blue slacks and a white shirt with his sleeves rolled up in what I thought was a bogus attempt to look informal. His face was unemotional but his eyeballs were clicking. Every now and then, as he looked over the crowd, he would ask someone to step out of line into a small room adjacent to the line where flash-pop another fellow dressed exactly like him would take the suspect's photograph and again run through his papers and licenses. The closer I got in line to this guy the more I could feel the vibrations like electricity coming off the back of necks in front of me as everyone tried to act cool, pretending he wasn't even there, shoring up the insides of their heads with inane conversation about far-out vegetables and microbiotic dope.

Occasionally a faint protest would register over the conversations of "Wow, did you see that!" as a friend or someone up front got picked off, but none of it struck home in either anger at the county man or sympathy for the freaked-out suspect. It was lost in the general low din of conversation. Everyone was cool.

Suddenly, though, from behind me someone was yelling at the top of his voice, screaming in fact, and so loud at first no one wanted to hear it for to believe in the sound was to bear witness. But the scream soon became audible as everyone else became quiet and "Goddam it, they never made me wait for this crap in Nam" flooded everyone's head with not only noise but also a strange sensation. The yelling was like a catalytic powder thrown into the air, a catalyst that turned indifference into—I hate to say it, because I am as political as a potato—revolution.

I turned, straining my neck, and saw Jorgenson for the first time. He didn't look like much. Short and stocky with red hair chopped short around his collar, in contrast to the rest of the hip daddies waiting in line that day with their locks flowing down over simple white madras prayer shirts, dusty serapes, or hopped-up Sears, Roebuck overalls fringed with iron-on embroideries. Jorgi's face had a rosy complexion; that and his hair were really the only touch of coloring on his external appearance, and they were natural ones. His face was punctuated with two dots of blue on each side of a short nose spattered with a few leftover childhood freckles. That was it. A soup can with a touch of color. The rest was plain bland American—bleached-out Levi's, a simple shirt that doesn't even register in my memory, a tan Levi jacket—the kind with copper rivets that glint dully in the sun. His only mark of external flamboyance was one of those cheap Navajo rings. Internally, who knows, did the bland can hold some rare court bouillon?

Janett was something else as she stood beside him, a grim look on her thin angular face with high cheekbones framed in straight brown hair that swept down along the side of her head. Except for her eyes, which were small and set too far back in her head, she would have been a classic tall, Slavic-looking beauty, but as it was she was a damn good-looking country girl with slim Levi's and a gingham shirt with an amply proportioned chest below her white neck. Her look was as fierce and determined as Jorgi's was rosy and indignant.

He yelled as loud as he could, pointing over the seraped shoulder of the freak in front of him, who had an expression on his face like he was trying to make his eyes and nose melt into his beard lest someone think he was doing the shouting. The freak's expression changed to anger as Jorgenson went on yelling. Jorgi yelled so hard he became an instant leader. The crowd hung onto his every word as he vehemently shouted—no, demanded—that "everyone should get his crap NO QUES-TIONS ASKED—we're hungry—and *right now* before everything donated to us is hauled to the dump or sent to India!"

That's all they needed. I immediately looked for an exit, a window to slip out of, but I was caught in the crowd that had by now joined in with lesser shouts and raised fists. Barefoot kids and babies were held aloft to be used as either proof of need or, I even feared, symbolic clubs shaken in the direction of the county man and his assistant. They couldn't control it. At first the county man tried to stare in a threatening manner at the original source of disturbance, but he was soon drowned in the wave of abuse led by Jorgenson. He split. Right into the room with his assistant, where they locked themselves in until the deputy sheriffs arrived. At one point they were totally freaked because the crowd was beating a very tricky drumbeat on the walls and doors à la Mick Jagger that made dust come through the crack on their barricaded door from the sheetrock that was loosened on the other side.

The county men were visibly shaken when the deputies got them out. They had to take one of them by each arm to a waiting patrol car before they zoomed his nervous body away. His assistant sought vengeance and with the aid of three deputies made a foray into the crowd, but nobody would rat. They arrested two lesser-looking Three-H'ers for possession and retreated to the county seat after only a few minutes.

"Hey, pal, lend me a hand," Jorgenson said as the sheriff's car drove off. "Someone's got to clean up this mess."

He called me and I went to him. Nobody wants to be seen hanging around a hero, certainly not me at any rate. But at that moment it seemed safer to join forces with anyone to avoid the melee that followed the departure of the police. The authorities were letting us stew in our own juices. Cans and bags were scattered all over the floor. The line of rollers containing several boxes of commodities was being tipped forward onto the floor and the volunteer ladies scattered, barricading themselves in the bathroom in fear. People were yelling and shoving, picking up handfuls of commodities, getting pushed, and dropping them again in order to hit back. The cement floor was covered with a mist of whole wheat flour and corn sugar. Kids were having a field day sliding through several slick spots of cooking oil while their parents scrambled for goodies amid the broken glass and scattered cans. Several more aggressive hippies were even ripping open cases of food still piled high on pallets as their country mamas cheered them on.

Jorgenson started yelling again, and since he had started it all I was sure he would be pleading and directing some sort of order to the anarchy that raged about us. But all that came out of his mouth was "That's mine!" He shoved bodies out of the way while directing Janett and me to pick up commodities. The three of us made several trips back and forth into the center, loading the goods in the back of an old Rustoleum-colored pickup before the deputies returned, this time in force. They alighted from four-wheel-drive Blazers and lit into the crowd with all the enthusiasm of their high-school football days, scattering hip, holy, and helpless alike. By then, though, Jorgenson, Janett, and I had already filled half of their pickup-truck bed with goods and I jumped into the cab, anticipating a quick getaway, but the two of them laughed at me.

"Friend, we've got our legal share coming yet and so do you," Jorgenson said and took me with them back into the orderly line that was re-forming under the watchful glare of the deputies.

It took some time for the ladies to reman their posts. Several of them had quit face-to-face charity work forever and had gone back to arranging flowers in their church and knitting doilies for the aged. My turn came and I filled my rucksack one more time, feeling guilty, but after I had unloaded it onto the floor of their truck,

Jorgenson had me return several times to help him and Janett with their fair share.

I didn't understand at first, for the three of us kept piling the rations higher and higher till there must have been well over four or five hundred pounds of commodities in the bed of the truck and I got scared, for I figured that maybe they were stealing it, holding knives to the throats of the volunteer ladies. Jorgenson sensed my uneasiness.

"Don't worry, buddy," he told me, "this is all our food, legal and by proxy. We pick it up on signed instructions for a bunch of lazy cats who live with us," which calmed me down. If I had realized how literally he meant what he said, I would have split that very instant, hitching back up to my tank as fast as I could.

That's how adventures start, out of a stupid favor or "What's the time of day?" I'm sure Ulysses must have pulled the same scam on countless fellows, never directly announcing "Hey, how about rowing across the sea with me to fight a war and get eaten by a bunch of pigs?" Before he ever said that I'm sure the sonofabitch had his eye out for any musclebound young man who happened down to the beach where from his stranded craft, feigning work, he would call out, "Hey, how about a hand with this oar, friend?" There was no doubt about it; I picked up my oar and joined the ranks of the world's vast multitude of rowers, with my back toward the destination and my only incentive the eyes of my captain at the helm, searching ahead for some unknown point in the distance, some curious goal known only to himself lending him his sureness that lent in turn to his crew a dull confidence to keep on pulling.

Away I went, with Jorgenson at the wheel of the old Chevy, for they had promised to take me home. Janett was between us and the back was full of government surplus food as we shot out into the woods through scrub pine, billowing white sandy dust behind us. Every once in a while I looked back on a big bump or curve to see why we hadn't turned over. An explosion of tan or yellow would appear as a sack of brown flour or corn-meal shook loose and hit the earth. The two of them only laughed when I said we should stop lest we lose the whole load.

"It's free, man, it's free," answered Jorgi above the noise of a broken muffler as we headed through the fir and fern forest.

3

THE HOUSE THAT
JUNK BUILT

They lived in an abandoned Aztec pyramid—well, sort
of. Not out of any deliberate weirdness, the kind that
seizes many of the younger inhabitants of our county
who build dwellings after any strange fashion that suits
their imagination and means in a competitive quest for
the most unusual house, much to the bane of the county
building department. Barns have become communal
homes; redwood-shaked three- and four-story towers
have risen above the woods like the ramparts of feudal
castles; caves have been boarded up and their interiors
sprayed with Styrofoam for insulation; there is even one
place which the welfare people chauvinistically call The
Snake Pit, where a dozen or so junk cars and wrecked
VW buses have been parked together side by side with
their doors removed so that their inhabitants might
move freely from vehicle to vehicle. Jorgi was simply a

master pragmatist. The home he and Janett built served him, and not he it. It warmed him while he rested, gaining energy for his schemes.

It was off the main dirt road and up another thin cut through scrub oak and second-growth redwood. We stopped next to three big black airport limousines neatly parked in a military formation next to an old Chevy panel truck that had been converted into a chicken coop.

"Whose Cadillacs?" I asked, but before the engine died Jorgensen was out of the cab to the back of the truck. Janett explained in a matter-of-fact tone that the cars had been part of a scheme "Jorgi cooked up to start traveling Alpha centers." Janett went on to tell me as straight-faced as could be that "Jorgi had been into making portable DC alpha caps that people could use to check on their brain waves to achieve higher states of meditation." It seems that "he had this idea to have these traveling centers in the back seats of these old Mission Street jitneys he picked up at a car auction in San Francisco for a hundred dollars each and the price of their tow bills. But nothing ever came of it because try working on the caps though he did, he never could get the electricity thing straightened out," Janett told me. "I was sure I had killed him several times. He'd sit in the back seat and yell to me up front under the hood to clamp the wires on the battery terminals. He'd come screaming out any door or window, holding his head, rolling around on the ground. Wow, it was awful."

I didn't believe her, but after we unloaded the commodities and they started feeding their animals with them I walked over to one of the stranded monsters and peeped into a back seat where from the ceiling there hung strands of wires like exposed tendons hooked up to what looked like charcoal-colored bathing caps cut from sections of old inner tubes. There were four or five speakers pointed in the direction of the seat and the hanging caps. It looked like a torture chamber rigged by junk dealers holding an inquisition. I quickly walked away as they called me to come in and have some tea with them.

We walked up a path followed by a horde of cats, two baby goats, a couple of dogs, and a bunch of chickens until suddenly there appeared before me a huge black and massive construction half the height of the nearest small redwood tree. It was their dome, their home, but it was a complete perversion of Buckminster Fuller's idea of freedom and space in architecture. Their dome caved in slightly at the apex and remained so in a twisting dent that meandered down the dark side to the earth, making the whole structure appear to be in two pieces. In fact it looked more like a giant relief of a stranded heart than the outline of a geodesic dome. Several galvanized stovepipes protruded from the structure like huge, fat needles in a pincushion.

We talked and smoked long into the night—or rather Jorgi talked, speaking to me of various schemes that were on his mind as Janett steadily filled Mason jars with grains, flour, and commodities near an old wooden stove in one corner of the interior of the structure. As darkness came on the interior of the dome assumed the appearance of a cheery spider's web, for the walls and ceiling were a network of cables. Jorgi stoked up a fifty-gallon drum converted into a fireplace; it crackled and lit the ceiling composed of four-by-four redwood posts set into large triangles that were held together by the cables and wires. I touched one near the floor; it was

31

so taut it virtually sang to my fingertips. Jorgi explained that he and Janett erected the whole place in only a few days after scoring most of the material off a movie set which, believe it or not, was in the form of the front of an Aztec temple that a motion picture company had constructed up in the woods. What the movie was about Jorgi and Janett did not know, nor did it ever play anywhere, because the company folded and left the front stranded in the pines until Jorgi carted it off piece by piece. Why a temple in the woods so unlike the Mexican plateau? Jorgi didn't know.

"Their reality didn't work out, so I just reconstructed their mess into my home," he said. "Their temple was nothing more than layers of roofing paper taped together to look like huge slabs of stone. These guy wires and cables were all over the place, attached to trees and concrete dead men." He went on to tell me the story of the ill-fated movie company. "They couldn't beat the breeze that comes ripping through the trees each afternoon during the summer and they couldn't shoot on the foggy mornings. The temple was forever falling down. Their wire to nature was short-circuited. It happens all the time with anyone who doesn't see the world just like it is, doesn't realize it's just all minerals and energy zapping around, you know, just real and all of it there for us to use, to make it with reality—rip off a little to keep going."

I had hardly any idea what he was talking about as he went on with fire illuminating his face before me in pulsating rhythms of warmth and, I must say, energetic frenzy. "There's really nothing new under the sun," he said, "just a big turnover of humanity. People think they need to see the world in a special way, need to run it down to themselves so they don't go bananas. It's a screwed notion. All they really need is to get some of those minerals and energy, to rip it off and pull it into themselves."

"Sounds pretty grim," I answered, no longer able to contain my skepticism.

"But it isn't, it's life's most joyous secret. It's the core of creativity, the nourishing sap of survival. Without it we're finished, and when we're finished here we'll take off to some other planet and turn it all over again."

"But this is the twentieth century," I interrupted. "The planet we live on has been bled silly by screwballs running around for the last three thousand years taking what they thought was theirs at the expense of others. What about a more cooperative way of life; what about Eastern thought and all of us getting it on with nature in harmonious balance?"

"Yeah, how about it?" Jorgi looked directly at me without any animosity at my having taken exception to what he had been saying. The uneven light from the fire showed a distinct smile on his face. He was even nodding at me in seeming agreement. Either that or humorous condescension.

"Check out your Eastern mystics. For every Buddha that lives in the forest, one hundred fat rich men must live in the city to keep alive the idea of the Buddha, for," he said, raising a finger in an upward gesture, "the ten thousand poor people who work for them must have some distant goal of attainment to make their lives of misery bearable. It all has a practical reason. The search for harmony is really the search for a full belly. The Hindus are hip to this in their own way. They've cooked up the idea that the holiest of holy men live off 'prana,' which is like eating air. It's a good idea, saves food for the hundred million other starving bastards. They spread the philosophy of withdrawal which cuts the national calorie count way down. Nature is never in balance, it's always berserko. Harmony in nature is an idea cooked up by a boring bureaucratic mind that insists on each and everything in its place. It's an idea conceived by simps too cowardly to face up to change. They want it to all hold still, as if time itself could stop. Harmony in nature is simply something thought up by nature's own most fearful creatures—men, scared shitless of death, insulating themselves in sameness."

"Hold it," I interruped. "You're jumping around a lot." And he was; he was into a syllogistic jitterbug that had my brain reeling.

"It's not me that's jumping around, Stanley. It's the universe itself. This forest all about us could be reduced to Tinker Toys or swallowed up by the sea or made into a gunnery range for meteorites. In the long run it means nothing to me at all. Before I was born I was dead. I was dead when the ground we sit on was molten porridge, dead when it was ice, dead when the ancestors of these trees first grew, and dead even when most of *them* first grew. All of it has meaning only while I am alive, and meaning in how I can use it. After that it's the same old story. It will change into something I will never know and can't have, and I can't see wanting to have anything to do with *that*. I'm just adapting to what I got right here."

"But what about future generations? If you suddenly decided to burn this forest down or level it because it suited your needs, they'd have nothing to start with. Nothing."

"Nothing, hell," Jorgi went on, treating my question as if it was ridiculous. "I'm only linked to the future genetically, and if I don't make it they don't even get a chance. If this forest doesn't do something necessary for me, then they won't make it at all, and that means if I have to reduce it to plastic in order to survive I'm going to do it. The true nature-lovers in our past are still climbing around the trees in Africa sucking bananas. Either that or we ate them during tough times. The next generation may thank us for taking out a forest because it might make it all the easier for people in the future to stick something else there much more in demand during those times. Like vast cabbage patches. Who knows what tricks nature has in store for us?"

There seemed no end to his screwball arguments, and I felt that it was senseless trying to go on countering him. At the same time, however, I was drawn subtly into Jorgi's misguided funhouse reasoning.

"That's the most screwed-up, selfish idea I've ever heard," I said with as much of a smile on my face as I could stretch under the circumstances of Jorgi's selfishly announced survival tactics. I didn't want to get beat up and thrown out into the night. "There's no reason behind what you're saying," I continued, but before I could say anything more Jorgi jumped right in on top of me.

"Reason, logic? They're the most fucked notions of all."

I felt sure I had overdone it. Jorgi was up and before me gesticulating forcefully, his face a soft red reflection of the heat.

"Magic, that's what you're talking about. Voodoo thoughts cooked up by queer Greeks thousands of years ago. A equals B, B equals C, so C equals A. Word games cooked up by a faggot warrior class sucking off the fat of the land, and teaching young boys how to chuck spears. Neat and tidy thoughts haven't produced a neat and tidy world. It's kinky chaos all around us. Order and harmony in the world are always cooked up by guys from small towns. Athens: population two thousand. Description and use, these are the only meaningful principles. Screw philosophy and ethics and all the other soulless dinks who think the world is not more than it appears to logically be."

He totally lost me. But his enthusiasm seemed to intensify as he talked on and on with his supermarket philosophy. I couldn't really care less about speculating on the nature of the universe. I was having a hard enough time just keeping shoes between my feet and the earth. But I was fully enjoying the energy Jorgi emitted as he did it. At a certain point I realized that I was not engaged in an aggressive argument with another man but was rather the singular member of an audience to whom he performed. I lived up in the woods with no cable television; Jorgi's getting it on with whatever was in his head provided me with a mellow evening. His enthusiasm was attractive. His manner and, I found out later, his schemes crashed right through life. Gusto and zest are its commercial names, but whatever, it enriched the dullish adventure I called life.

For what was I before I met him? A Thoreau without a neurotic fixation for detail, a voice unto myself without notebook stuck away in my tank while the seasons changed about me in a screwy world. Surely at the bottom of my soul there stood some sinister roadsign indicating "All is accident," which kept me from playing in the traffic of life or joining some rural cult of insanity in the nearby woods. I really had no stick of conviction to beat down his nut-pie argument. Perhaps vitality could cut through any mess in which reason despairs. That was what Jorgi seemed to be saying. I took off after him, for he awoke in me the possibility of being able.

The night wore on. Janett fixed us some hot natural apple juice with cinnamon sticks on top of the fire drum and laid Jorgi back a bit by sticking a joint in his mouth in midsentence.

Lorraine needed firewood, but somehow the tranquility of my tank slowly slid under the stern of my brain as Jorgi went on and I basked in his enthusiasm, an enthusiasm I hadn't experienced in a long, long time. Later, in the early morning hours, the three of us talked of whales. Jorgi had a wild idea for watching their migrations along our shore.

"If I could just get the backing," he said enthusiastically, "then I could construct ferrocement boats with huge plexiglass windows below the water line. I'd anchor right in the middle of those gray-whale freeways and run rich whale-watchers out for ten bucks apiece. A string of them all along the California coast, complete with seafood restaurants. It's a natural."

"But the whales only migrate during a limited part of the year," I added skeptically.

"So what? We dump garbage and commodities off the restaurant and the customers watch sharks tear each other to pieces the rest of the time."

By the time he drove me home with my handouts the glow of morning was already in the east and Cassiopeia's chair was to the west of the North Star, eternally hidden to the ancient maid's view by her mirror of stars.

4

THE JOY OF COOKING

We all hope to be more than we are and live interior lives that reinforce those hopes with only the chill reality of money pulling the covers from our sleeping bodies, awakening us to our personal desperate situations.

I had slept long into the afternoon. Little lines of light were shining through the cracks of my shake roof. As I swung myself slowly out of the loft, I noticed several of the little beams illuminating Lorraine's note which I had found nailed to the door when I had returned from Jorgi and Janett's: *Cut wood or cut out.*

After a breakfast of commodities oatmeal and Canned Pork Parts Water Added I felt I had the energy to face her. I walked up to her chicken-coop cabin along the old logging road that ran down through the middle of her property. It was a beautiful afternoon. Robins and bluejays were perched in madrone trees along the way munching on the red-barked trees' slightly intoxicating berries. My feet crunched along through tan oak acorns that lay all over the place. The smell of pitch from green fir medicated my nostrils, but when my landlord and lover's cabin came into sight my stomach did a flip. Zip, Lorraine's little Scotch terrier, came barking out from under her place like a string of exploding firecrackers, but as soon as he got my scent he melted into leaps and licks, practically knocking me off my feet.

Lorraine yelled "Who's there?" and I sang back in as cheerful a voice as I could muster "It's me, baby," but she turned from the door without a hello, leaving it open with just a crack of invitation. I noticed the bareness of her firewood pile, only a few bonelike sticks remaining, as I walked up the redwood stump that was her front porch.

Lorraine stood with her back toward me as I entered. She wore one of her flowing mumus, one with a Chinese print of red silken birds. She was stirring a big pot of noodles on her woodstove, but I took this backside indifference as a signal that perhaps she really missed me and was only afraid or embarrassed to show her true feelings. She had nothing to worry about, though; after several celibate days beating about the county searching for work and standing in welfare lines I was fully prepared to pay my dues. I'd even chop wood again to get the fires going. Lorraine's broad silhouette near the firebox door of her stove warmed me internally and I hurried over to her, putting my arms around her, and gave her what I thought was an affectionate hug.

"Fuck off, Stanley." She quickly moved her arms upward and broke my grasp just as my hands came gently to rest on the large softness of the toasted front of her mumu. I moved back startled—and just in time—for with the hidden quickness of a Sumo wrestler a hot wooden spoon came steaming by the front of my face.

"And don't give me any of that crap about you missed me, Stanley," she screeched, rocking me back on my heels. I upset a large bowl on a table behind me, sticking my fingers into some sort of gooey mess to keep from falling. I ducked under the blow of the second theatrical swing of the spoon and moved in while she was quickly off balance, putting my arms around her solid warm body and kissing her on the neck.

"Screw off, creep." She still hadn't settled down and I pulled back again just in time. All this sham anger and hatred, I was sure, was just a cover for the fact that she had missed the hell out of me and not solid chunks of firewood. Alone with her goats, Lorraine had had no one for several days to pour her heart out to and her unfulfilled emotions had gotten the better of her. I knew if I rode out the storm of discontent I could anchor later in her snug harbor. I retreated to the far corner of the cabin. I was going to have to listen for love.

"Stanley, you're a blood-sucking leech, a bum, a typical male pig. I've baby-sat your ass for nothing. Cooked your meals whenever you decided to show up. You're a threat to the sisterhood."

The last word came hissing out of her mouth like a live cobra, and a venomous cold hit my heart.

"What sisterhood?" I asked in a calm voice.

"The Sisters of Survival, jerk. The women's commune on Albion Ridge dedicated to the protection and propagation of women's rights. I've joined. And the first thing I've learned is that you just can't come jacking off around here treating me like a sex object. I'm a real live human being, Stanley. I've got rights against men."

A den of welfare witches before a bubbly cauldron with screeching children running around in a dry-ice fog flashed through my head. I stopped and scrutinized Lorraine much more closely than when I had first come in, looking for a dried chicken leg or obscene amulet strung around her neck. I noticed nothing except that she was a bit neater and tidier than she had been before and she had made an attempt to do something with her usually disheveled hair with a gay ribbon that pulled it tight behind her skull.

"You mean you've thrown in with the butch town mamas, Lorraine?" I knew it was stupid even before it flowed out of my mouth. Lorraine knew it too, for immediately a cynical "I told you so" suggestion of smile appeared on her lips.

"All right, Lorraine, I know that they are the leftover ladies and children of a disappeared string band and how they've taken care of themselves is great and they aren't dikes, but what does that really have to do with you and me?" I was trying to cover the messy tracks my mouth had made.

"Nothing has to do with me and you, Stanley. You're a goddam oppressive oppressor, or at least you would be if I let you, and the sooner you learn that the better."

I could see that there was no stopping her now. When Lorraine got into something it was always past the point of no return. There was no doubt about it, her life was oppressed, but whose wasn't? While she turned back to her stove to stoke it, I hurriedly ran down my troubles to her, my poverty, my inability to wiggle into the mainstream of life. I even put in a plug for the rest of mankind and told her again about the unfortunate money junkies I had run into at Friendly Finance.

I decided to get the hell out. The tide had receded in my erogenous zone and I was in no mood to refute Lorraine's arguments against the devilish male. I had no reason to find her wrong. She had reduced me in one quick onslaught to the eunuchlike state I had existed in back in the city. I hastened quickly into the main posture of my existence—escape. But I didn't make it.

Her electric command short-circuited my steps. I had hoped to make it to the outside while she ranted on about the plight of women so that I could go hide in the spidery recesses of my tank, contemplating the plight of man, before she had a chance to bring up the subject of money, wood, and work I owed her. She had laid a righteous case of guilt at my feet and it became a ball and chain that prevented me from fleeing. I owed her newfound consciousness at least that much. My continued presence would pay the interest on my debt.

"You've got to learn, Stanley," Lorraine said firmly but with a hint of compassion.

She wanted a sincere talk about our relationship even though I wasn't sure we had one, and in a few minutes the lingering fear of eviction allowed my brain and speech to be mesmerized into "Yes, Lorraine; No Lorraine" as I promised to shape up: cut firewood, reshake her roof, milk her goats when she went to town, tend her compost pile, clean out her springbox, and repair her garden fence the deer had broken down—to all of this I nodded yes in between her declarations of emancipation, equal rights, and the general plight of the world, for which she blamed the male sex. In short, I silently let her believe I consented to the confessions of universal guilt undeniably recorded in the dossier of men. But throughout the whole thing what little was left of my true dignity remained unseparated from the secret compartment in my soul.

Her mood mellowed in direct proportion to my humility. She had me sit down at her gateleg table before the stove and fixed me a pot of tea with the skill of a pharmacist and the flair of a missionary with a soul to save.

"It's Mu tea, Stanley. It goes right to the central nervous sytem to release high-tension nerves."

It tasted like ground rubber tire, but I smiled back my contented approval while she rolled us a couple of organic cigarettes. In a few minutes I did seem calmer, the room warmer, and Lorraine less vitriolic.

She continued to busy herself with conversation, conceding that she didn't hate men at all. "I just want them to join the civilized world to give as well as take from it."

Evening came and Lorraine stoked her stove and left the metal door open so that the flames lit the cabin with a flickering warmth that pervaded my mood, which had become liquid and accepting as the smoke and tea flooded my body.

I watched the flames dance and before the words deciphered themselves in my brain Lorraine was into a totally different subject. Or was it the same one? She was sitting across the dim table from me now, her face reflecting the reds and yellows from the stove. From a drawer in the table she withdrew a thick white book and told me "Stanley, this is the *Recipe of Sex* book. It's a guide to liberated sexual experience. It helps to unlock our souls from the torture society has placed upon our bodies."

The legs of her chair screeched as she slid it on the floor around and next to mine, placing and opening the book before us with her shoulder bumping me from time to time as she turned from page to page.

At first I couldn't see because of the poor light, but soon Lorraine had a candle lit before the pages that were arranged like an expensive cookbook with scroll-like whorls and fancy decorations along the margins and headings. On the cover of the book was an embossed picture of a cornucopia with hundreds of skinny naked men and women streaming forth in a misty dance and heavenlike setting. The "recipes" were mostly pictures that filled the pages with people in various sexual poses topped with a "list of ingredients" captioning the top of the pictures.

At first it looked real good. A warmth that hadn't been there in weeks returned to the center of my body. After having beaten me to the ground with her equal-rights proselytizing, Lorraine now had my eyes lapping up her every turn of the page. There was a naked young male with beard and long hair doing it to a lovely lady with short hair under the recipe of "au naturel" and "service for two." But as the pages fluttered by the diet changed.

"A true total experience of sex," Lorraine said, in a strangely hushed tone that seemed almost to paraphrase the language of the recipes, "a true experience of love comes from inside, the totality of the individual, what we truly are, the oven of the soul."

To which I could say neither nay nor yea, wishing she would turn the page to the chapter on Foreign Desserts.

They were a delight, but then the bill of fare became more elaborate. A Feast of Plenty depicted an orgy with beautiful bodies choreographed in a field of grass and daisies. A section on TV Dinners showed how to perform quickie concoctions on motorcycles, desks, in bathrooms and small cars. More and more as the illustrations leapt off the page the desire in me became stronger to do my own cooking. Lorraine must have felt the same way, for she was nudging me frequently with her shoulder as she turned the pages. However, every time I thought something was funny (like "Crepe de torture," which depicted a tied-up man having to watch his lover masturbate before him), every time I started to laugh at any of the recipes Lorraine's mood would change to lecturer again and she chastised me for profaning the beauty and liberation of the depicted experiences. She explained that the bound man should not feel the woman was his special sexual object that he alone was allowed to manipulate.

Then she turned to Specialities of the Heart: Advanced Psycho-Sexual Therapy; or The Banquet of Being.

"Stanley, baby, you've got to do something for me, for both of us." Her voice had been completely mellowed from that of teacher and was now embellished with cajolery.

"What's that?"

"Stanley, let's get it on in a way that promises complete release, an experience that transcends the normal bounds of sexual relationship, something that liberates the true creative process of our being, immortalizing ourselves against time and sameness. Will you help me, Stanley?"

Hell yes, said my brain, but something inside me made my voice answer with a cautious "Sure, Lorraine, whatever's right." I knew she was borrowing her language from the sex book, but I wasn't sure where she was borrowing her desire. Her voice had taken on a desperate, superserious hushed tone like it was coming from someone other than my crazy Big Lorraine. And before I knew it she had stood up and was pulling her mumu over her head in a passionate tangle of cloth, revealing her two-piece undergarments of thermal underwear while she fumbled with the buttons below her neck.

"Help me," came a muffled voice, and my body quickly changed from passive observation to action. I stood up, thrusting my hands and arms under the mumu until I found her fingers trying to get at the inside-out buttons. She pushed my fingers away with "No, goddam it," and had me hold the mumu over her head instead so that she could have unhindered access to the buttons, which were soon undone. With the mumu off and lying on the floor, Lorraine stood before me like a small erect polar bear in her white thermals. I immediately moved in a blaze of passion and tried to pull the thermal top up and over her large breasts, but her voice pierced my ears with a command of "Hold it, Stanley," which I was trying to do, but my hands slipped up and began feeling her breasts. She unexpectedly pushed me backwards.

"Not yet, dammit." Her voice was harsh and commanding but it quickly changed back to a reasoned seriousness like a teacher reprimanding some over-eager pupil.

"It's not going to be the usual old way. I've told you,

Stanley, what I wanted you to do. Do what I say and the experience will carry us both to our true beings."

She hadn't told me anything. It seemed enough to me that my body wanted to take over.

But she wouldn't allow it. First she had me clear everything off the table we had been sitting at. While I did she consulted the back of the recipe book again and then went over to the shadows next to the woodstove and got something that scared the hell out of me when she came back. In her hand she had a large French knife, the kind that begins with a needlelike point and widens to a broad triangle at the base of the handle. She also had a rope. A flood of castration fears drowned the center of my body and bubbled into my throat. I backed nervously into a chair. Terror filled my heart and my eyes searched for the door, expecting other members of the ritualistic murder cult she had joined to burst forth into the cabin to catch and impale me on the table. I tried to speak but the words solidified in a hundred questions in my throat.

"Now take it easy, Stanley; this experience won't hurt either of us. It will help give us a wholeness we have never known before. Just do what I say and you'll enjoy yourself."

The complete takeover in her voice damped down my fears but the initial shock of the knife and rope was still with me and the afterglow of fear was undoubtedly the reason I was so pliable to her commands. Besides that, having spent a life that never seemed to know exactly where it was at, a life that always expected more than the hand dealt it, I was a complete sucker for cheap thrills.

"People must be allowed to find their metaphor of

love," Lorraine said in a reasoned tone as she stood before me in her long underwear with the knife and rope.

"I have always felt bound down to a soul that quested for release, Stanley. You were never much help—nor any other man, for that matter—with your quick desire to satisfy yourself. I've always been left stranded on the precipice of ecstasy and nobody's had enough push to get me over. That's what we're going to do, Stanley, get me over."

With that she solidly placed her buttocks on the cleared table and carefully handed me the knife and rope, which I had no intention of using, no matter what she told me to do. But my thoughts for her safety and my sanity were soon befuddled by her continuing spiel.

"As a woman, Stanley, I am bound down to my own body." She carefully lay back on the table with her feet and toes protruding over one end. Her voice was taking on a more solemn tone. "Only through releasing that bound body can I escape and break through to a transcending experience. Stanley, I want you to bind that body to this table, tie my arms and legs securely as my sexual soul is tied to my being."

No way, said my brain. But she was so completely intent on what she was doing, theatrically laying her head back and thrusting out her arms and legs in one big twitch It seemed sacrilegious to break her mood. Besides, some hidden urge tingled up and along my spine, spurred on by her broad exposed stomach and deep dark navel that was now revealed between her thermals, spread out on the table before me like an unexpected feast. Reason dictated that I go along with the joke, tie her up, tickle her half to death and split, letting her desire cool through the night with the embers of the woodstove. But as I slipped the rope around her wrists and ankles and secured it to the legs of the table, a strange sensation filled me, a sensation of power.

"How do you feel, honey?" she asked. Her hair was streaming electriclike away from her head over the end of the table.

"Like a freak."

"Don't feel bad. You see, that's so correct. We're freaks to convention, conditioned to revolt against the unusual while all the time that's what we truly desire. These are the very ropes of civilization and culture that bind me."

I had no idea what she was talking about. Alone and stranded in the woods on top of her goddam mountain, it was no wonder she was weird. But her weirdness was deadly infectious and the sight of her now-bound body made me feel strangely confident, much more than I had ever been in her presence before. I hardly had time to think about that since next she told me to take off her clothes, which seemed to be much more where it was at, and my hands started to pull down her drawers and lift her top while my mind tried to figure out how I would get them by the ropes. But almost as soon as I did she yelled, "No," and before I knew it had directed me to *cut off* her undergarments!

"Take the knife, Stanley. Cut my body loose from its earthly clothing, with the sharp edge of the knife up and the cold dull edge of the steel down and along my skin; cut me loose."

I did it. I slipped the knife under the tight thermal band at her ankles and sliced up one leg and then the other; both slits met just below her navel, laying back and exposing all of her body from the waist down as if I were skinning some great sea mammal, exposing its fat warm insulated flesh.

"Now the top," she said, her voice quick and excited. So was I. My brain was short-circuited between fear and delight as the blade slipped delicately up alongside her rib cage, parting the top and exposing her fleshy breasts that hung in rounded folds just over the passing knife. When I finally cut through the collar at the neck I was practically paralyzed with fear seeing her blue jugular vein pulsating. With the last cut I threw the blade to the floor.

At Lorraine's direction I worked on her body half the night, taking off my clothes, massaging her with warm salad oil, making her tingle with light deft swats of a bay-leaf branch; painting her with food-coloring designs, licking clover-flower honey off her kneecap and other delicious places. I did everything asked of me, but each time I tried to join her for the main course I was admonished not to, although she was at my complete mercy. I had power over her, yet I felt as helpless as she was. She had a strange hypnotic control over me, restraining me with words each time I tried to mount the table. "Not yet, jerk, not until I'm ready, not till we're both soaring. No, Stanley, your true release will be in your total control. Deny yourself, help me."

It was as if I were a mad scientist commanded by his own creation. I let myself be directed by her every wish, but the early hours of morning found me increasingly frustrated and both of us more physically exhausted than contented with the promised ethereal heights. The first light of dawn shone on my cold ass as I tried to stoke the stove while Lorraine shivered on the table, having just had her body turned a horrid pink with a demanded bath of ice-cold spring water "to better experience and contrast the inner glow that is beginning to spread from the core of my existence," she said. But I was truly dogged. I couldn't hold back any longer. I quickly joined her against her protest for a cold breakfast of her body, having a hell of a time not sliding off its slippery chill. It was all over before she had a chance to yell "son of a bitch" a second time, but I was so tired I could have cared less. I hurriedly dressed against the chill, cut her arms and legs loose after making her swear not to try anything, and got the hell out of there back on the trail to my cabin hunched over Quasimodolike in gloom, exhausted, and mentally shrunk into the small proportion of a creep.

5

HARVESTING THE SEA

I was elated when Jorgi told me that we would become fishermen. I was performing only the most perfunctory of chores for Lorraine, chopping wood, and then only when she was away from her cabin so that she couldn't pin me like a butterfly to her organic piece of the earth. She had very little to say to me after I had fouled up her recipe of love. Besides, I had my own wood to cut, for each fall day brought a night more chilled than the one before it. Most of my time was spent at Jorgi and Janett's or roaming the beaches of the county kicking at bits of driftwood and watching the waves beat themselves senseless on rock and sand. There were no whales in sight, although their promised southern migration should have passed any day now. The sea seemed gray and wintry even when the sun shone on it. I had totally given up on a job. Ours was a county of seasonal employment, and even the loggers were cast adrift by the wet woods to punch themselves silly in the numerous bars that thrived in the towns.

"We'll harvest the sea, Stanley" was what Jorgi said. I would have harvested the snows of Mount Everest had he suggested it, so desperate was my financial situation.

Abalone. One of nature's strange creatures. A huge oval shell placed in the sea like an upside-down ashtray full of sweet white meat and, fortunately for Jorgi's scheme, protected on our north shores by the Department of Fish and Game. The commerical abalone operation in the southern part of the state had been all but wiped out by a hundred years of overfishing by first the Japanese and then our own industrious fishermen, followed by the coup de grace in the form of one frail little woman, Mrs. G. Trumbell Black, wife of the late founder of our state's largest banking system.

Mrs. Black, from her lofty estate and perch on the cliffs of Big Sur, fell in love with the elusive and thought-to-be extinct sea otter whose fur once graced the neck of European royalty. Through her efforts with the state legislature she succeeded in closing one area along the southern coast after another as sea otter sanctuaries, slowly backing the professional abalone divers into smaller and smaller areas, for the little seagoing furballs' favorite diet was abalone. The price of abalone went up at Fisherman's Wharf and in all the other fine seafood restaurants surrounding the yacht harbors of our state, and the abalone fishermen and their families were forced off the sea and onto unemployment rolls, helped somewhat by their own actions and the publicity Mrs. Black received through the media as a result of the massacre of thirty-one sea otters by angry divers beneath the cliffs of her villa. The whole event was seen in our state as the first instance of establishment and youth getting back together: through her efforts several protest marches were staged around the Morro Bay plant of the El Morro Shellfish and Oyster Company, a leading abalone buyer. Three abalone boats were burned at the docks and several junior-college students were badly beaten by the divers, but the good fight prevailed and ecology won out. The otters were saved, the divers all but eliminated. Jorgi's idea was to steal the abs off the rocks of the forbidden Mendocino Coast where they were virtually dying of old age one on top of the other "to feed the hungry mouths of the rich," he said, for abalone was strictly in the realm of the gourmet belly at $7.95 a pound or $45 a dozen on the black market. His plan was simple enough. We would pry them off the rocks during low tide after dark in hidden coves along the coast.

We, or I should say he, worked furiously at his dome for several days before the great poaching scheme got under way. Jorgi was all over the place and Janett and I more or less just handed him things as he put garden hose, pipes, ropes, sacks, an old paint compressor, wires, and a naked sealed beam headlight out of one of the Cadillacs together in the back of the pickup. None of it made any sense to me as his raw native ingenuity screwed and tied, connected and cut away. He was insulated in his creative drive and oblivious to the fall chill that had come to the woods. Millipedes had emerged from the ground and were crawling with shiny backs over the wet junk and car parts, chased by Jorgi and Janett's chickens, whose feathers had taken on a thick, full look in anticipation of the coming winter. One or two rains had fallen and solidified the dust of sum-

mer. The woods were fresh; leaves of deciduous trees
had turned and fallen, revealing the stark cleanness of
branches and limbs. Each deep breath swelled the body
with air chilled ever so slightly to create an almost
pleasant pain around the edges of the lungs. Winter's
gloom was undoubtedly on the way but everything was
cleared away, exposed, trimmed of summer's opulence,
ready to face nature's worst—as was I, now that Jorgi
was leading me in a plan for survival.

Jorgi worked on the fishing gear furiously for three
days and during that time I was of little help to him. He
repaired an old paint compressor. Piled up coils and
coils of garden hose, and at one point I helped him
extract his head from a large warm pan of plaster of Paris
in which a death-mask image of his face remained.

"What's that got to do with fishing?" I ventured.

"It's a mask, stupid, to make me look like a fish so I'll
stay hidden from the abs. Before they know it, I'll have
their ass."

Later he used the plaster-of-Paris mold of his face as a
foundation for pouring and constructing a fiberglass
mask into the front of which he molded a circular piece
of safety glass, using one of Janett's pie pans as a
template. Where the chin and mouth should have been
on the front of the diving mask he molded in a regulator.
When it was finished he put it on his head and moved
about testing it, a Cyclops of the junkyard. Air hissed
from his head as he walked through his stranded
Cadillacs.

Jorgi's pragmatic insanity had little room in it for me,
so while he worked I helped Janett.

Janett wasn't always easy to get next to. To someone
who didn't know her, her manner seemed one of

reserved hostility. But this wasn't true at all. On the first day I felt like mother's little helper, for she was busy canning and I made myself useful by preboiling jars and wiping lids at her direction. Janett was efficient. While Jorgi worked on his harebrained scheme outside, inside she put away a delicious larder of stewed tomatoes, pickled eggs, string beans, and various other staples that would see them through the winter no matter what happened to our plans. She and Lorraine were polar opposites. Janett's life seemed more ruled by reality and a rational practicality. At first I thought that she was simply a farm girl grown up, but I was wrong. In fact, it was the opposite. Janett came from a well-to-do family on Long Island and had spent her youth in expensive schools and travels until one day she met Jorgi and left with him for the wilds of California, much to the consternation of her family. She was blunt about the whole thing as she related her love affair with Jorgi next to the steaming pressure cooker.

"They were not 'big money,'" she said, as she energetically stirred a pot of boiling tomatoes, "but my parents were more than comfortable. We always had what we needed and a whole lot more. When I met Jorgi, since he had never been around any kind of money I think that he took my comfortable background as one of true wealth, and it was something that worried me for a while after I first ran off with him. But he stayed with me even after I received absolutely nothing from my parents ever again. We love each other and we're totally on our own in this world. At the time I was all set to marry a promising young psychologist and spend the rest of my life in comfortable urban therapy."

Janett seemed much more down to earth to me than my Big Lorraine, in spite of the fact that Lorraine was always making a fuss about getting down to earth in one way or the other. Janett took life as it came and stepped out smartly against all tasks. She was an intelligent first-string woman, and although I knew she loved Jorgi I also sensed that he and his schemes didn't control her destiny. They each had their own canoe as they paddled in tandem down the river of life. As usual I felt like a spectator on the bank as they busied themselves at their respective tasks, Jorgi inventing weird paraphernalia to capture and kill life and Janett cooking and canning to sustain it. I was of little enough help to either one, especially on the second day when several of Janett's country-cousin girlfriends showed up for quilting.

They arrived early in the afternoon while I was testing the vacuum seal on a batch of pickled zucchini and Janett was presteaming fresh corn. Jorgi was outside experimenting with his diving apparatus. In his black wet suit he looked like a phantom in a bowl of spaghetti: he was sitting in a huge pile and snarl of garden hose trying to coil it into some sort of order.

It was truly a raid by the maternity brigade. Janett was "quilt mother." Apparently she and all of her girlfriends who lived in their neck of the woods would get together periodically to make a quilt for one of their number who was pregnant. But after they got situated on her dome floor, spreading their brightly colored materials before them, and proceeded to quilt away, they reminded me more of a hot-rod club, except instead of talking about sleek or fast cars they discussed skinny or plump babies, maternity dates, missed periods, pills, diaphragms, diaper rash, breast-feeding, and a host of other reproductive topics.

I found myself pinned between two of Janett's friends, one of whom was demonstrating how to nurse correctly by switching her little bundle of flesh and bone from teat to teat, showing me how each breast shrank in size during feeding. The large woman on the other side of me was wiping vomit off her little baby peek-a-boo's face. If there was a national program to limit population Janett's friends definitely didn't give a shit about it. I know they didn't, because after being around me for a couple of canning days Janett was quickly attuned to my likes and dislikes and sensed a certain revulsion with all the reproduction madness that surrounded me. Sure that I was within hearing, she told one of her quilting mamas as they stitched away that "the people that breed together succeed together," but I was on my way out into the safety of the yard to escape their babyland madness and diaper jingoism.

Jorgi was sitting and sweating in his wet suit on the back end of his pickup truck with an inner tube looking like a giant black doughnut resting across his lap. He was lacing an open sack to the inner tube with gray clothesline.

"Stanley, do you know how an abalone breeds?"

I confessed that I hadn't the slightest notion.

"It's the dumbest fuck in the world. They sit sucking away at a rock eating seaweed and every once in a while when the mood moves them they release sperm or eggs into the ocean and hope for the best. Can you imagine? It would be like for you or me to stick our cocks through the porthole of a 747 at 40,000 feet and hope to fertilize a woman somewhere on the earth below."

"No, I can't imagine it," I said. "I can't even figure out why I should care."

"Well, because," he went on in a tone that implied I showed a complete lack of awareness, "dumb fuckers like that, animals so low on the order of love, must be the stupidest things in God's creation, and that should make them all the easier for us to catch."

I was glad when the night of the third day came. I was starting to feel like a useless domestic hanging out with Janett's jars and baby-crazed ladies. It was early evening and we had just finished a commodities omelette, fresh eggs with a side of fried farina full of onions, covered with a yellow coat of shiny hot U.S. Donated Butter. Jorgi was consulting a tide book and sketching our plan of attack on the back of a paper bag. A place called Cuffy's Cove was our target area. With a note of conspiracy in his voice Jorgi explained what we were supposed to do.

"We drive, lights out, off the highway through the Catholic cemetery on the north end of Elk, through a hayfield, up a rise in the ground, and down right to the edge of the cliff. The cove's below us. Stanley, you're my lifeline and sack man. Janett, you're on the truck. I take the gear and go over the cliff; Stanley, you follow. We hit the beach, I wade out into head-high water, we switch on the light, I vacuum up the abs by prying them off the rocks with a tire iron, you pull them in, and we're rich."

I turned to Janett, thinking it would be proper for her to be the one to tell him he was insane. The look on her face scared me as much as his plan. Her eyes were set immovably back in their sockets, a faint smile of satisfaction betrayed her lips. She was nuts, too. There was no way I was going to drop over a cliff at least a hundred and fifty feet high in the dark to get drowned on a deserted beach. I would have split if Jorgi hadn't anticipated my fear.

"Man, you have got to be one of the faithful," he said. "You don't righteously believe in yourself enough to dare the different, get it all together, and take on reality. It's life you live and life alone. Your blood's too thick; thin it out," he went on, but the only blood I could see was mine splattered all over black seaweedy rocks lapped up by sea anemones. Jorgi was not calling me chicken, for if he had I would have split right there and then, since it was already an established fact in my mind that I was. I think he sensed that. His message went deeper and he knew it. He was calling me out of the woods and the lonely cabin of my soul into the world where a multitude of chance could shatter my very being and project it into a life that I could feel. Adventure therapy if you will, but more than that. It struck me for the first time in my life, as the two of them stared at me awaiting my answer, that perhaps after all, my own logic, that reasonableness itself was unreasonable to the organism that had to endure it. Besides, I needed the money.

A few hours later I helped Jorgi climb into his black wet suit as Janett sprinkled and rubbed cornstarch over his naked body. We piled into the truck to take on the Pacific Ocean. Jorgi sat between Janett and me looking like the creature from a bottle of blackstrap molasses. The only protection I wore from whatever wet fate awaited me was the clothes on my back and a heavy woolen sweater. It was very dark out now. Janett drove and Jorgi kept his mouth shut over the roar of the muffler as we headed through the woods down to the coast. I began to hope that perhaps he would have second thoughts and we'd turn around and all drive back to the dome and get loaded, but we didn't.

We hit Highway 1 and found that the dark night was further compounded by the thick fog that had crept up from the sea, covering the town of Elk as we cruised through it seeing only a dim light here and there in a couple of houses. It was one in the morning. At the north end of town the fog was so thick that we had to slow down to a crawl to find the gate on the edge of the cemetery, which we drove through, switching off our lights and sending my brain into vertigo swirls as we bumped over the black field that led to the cliff and the cove. Janett found the way. She stopped the truck and Jorgi slid behind the wheel while she climbed up onto the bumper and hood like some banshee we had impaled in the mist. Her back was hardly visible to us in the reflection of the headlights as her eyes felt out our path in front of us. She banged on the hood—once for left, twice for right, and then a metallic staccato as we eased up to the edge of the cliff. I heard the ocean before I saw it, as way down below us in the fog the waves gargled over the rocks through the throat of the inlet.

The descent was a hideous experience for me, but I followed the leader after Jorgi, who with rope in hand and coils of garden hose about his body slipped over the side and descended to the beach below. Luckily, when he tugged the rope to signal that he had landed and for me to follow, I found at first that the cliff was not a sheer ninety-degree drop but rather a rocky, shaly, rootsy seventy-five, which I felt out with my sliding ass as I let the rope slip cautiously through my fingers. The rest was a nightmare. The last ten feet was a sheer dropoff where the sea had eaten away the cliff, and Jorgi's voice was already coming up to me before I hit bottom with something about "Man, this tide won't wait." Out of one of the sacks I had tied to my waist he pulled a flashlight. The lens was covered with thick red cellophane. He clicked it on, illuminating both of us in a dull fire-glow aurora of light in the mist.

We were standing on a little rocky beach. Two steps forward to the surging water, two steps back to the cliff. My body was already numb with the cold. Next, Jorgi took out his breathing mask, the grotesque fiberglass face piece with the pie-plate window in front. He attached the garden hose to it and then pulled out the car headlight sealed in a waterproof box and attached it to a cord wound around his air hose. He gave three tugs up the rope to Janett; moments later I heard the sound of the small gas engine on the compressor waterfalling down the cliff, which was followed by a hiss coming out of the mask. An instant later the sealed-beam light came on as Janett attached its cord to the truck battery high above us. Satisfied that it worked, Jorgi quickly snapped it off but it had in that quick instant floodlighted the two of us and the absurd situation we had climbed down into. How could I have done this to myself? The sound of the surf, hidden by the dark and fog, exploded nearby. I expected a wall of water to obliterate us from the surface of the earth at any second.

Jorgi's red face, illuminated by the flashlight, came close to mine and he whispered over the hiss, "Stay cool, Stanley. Two tugs you pull in the rope and abs, one on the hose means throw the sack back, three on the rope means the line is fouled, and four tugs on anything means my ass is stuck. One short tug—that's goodbye forever." And with that he sort-of wheezed a chuckle from out of his chest, constricted by the suit, and placed the mask on his head, fastening it on the sides with strips of inner tube, which gave him an even weirder Medusa appearance. He slapped the red flashlight in my hand and waded out toward the depths. He must have already been chest-high when the sealed beam came on underwater.

Failure lies in the conception, however heroic the action. I was up to my knees in ice water. I couldn't see, slipping over seaweed onto knees and elbows down into the living primordial slime itself as I followed my heroic sea king to disaster, demonstrating to myself that one thing and one thing alone in the whole conscious universe proves that we are real and not just a conception of our brains—pain.

I slipped and twisted in the dark. My clothes clung to my body like cold, wet cement. I went down and was wedged between rocks and tidepools until cold surges of water rocketed me up again as I dimly followed a light out in front of me emanating from underwater where Jorgi harvested the sea, somehow swimming or sliding like a snake over the rocks.

Two strong jerks came telegraphing along the rope and I strained and slid as I tried to pull in the sack, but the harder I pulled the closer I advanced toward the depths, for it was as if I were trying to pull the sea bottom inside out. In my straining I lost track of Jorgi's light. He had either gone farther out or around an underwater ledge or rock, and a shiver of panic raised the hairs on my frozen back as a vision of me pulling in his drowned body flashed across my eyes. I was going to be an accessory to suicide.

He must have tugged and tugged at the rope, giving the signal to throw back the sack, and when it never came he surfaced with that weird light of his illuminating the whole cove. He switched it off, yelling as he did, "Goddam it, it's a bonanza out here! Throw the sack, throw the sack!" But I didn't, for I never got it in, and when I yelled that back to him, he came splashing and cursing ashore to give me a hand.

An abalone has to be the most docile, simplistic of nature's creations, two pounds of meat and guts served in a half shell for the predators of the world to simply pluck from the rocks. But with neither tails, eyes, legs, teeth, jaws, nor arms, they were putting up quite a fight, because the harder we pulled the more the sack seemed to resist our efforts. I was up to my waist in water; Jorgi was pulling with me and mumbling dollar signs about their worth when the first freezing wave of the incoming tide swept over us in the dark, filling my throat with a painful salt taste.

That was it for me. "Come on back," Jorgi yelled. "We'll use the tide to bring these babies ashore," but I was gone, pulling myself out of the rocks and up to the cliff where on my hands and knees my stomach tried to convulse that portion of the ocean still swirling around inside me.

We struggled through the rest of the night, letting the tide slowly bring the bulging sack ashore, taking up the slack each time a wave came crashing in till by the dawn's light spreading its first gray glow through the fog above us we had the sack of abs up against the cliff with the water not far behind.

"Jorgi, let's get out of here. The hell with these scrambled fishburgers, let's save ourselves," I yelled, but he wouldn't quit, and by the time the morning was completely upon us, breaking through the fog with religious-looking rays, he had Janett slowly backing through the field above with the rope tied to the front bumper towing the sack, hose, and us up the cliff with the power of the old Chevy truck.

"We've got 'em now, Stanley," he yelled as he guided our stolen bounty up from the sea. "There's almost a hundred abs in there, three or four hundred dollars! We're rich!"

There is no such thing as a sleepy little town. Who knows what blunted desires breed the closet insomniacs that lurk in the quiet places of America?

They were on us before we knew it, on us while we clung shivering to the rope halfway up the cliff. And they were wild, shouting and yelling "private property," "thieves," sticking their heads and shoulders over the edge cautiously, hurling insults at us. But their threats of beating and death meant nothing to me in the face of the fact that they had apprehended Janett, which left us hung up above the real thing—the crashing, drowning sea below us.

Of course, later it was written up in a much more exaggerated manner in the *Mendocino Beacon,* the weekly put out by the next berg north of Elk—STRANGE LIGHTS FLASHING UNDERWATER, TRESPASSERS PLUNDER GAME REFUGE, ASSAULT ON A PUBLIC SERVANT, all of it designed to prejudice our court case. The public-servant thing was the biggest lie of all.

He stood on the cliff's edge above us and shouted the loudest in his green uniform. It was the game warden, gesticulating wildly down at us. Jorgi couldn't take it any longer; he leaned back on the rope and, half-rising off

---

65

the steep slope, yelled back up at the crowd of outraged citizenry and the warden, "If you want our asses, you'll have to haul us up." Instinctively I ducked, expecting a barrage of rocks or worse to come blasting down at us. But after a few silent moments they took his suggestion and I could feel movement along the rope, slowly at first and then solid as they all got into it, hauling us up like two flies caught on one slender strand of web.

Christ, I thought, Jorgi was going crazy. As soon as the first tugs started us back up to the safety of the mob, he pulled a knife out of the scabbard strapped to his leg and in one dizzy flash I thought we were going to make our getaway with a suicidal slash at our lifeline and plunge downward. But Jorgi only cut the rope below us, and like a lead ball our plunder and the main sack of evidence went shooting back to the sea where it came from. It was in that instant of cutting loose that Game Warden Glover was injured. He hadn't been pulling on the rope but was keeping an eye on us from above when Jorgi made his move, and the moment he realized what Jorgi was up to he waved his arms and yelled at us—leaning out too far, slipping off balance, and hurtling over the edge, where he tumbled and rolled right at us in a swirl of dirt and rock.

If he hadn't hit us and if Jorgi hadn't held on to him, he would have followed after the sack and with an arm fractured in three places would have been no match for the sea and incoming tide below.

The rest was an unbelievable legal hassle that at times had me feeling I would never have to worry about money again as I stamped out license plates forever in the state penitentiary.

We pleaded our own case—or rather Jorgi did.

His reasoning was this: The three of us together couldn't raise enough money for an attorney for even one of us and the public defender was a thrill-seeking idealist whom Jorgi had once seen at the Apple Fair in Boonville taking a turn at wild-horse riding.

"He's one of those dropout lawyers picking up on an alternative lifestyle here in the woods, bored to death handling the Friday-night fistfights of drunk loggers," Jorgi said. "He'd jump at our case—but only if he could make something more out of it, like poor hips versus the straights of Elk. He's a nature-lover; we'd only be a side issue to him. In his soul he'd never forgive us for upsetting the ecology and plundering the shoreline. Secretly he's got politics on his brain, subverting the system from within. We could get lost in the shuffle of his fantasies."

Jorgi felt that the only way to win our case was to play it straight, have nothing to do with the public defender or the welfare rights law commune, which was another alternative. "We've got to seem right out front, stick to the same basic lies straightaway, and hope for technicalities."

Which is what we did.

Justice was swifter than I thought. We were only out on bail for three weeks before the hearing and trial came up, and during that short time the people of Elk turned their thoughts away from the underwater invasion hysteria. I saw Jorgi and Janett only once or twice because the truck and all its equipment had been impounded as evidence and I spent most of my time outside my cabin in the surrounding woods and clearings stalking the wild mushrooms that were resurrecting themselves from the earth after the first rains of October. There were a few blueberries left on the bushes and one morning down near the road a valley quail chased by a red-tail hawk struck a barbed wire fence in midflight, exploding in a puff of feathers and breaking its neck. The roast quail, stuffed with wild mushrooms and glazed lightly with the blueberries, was a welcome relief from my usual fare of starchies from the government. However, this gastronomical diversion was the only mild relief I had from the nagging paranoia that hung low like a tule fog, diffusing itself through my soul as thoughts of slammed barred doors and locked handcuffs rattled in my brain. I stayed away from everyone during that time, even Big Lorraine, letting my hermit's nature get the best of me, perhaps preparing myself for the worst.

But it was okay.

Jorgi stood there looking up at the judge with Janett and me right behind him. There was no jury. Jorgi decided that ".we'll let it all go on one roll, waive the jury bit. We might suck one egg but not a dozen."

In a way, Americans are such saps for initiative and the appearance of integrity. Jorgi admitted right out that our intentions had been to get some abalones. He took full credit; in fact he delighted in admitting he had invented all the outlandish equipment that was now in the court's hands and spread out on a table before us like items in a garage sale.

"But, Your Honor, we did it because the wilderness is disappearing; it's all private property, which is all right with me; it's just that all of the good old out-of-doors places where people can go to hunt and fish are locked up." Jorgi had guessed right as he stood there as sincere and honest as a Protestant converting in the face of the Inquisition—the judge was a sportsman too. And when

Jorgi got down to the "our foolishness didn't even pay off, sir," I saw in a flash that the private-property thing had only been smoke. "Your Honor, we did not take one creature from that beach except for ourselves, and even at that when Game Warden Glover apprehended us we were still well below the mean high-tide mark, if you count the waves of winter that bust up that cliff. We were still on state property, not private."

That was it. The breath I had been holding for three weeks finally exhaled when the judge finished dismissing Jorgi and me. Assault charge dropped, for without the evidence, Game Warden Glover's broken arm in the line of duty was something he'd have to figure out by himself with Workmen's Compensation. Fishing without a license dropped. The taking of mollusks out of season dropped. And, except for Janett, trespassing on private property dropped, because when they got us we weren't on private property. Since she was with the truck she was fined fifty dollars or five days for trespassing. Jorgi visited her during her second day in jail when he went to get the truck back.

Expecting a release and victory party on the fifth day as Jorgi promised, I hitched over to their dome to find nothing but screams and sobs coming from the interior. I beat a hasty retreat back to my neck of the woods. I returned the next day and found that all apparently had been forgiven. They were frolicking in the nude, taking advantage of the short burst of Indian summer, throwing chicken feed at one another around the old Cadillacs. The noise of the tiny pellets striking the metal was interspersed with delighted shrieks. They waved to me and went right on playing.

6

FALSE SPRING AND
CABIN FEVER

False spring arrived. It was already late November, but grass was sprouting everywhere, making oak trees in the hillside meadows look like masts on old-time sailing vessels at anchor in a green sea, their branches denuded of leaves, their bare yardarms reaching up to a spacious blue sky. Already into the fall, a warm deception had spread over the county. Several blossoms appeared on my plum tree, the swimming hole under the Navarro Bridge was daily filled with naked bodies who should have been laying away cords of fir and redwood for the impending rains. Big Lorraine had begrudgingly forgiven me, and we got together once or twice, but for the most part I still hung around Jorgi and Janett as much as possible in spite of our fiasco with the abalones. A few cedar shingles needed replacing on the top of my tank, but I never got around to doing it. I secretly hoped Jorgi would come up with some scheme or idea that would send us once more out to do battle with life. The profit I hadn't realized was nothing compared to the turn my own existence had taken during those past few months. I was infected with a lack of stability and it felt good.

The Arcadian concept, an ideal landscape inhabited by simple, virtuous people, is derived from Virgil. In my tank I had a lot of junk books which I had purchased at the People's Trade Fair held monthly at the old school-grounds over near Albion. They went for ten cents a pound, and what I didn't read I used to start my morning fire. In his *Eclogues* Virgil has the lovesick Gallus say, "Arcadians, you will sing my frantic love for Phyllis to your mountains, you alone who know how to sing; for you have cool springs, soft meadows, and groves. Among you I shall grow old now that an insane love enchains me, and in the forest amidst the dens of wild beasts carve the story of my loves on the tender bark of trees; as they grow so shall my loves." It's a great idea so long as you've got the money. We didn't, and as a consequence spent several weeks looking for space-age metals, as Jorgi called them.

"It's bound to be all over the place," Jorgi said. "Throughout these woods there are piles of lead and copper. You take one ounce of lead, cover it with copper, and you have your basic bullet. The war used up zillions of them. It's as good as gold, Stanley, fifty cents a pound for the lead and up to seventy-five for the copper."

We blasted about the woods in the pickup with crowbars searching for abandoned homesteads and logging camps, hoping to salvage as much scrap metal as we could. We tore into old walls for the lead in the plumbing but discovered for the most part vicious nests of bees and spiders. Most of the abandoned mills had already been picked clean by bottle collectors, a strange cult then sweeping the West—largely straight and acquisitive by nature and driven by a curiosity for finding something that contains nothing. We could always tell when they had reached a site before us. The old latrines and outhouses were pitched over and unearthed sometimes down to bedrock, for it was this cult's belief that old-timers spent most of their time getting loaded on the john, pitching empty double-eagle bourbon and ceramic beer bottles into the void below. The best we did on the copper was not at an old lumber camp at all but rather at a lookout post on a coastal mountain called Peek-a-Boo Top. It had been manned in World War II by the Coastal Defense forces on guard against low-flying Kamikaze planes. The walls of several cement bunkers were filled with copper wire encased in conduit. We beat and chipped a hard profit out of the concrete. Finally the axle on the truck broke trying to pull down two miles of old telephone cable that stretched from the coast road up to the bunkers atop Peek-a-Boo. I was glad it was over. There had to be an easier way to make a buck in the woods.

Jorgi brooded. It took days for him to repair the axle on the truck and during that time, except for handing him a tool he growled for from under the truck, there was very little communication between him and me.

Janett spent most of the time inside the dome industriously baking bread, canning blackberry preserves, and pickling mushrooms, adding them to a glittering glass-jar winter larder that occupied an entire shelved wall on the kitchen partition.

Finally thinking that I had said or done something wrong, I asked Janett as she made bread, "What's bugging Jorgi?"

"Himself, that's all, Stanley. I love him, but sometimes he's a complete asshole like that. He won't talk to anyone, not even me, for days. He broods and tinkers and dabbles at meaningless jobs and it's impossible to approach him."

"But you must have some idea of what's on his mind. You're the closest person in the world to him."

Janett looked up from the counter near the woodstove, her hands thick with a gooey tan mass of dough she was strenuously kneading.

"Stanley, as far as I know, Jorgi's biggest problem is just like your biggest problem. He's broke, you're broke. We're all broke. We've all flown to the woods to find paradise, checked out of cities because we know down deep in our hearts that something was disastrously wrong there, that sooner or later it was all going to come apart. We wanted to be survivors, to find ourselves in nature, not at the end of a food line eating the leftover garbage trucked to us from the cities we've tried to escape. Wake up, Stanley. Just about everyone you've met since you've been here—I mean just about everyone who has got it all together with a little house and garden in the woods and lets it be known to you that they are living off the land or groving with nature or such crap—all of them are doing so because someone has a rich relative somewhere else. It's hard for Jorgi to accept this, especially since he has so much more brains and energy than the average homespun millionaires that surround us. Penniless pioneering can be a real bum trip. The unemployment in the woods is twice what it was back in the city. You're either rich or on welfare. Never before have such opposite groups of people lived so close together. Three of the women in my Sufi class have trusts of well over a hundred thousand dollars. Fifteen hundred acres right next to our three were just bought by a young couple who are heirs to the Seagram whiskey fortune."

Everything that Janett said was making me both agitated and despondent at the same time, but she had remained calm throughout, kneading and pounding her bread. I felt very sympathetic to Jorgi's bad mood; I was beginning to feel the same for myself. I was beginning to wonder how Janett could remain so serene about a situation we shared, but before I could say anything she went on.

"Listen, Stanley, since you've already gotten me all wound up, you might as well know I'm pregnant. I know the world is full of people and intelligent people aren't supposed to breed, but I'm twenty-nine years old and I want the child. It's put Jorgi in a bad spot. He knows what I want, and I think deep down inside himself he wants it too. He's complained several times that only the idiots are breeding any more on the planet, but I knew it was just his way of saying he wanted a kid. The only thing wrong about the thing is the economics of the situation. We're broke and he's desperately trying to come up with something. I refuse to go down on my knees to Aid to Dependent Children, skimping along beholden to our own offspring's existence for one hundred and forty dollars a month. There's got to be something better. I don't know how he'll work it out, but I've already made my decision about keeping the baby."

I didn't know whether to congratulate or console her. All I know was when she said "I've already made my decision" she smiled directly into my face and I saw a maternal force there that made me turn away.

Janett's confiding in me filled me with a mood of well-being and I attempted to spread it around by confronting Jorgi directly to see if there wasn't some way in which I might console or help him with his ideas.

"Jorgi," I asked when he finally pulled himself out from under the truck, "what's eating you?" I expected to see him respond with a face indulging itself in my sincere sympathy for his condition. Instead he turned on me with "What you don't understand about living, Stanley, is that everything's a trip. When I'm up, that's cool, everything's an ease of energy, but when that runs out and I'm down I dig that too. I like being bored, depressed, lazy, and moody; it's healthy, it lets my tissues rest and my batteries recharge. My brain gets washed out and I figure out where I made my wrong moves. When that plays out, I'm up again, using all you level heads of the world to freeway over."

With my failure in client-centered brotherly love I left him to his turgid masochistic therapy and didn't see him for several days. I last saw him mounting the roof of one of his stranded Cadillacs, where he sat half-heartedly taking small pebbles out of his Levi jacket, tossing them at his foraging chickens plucking about the ground beneath him.

Internally I know I was offended, I who had tended his lifeline and substantiated his lies in court. Cast out, I retreated to my tank, sought solace in Big Lorraine, and made the mistake of waking up in her coop after a night of rather uninspired and half-hearted lovemaking. Perhaps it was the fact that my continuous companionship for the past months with Jorgi and Janett had infected me with a desire for continued human companionship, but whatever, I paid dearly for my need. Lorraine, sensing my pensiveness and put off with our night's labors, immediately with the first rays of morning sun began an effort to cultivate me as she did her vegetables.

"Stanley," she said, trying to fertilize my soul with her organic philosophy, "what you lack is a righteous diet." And with that she pulled from her bookcase filled with volumes of the *Organic Gardener* a slim purple hardbound book entitled *The Perfumed Garden of the Shaykh Nefzawi.*

For breakfast she fed me a small bowl of very thick honey accompanied by twenty almonds and an even one hundred pine nuts that she counted out of a Mason jar while glancing occasionally into *The Perfumed Garden.* My gums still felt like they had been bathed in turpentine when at lunchtime I was fed green peas boiled carefully with onions, powdered cinnamon, ginger, and cardamoms. My nausea had hardly worn off late in the afternoon when she approached with *The Perfumed Garden* still in her hands, mumbling more to herself than to me, "It says here to rub the virile member with asses' milk or the marrow of the hump of a camel, but since there isn't any of that stuff around here I'm sure a goat will do just as good. Hold on, baby." She split for the goat shed with a plastic bucket and I got myself together and slipped back to my tank, wondering what the consequences would be if Lorraine and I ever created a child.

False spring disappeared one night as I awoke to the sound of rain splattering my roof. It didn't stop for two weeks. On the first day I felt very woodsy, toasting my feet up against the woodstove, sipping hot chocolate laced with carefully measured amounts of bourbon out of a bottle I had saved for winter's first onslaughts. The second day I read some of the junk books and looked out the window at my soggy woodpile. The third day my body felt the strain of inactivity and I did exercises, chinning myself on a loft beam fourteen times in succession. On the fourth day I noted the first signs of a serious attack of stir-crazy. For lack of anything else to do I was bringing firewood into the cabin and splitting it in half and then those two pieces in half and so on until my hatchet would come swinging down through the air at a sliver of wood held delicately with my fingers, which I pulled away at the last moment before the hatchet hit the balanced wood. I entertained myself with the tingling thrill that spread from the palms of my hands through my wrists and up my arm. Fearing that on the fifth day I might progress to actual self-mutilation, I awoke early and tramped through the spongy woods to Lorraine's.

She was entertaining Michael Smith, the local mushroom freak. As far as I was concerned he was totally suicidal. He went about the woods with coffee cans collecting bits and pieces of the Aminita Mascara dimunitive, hemlock roots, and God knows what else in search of an organic and cheap high. When I saw him there I must admit that I was jealous, an emotion I thought I never would be able to experience in relation to Lorraine. I knew I was being punished for running out on her five days before. Michael had a Jesuslike face, thin and dark, but very short hair, almost a crew cut, which also gave him a sort of concentration-camp appearance. His face and neck, every time I saw him, were scratched or healing with long thin scabs that were undoubtedly wounds from branches and blackberry vines. Michael was often seen careening through the woods on foot in various stages of nudity, screaming and babbling "in tongues," as he called it. At any rate, I returned to my tank and faced up to my isolation rather than brave his dares to dip into his coffee can. He and Lorraine both looked like they had just arrived from another planet anyhow. I split some more wood, banked the fire, finished off the bourbon, and drearily settled myself away in my tank hoping I would pass out before nature's incessant damp pounding on my roof and skull drove me bughouse. Screw Thoreau.

7

THE WHALE

Salvation came early the following morning. I was awakened by Jorgi's repaired pickup spinning and sliding up my road, its engine revving and gunning wildly.

He could hardly contain himself.

"This is it, Stanley; get your ass moving. We are gonna make it. No more rotting abalones, or junk metal. This is it, real American money. I've found the white whale, baby."

All the fiction in the world I believe is but a heroic attempt to blunt and dull reality—an ass-backwards theory, I realize—but one from that moment on, and forever, I will always believe.

Jorgi was back in his truck almost as soon as he had gotten out, assuming I'd be right behind him plunging, without question into his latest scheme. And he was right; there was really no decision about it. The physical security of my tank and the tranquil solitude of my head were making me a nervous wreck. Besides, I had ten dollars left to my name. I grabbed my jacket, threw on my face some water that had collected in an open five-gallon tin off the eave of my roof, said goodbye to the trees, and jumped into the cab that was already rolling.

"Right, Stanley," Jorgi yelled as we careened back down the hill, "all that ain't movin' is dead."

He could hardly keep the truck on the wet county road as he raced on, filling me in as he went about the whale.

"I gotta get back to him, Stanley, before some dogs or scientists set upon him. You won't believe how I captured him. There I was way out on the beach at Ten Mile looking for weird pieces of driftwood—you know the kind, the ones that look like naked men or women or parts of their bodies. Janett and I lacquer them up and take them down to Chinatown in Frisco to the tourist shops. There I was, early in the morning, miserable and wet with only a few torsos and some rough-looking crotches in my sack when all of a sudden down toward the end of the beach near the rocks and out beyond the breaker line near the kelp there were six or seven huge dorsal fins like giant arrowheads cutting through the water."

He was excited as he went on, speeding north on the twisting curves of Highway 1.

"They were killer whales, Stanley, big ones, but there was one out in front of the pack even bigger, and almost as soon as I saw him something leaped out of the water in front of him about the size of a full-grown man. In a flash there was a swirl of water and spray as the big one's dorsal fin cut after it, hitting it dead center and driving it up and out of the water. He had latched onto a big sea lion. It must have weighed four or five hundred pounds, but the killer whale was shaking it in the air like a puppy shaking a rag doll.

"In a flash the rest were up to the big one and breakfast was over in seconds. They circled the spot once or twice and then started off again, slowly cruising just outside the kelp line. Wham! I heard a shot coming from above me near the road and I looked up to see these two sportsmen next to the side of a camper, both with rifles in their arms, zapping away at the whales. They must have been having breakfast. They had the big whale dead on. And I swear, Stanley, almost as soon as these guys started shooting, that big baby made a target out of himself while the rest of the pack slipped out to sea. He leaped out of the water twice and rolled his head several times as little geysers of spray hit around him from the rifles. Then *pow!* One caught him. And his head slipped beneath the water and his huge body slowly rolled over on the surface, showing his white underside and blue top in a revolving motion. It took the bastard at least a whole hour to kick off. The hunters split. Toward the end one of the other whales suddenly broke the surface near him and circled him several times like he was trying to help or keep the big, dying one from drifting into the beach. When he understood that the big one was finished, drifting like a huge log in the sea with the tops of swells washing over him, the other one took off. I waited for about an hour and before I knew it the whale came rolling in with the breakers, the high tide stranding him dead on the beach. That's when I claimed him; he's all mine."

And Jorgi wasn't kidding.

We parked the truck at Ten Mile Beach and I jogged after Jorgi as he ran down along the wet sand.

I saw it from at least two hundred yards off. The dorsal fin protruded into the air straight up, dark and sinister on a massive, glistening, blackish-blue body. Jorgi was way ahead of me, and by the time I got up next to the huge carcass he was up on its back, holding himself in place with an arm grasping the dorsal fin, the tip of which was a good half a foot over his head. It was sinister and big, and even in death I approached it slowly as if its monstrous life hadn't yet flowed out of it. Its pointed beak was aimed at the sea. Above the beak and mouth there was a large blunted forehead and lidless eyes as real as life staring out at me. Its underbelly was a brilliant white, but it met the sleek blackness of the upper portion of the body in a line that started at the mouth and curved back in a hard edge along the middle of the beast to the underside of the flat tail, which was the size of a large table. Just behind the eyes on each side there was a strange oval patch of white, as if the thing was done up in some sort of decorative war paint, and again just behind the dorsal fin a strange swirly sharp-pointed streak of white curved forward like a sickle on either side of the animal.

Jorgi jumped down, poking about the whale with a driftwood stick, completely hidden from my view on the other side of the huge whale. He appeared by the head and yelled for me. "Look at these choppers!" He pried the stick into the jaws, which slowly opened to reveal hideous rows of conical teeth, each at least four or five inches long. Next he was down along the side poking his stick into the whale's death wound, a small hole I had completely missed about three feet above the flat, broad front flipper.

"Man, it must have been a thirty-ought-six, lookit here," and he inserted the thin stick into a small, bloodless hole hardly bigger than the diameter of a penny. "It had to go clean to his heart or right through his lungs, a lucky shot." I couldn't appreciate the marksmanship of the great hunter who had slain the beautiful whale from the breakfast perch of his tin camper and I told Jorgi what a waste it was.

"Don't get uptight, Stanley," he smiled back at me. "You and me didn't shoot him, but the fact he's dead is real—what we've got to figure out is how to get this monster off the beach so we can cash him in."

"Cash him in? Jorgi, you're out of your mind," I told him. "This thing's at least thirty feet long and it must weigh ten tons. Just who in the hell buys whales these days?"

"Well," he answered, "the Dr. Erik dog-food factory for one, down at the old Oakland whaling station. Legally they can't buy whales any more for dog food in America, so they've switched to wild horses from Nevada and old plugs that were part of expensive cowboy fantasies of surburban Californians. All we'd have to do is figure out a way to load him off this beach and haul him south before he starts to rot. But the way I figure it, that would be small potatoes. There's much bigger money in this baby."

I certainly wanted no part of reducing the sleek, powerful creature in front of me to cans of dog food and I half turned away from Jorgi, but it was as if he read my mind, and before I knew it he was launched into a scheme that sucked me in as being worthwhile.

"Stanley, what we'll do with this monster is fix him up so he won't rot and take him around the state, up and down the coast to show the people of this land man's brutality to nature. Buddy, it's a natural. We'll create a Save-the-Whale club or movement or what have you. We'll park it in supermarket parking lots and shopping centers and let people look at it absolutely free—even fix it up so kids can climb up on its back. The kicker will be bumper stickers and donations. SAVE THE WHALES in white over a dark background with the silhouette of our whale, all for just a minimum donation of a dollar. Just a basic dollar so that whale-watches or something like that can be set up along the coast of California to keep an eye on whales and the idiots who try to kill them. There's no end to it, Stanley! We can hook into all the schools, the media, and we will be right out front; I mean we won't take the bulk of the money, just skim fifty percent for expenses, which in itself ought to make us rich while at the same time helping out nature. Can't you see it?"

Unfortunately I could. With Jorgi's scheme in mind we undertook the resurrection of our whale.

It was a bitch. But there is both art and mystery in utility, and Jorgi was a poet of pragmatism. He told me to guard the whale while he took off after Nog Johnsen, a cousin of Race Hubbard's, the junkman we had sold our precious metals to. Nog was a cat-skinner and had access to logging equipment. Jorgi ran off down the beach to get him. He was gone for three hours while I stood watch over the carcass, but no one disturbed the whale's and my solitude on the lonely prewinter beach except flocks of sandpipers delicately running back and forth on toothpick legs, racing the foamy far edges of waves, oblivious to the presence of man and stranded monster.

The sandpipers exploded into the air with shrieks at the first approach of the tractor, a gigantic machine with

Jorgi walking ahead of it, his body weighted down and covered with the coils of a huge rope. The tractor was only half the size of the whale, but its power was enormous. Jorgi and I tied one end of the huge hawser to the thick muscle and flesh of the whale between its main body and tail. The other end we attached to the rear of the tractor, which vibrated the damp sand with a roar and surge of power as the tracks dug into the beach. I felt for sure the tractor was going to bury itself up past Nog, a skinny-faced guy with a plaid shirt and black skullcap. He had to back off the rope two times so that Jorgi and I could give him more length and he could get farther up the beach to firmer and drier footing, and even that wouldn't have worked if Jorgi hadn't thought of putting flat pieces of driftwood under the cat's tracks.

We progressed in slow stages like Egyptians moving a monolithic block of stone, with Jorgi and me running back and forth on each side of the tractor picking up the wood that the cat had run over and laying it down again in the tractor path. The dead whale slid along behind us, leaving a track as wide as a truck in the sand.

It was dark before we reached the dirt ramp that led from the beach to the parking lot. The cat started up the ramp but the whale wouldn't budge on the dirt. It would have remained there until it rotted if Jorgi hadn't hit upon the idea of laying plastic under the belly of the brute and wetting it with water to make it slide. We spent the better part of that night riding around looking for plastic, but we had to settle for several rolls of tar paper we stole from a construction site, which worked just as well.

The dawn found us hard at work again with Janett serving hot coffee out of a thermos as Jorgi and I ran back and forth to the edge of the sea to fetch buckets of water to lubricate the whale up to the parking lot. Needless to say, by noon we had attracted a considerable crowd of onlookers, which delighted Jorgi and spurred him on to greater energies.

"You see," he said, "look at the crowds. This baby's a natural." And so it was, but at that moment I felt more silly than successful as I sloshed buckets of salt water under a dead whale's belly button.

Around lunchtime Game Warden Glover, the one we had almost crippled while in the abalone business, showed up in his green cruiser. He maintained a polite distance at the far end of the parking lot, where I saw him rapidly flipping through several pamphlets and books before he moved in on us. He was obviously checking out which laws we were now breaking against the flora and fauna of California.

I was all for making it out of there and leaving the whale behind in the parking lot, but Jorgi reassured me before the game warden reached us.

"Moving on to bigger Fish and Game violations? I don't think the evidence will be as easy to get rid of this time," Glover said sarcastically.

But apparently we had broken no law. He searched Jorgi's truck and found no rifle. He even climbed up on Nog's tractor and poked around. We were clean except for twenty thousand pounds of cetacean we were stringing along on a rope, but as it turned out Jorgi ended up putting it to Glover.

"Officer," Jorgi told him, "we are removing this deteriorating mammal from the beach to protect the public from disease and stench. It's the same law that lets anyone who burns a dead sea lion on the shore get twenty-five bucks. We're putting in our claim right now."

I had never heard of any such law, but apparently Jorgi was right and Glover ended up reluctantly filling out a yellow form and handing it to him.

Evening brought on the dispersal of the onlookers. Our first day's labors had succeeded in fetching the whale from the sands and we had him high and dry in the center of an asphalt parking lot.

"Jorgi," I complained as Janett, Nog, Jorgi, and I sat on the flat expanse of our whale's tail eating our dinner of burgers and shakes Janett had run into town for, "we can't tow this thing around the whole state with a tractor and buckets of water. There's just no way."

The immense improbability of our task was filtering down from my brain, adding further numbness to my fatigued body, but Jorgi put my short-lived mutiny to rest by revealing to me the next stage of our operation.

"We're putting wheels under this baby, Stanley. We'll be rolling across the land tonight."

His plan was to have Nog take the tractor back to the lumber-company logging operation where he had borrowed it. In its place he was going to bring back a giant log-loader, a huge machine with two massive lobsterlike claws suspended in front of it. With that we would lift our catch onto a flatbed trailer and truck that Jorgi was going to rent. Jorgi, Janett, and Nog disappeared on their various errands, leaving me to baby-sit with the whale once more. Several curious cars appeared from town and cruised around the whale in the parking lot, sweeping and illuminating it with their headlights. I was offered several beers as I guarded the beast in the night and two guys had their pictures taken to the blinding pops of flashbulbs as they leaned on either side of the head. I stopped a teenager from hacking off a souvenir piece of our whale with a hunting knife. Around ten Glover came back with a guy from the Beach and Recreation Department, who ran down some scam about no overnight camping and parking. He gave me a twelve o'clock deadline, citing an obscure ordinance.

Everyone finally split except the whale and me. I was worried and cold under the expanse of the stars and the chill wind coming in off the ocean. I attempted to read some answer in the constant heavens, but the little blue-and-white twinkles beamed down at me and our dead monster without providing either inspiration or illumination on my condition. Was I just part of some nickel-and-dime scheme or was I repeating some time-less duty, guarding prey from other predators?

Jorgi, Nog, and Janett spent the rest of the night rounding up the truck, trailer, and the log-loader. Mean-while, at about one in the morning, Glover's Beach and Rec man returned and our whale got it's first parking ticket.

One thing was certain: there was no adept and dominant Ahab among us capable of dealing decisively with that whale. Ours was a committee of Ishmaels, greenhorns to the whaling industry, observers of our own blunders. Jorgi's commands were innovative but hit-and-miss as we struggled to secure our fortune.

It took all of the next day to load the whale. Jorgi had rented the old truck from Race Hubbard for twenty dollars a day, using for the deposit Janett's packaged bay leaf sales receipts that had taken six months to accumu-late. The monstrous log-loader kept placing its giant tongs around the creature, but every time it was lifted it would bend and slip out of the pincers. We finally had to bring in several three-by-twelve planks twenty feet long onto which the log-loader rolled the whale, creating a rigid cradle with which to lift the creature.

A busful of high-school biology students arrived after lunch, flooding the parking lot with frantic juvenile note-takers who swarmed over our whale, impeding our progress further. One boy and girl stuck a long needle into one of the creature's eyes. The leader of the scientific expedition—a rotund, square-headed and half-bald bespectacled young fellow wearing baggy Sears, Roebuck gray twills and a knit sweater depicting two stags meeting head-on on his chest—kept yelling at us to hold up our operation each time we had the whale on its side so that he could locate the creature's anus and sexual apparatus.

Jorgi was furious, and his screams and threats finally created a slight no-man's-land around the whale as we worked. But each time the creature slipped out of the pincers of the log-loader and loudly plopped back to the pavement, we were met by shouts and taunts, even boos from the students when the whale's hide was ripped open a little in several places.

It was dark before we finally got it loaded onto the trailer, head toward the rear and tail crowded up against the back of the cab. Jorgi was frantic with delay and cursed my slowness due to lack of sleep. "This is a race against decay, Stanley," he said to me. "Either we pickle this thing soon or we lose the whole Mary Ann."

I did what I was told, but noticed in my funk that Jorgi's personality had slowly inflated during the day to meet the immensity of his task. Janett was on pins and needles and Nog had had his share once the whale was securely on the trailer. He split. As the afternoon wore on he had become increasingly worried about someone at the logging operation he worked for showing up and finding out that their biggest and most expensive piece of machinery was on loan to some crazies who had caught a whale.

We finally lashed the creature to the flatbed trailer with ropes, climbed into the cab of the rented truck, and took off at a slow pace down the twisting curves of the coast road. Our crusade to save the whales was launched, and once we got moving Jorgi became more jovial again, getting Janett and me to sing with him, "This whale is your whale—this whale is my whale, from California to the New York Harbor, this whale belongs to you and me," but I soon nodded off to the drone of the truck's engine while Jorgi and Janett planned and schemed away the money they'd have when they were rich.

8

DANCE AGAINST DECAY

How do you preserve a whale? Certainly not all at once. The next morning the three of us stood along side our whale, which towered above us on the trailer, parked on Jorgi's property. A cold southeasterly wind was skimming across the tops of the fir trees around us, boding rain before nightfall, so Jorgi didn't waste any time preparing the whale for the road. He got a ladder; climbing up on the whale's back, where on his knees and with one hand holding the base of the huge dorsal fin, he minutely examined the small wounds and abrasions on the animal's hide picked up in the loading, yelling down to us at the same time in a panicked voice, "Quick, Janett, get some Clorox. I've already found a maggot; we've got to sanitize our investment."

So the three of us spent the day crawling and slipping

over the whale's body, giving him as cosmetic an appearance as possible by scrubbing him down with detergents, rinsing him with Clorox, and pasting epoxy glue tinted with blue and white paint into the animal's wounds to restore his original deep-sea appearance. Once the holes were plugged we discovered that this was best done by spraying water on the brute to bring out the natural sheen of his skin.

"Hosing him down for appearances won't stop the rot," I told Jorgi just after he finished his water idea, for it took hundreds of gallons to maintain his luster, which wasn't exactly an ecological plus in drought-ridden northern California. He answered back from on top of the head, where he was trying to fix the punctured eye.

"Stanley, you're just a jackrabbit liberal. The issue at hand is to save our asses using whatever chunk of meat we can rip off from Mother Nature. Do you want a planet filled with beautiful parks, clear lakes and streams, and nothing but bugs and polar bears to enjoy it? After we're rich, baby, after we're rich—that's when we'll slap ass and wrists for throwing beer cans; till then we need every drop of water and available atom to make it."

But he took my suggestion nonetheless, in spite of his brief minute of robber-baron madness on top of the whale's head. We drove down to Mendocino and bought twenty gallons of quick-drying Varathane, a clear paint-like plastic liquid. Jorgi made the purchase with a stolen credit card he got off a local dope farmer who owed him a favor.

The finishing touches were carried out that night. Jorgi had already discovered that the price of formaldehyde was out of sight and mortuaries didn't take credit cards. So around eleven we drove into Mendocino again and parked a block away from Dutra's Funeral Home. The back of the place had a convenient exit to an alley through which we crept, reaching the back of Dutra's and a loading dock upon which four fifty-gallon drums of the chemical were stored. It wasn't even locked up, for what mortician could even imagine the theft of death's own bathwater? We tilted the drums over the edge of the dock and rolled them away on their edges through the dark to the waiting truck.

Back at Jorgi's it was only a matter of seconds after arriving that he was in and out of the dome carrying in his hand two large horse syringes into the glare of the truck lights, which were aimed to illuminate the whale. It looked more alive than dead in the dark.

"These were left over from my fish business," Jorgi said, holding the giant needles over his shoulders in the truck's light, giving him the appearance of a mad Nazi doctor.

"Janett and I had a fish route to all the communes. We shot the fish full of water to get better weight."

In a flash he was onto the back of the truck, filling the syringes and handing me one, signaling the start of the night's ghoulish work.

Each shot held about a cup of formaldehyde, which we plunged beneath the whale's skin, releasing the preservative chemical. But it was like two mosquitoes attacking a Greyhound bus. I must have poked ten thousand holes myself and spilled enough of the stuff on my hands and arms that archeologists digging up my body a million years from now will find two perfectly preserved arms in a box of dust. We slipped and slid over the whale's body for several hours, inoculating him against deterioration.

Then we gave him a paint job. We covered the entirety of the whale's carcass, using paint rollers dipped in Varathane. The finish was as slick as the paint on a new car. The killer whale sparkled in his orginal underwater tone, lit up by the headlights.

After a few hours' sleep curled up like a dog inside the dome near the gas-drum fireplace, I awoke to a low staccato of outlandish chants. I walked outside into a morning as crisp as cellophane and was visually knocked on my ass, for there were twenty or thirty people dancing around the whale emitting guttural sounds from deep inside their throats in unison to a large bongo-drum-looking instrument played by a hippie naked from the waist up. "Oh, yah, yah, yah. Oh yah yah, oh yah ohmmmmmmmm," they chanted around the whale and truck while they slowly shuffled away with a little foot movement resembling a Japanese folk dance.

In a flash I recognized Lorraine's breasts, practically purple at the nipples in the cold morning air, but she was as oblivious to me as were the rest of the half-nude, long-haired participants.

"Over here, Stanley," Jorgi called. He was on the front fender of the truck with the hood up, yelling at me over the din of the dancers.

"Ain't this a mind-blower?" he said as I reached the truck. "It's Janett's Sufi school—wow, what a sendoff!"

It was true. I climbed up and helped Jorgi change the oil filter.

"I forgot all about it," Jorgi said, as he fiddled with an oily wrench and nut. "This was Janett's temple day. Christ, it's beautiful. What a far-out bon voyage party!"

Jorgi was in great spirits.

So were the celebrants' bodies as they twisted and

turned to the beat, although their faces were curiously
vapid—like the surfaces of unlit, milky-white lightbulbs.
Undoubtedly some inner light burned in their souls
unobservable to the beholder. The drum suddenly
stopped, but the dancers went on in silence except for a
soft tramping of the earth with their bare feet and
occasional curses and metallic knocks coming from Jorgi
and me as we labored under the hood of the truck.

"Reee-verse po-lar-i-ty!" one of the participants sang
out chantlike, and in a flash they all were going back the
other way to the renewed chorus of the drum around our
dead whale. But this time the tempo was more upbeat
and the dancers gradually broke into their own thing,
skipping and gamboling faster and faster in an ecstasy of
movement. I felt like I was observing some forbidden
ritual and kept as low a profile as possible up under the
truck hood.

A strange feeling swept my body as I watched them
cavort in a more and more uncontrolled fashion, a
feeling not exactly like, but somehow resembling, em-
barrassment. Perhaps my basic nature has always been
uptight, but the dance they performed had taken a new
turn; each participant seemed to be attempting to outdo
the other. One fellow, jumping higher and higher in the
air Zulu-fashion pretty much in one spot, faced off with
another guy who looked like he was bumping and
grinding on a tightrope. Big Lorraine was making short
running dashes punctuated with quick stops that sent
her torso into convulsive shakes of shimmy. Even
Janett, normally placidly practical, was taking great
bounding ballet leaps into the air, deftly landing next to
the rolling body of Michael Smith the mushroom collec-
tor. I feared for the life of little Jorgi in her womb, but

she danced on while big Jorgi fumbled away at nuts and bolts.

Outside the ring of dancers several people, all revealed in their shirtless state to be fatter than the rest, were drawn up together in a semicircle rocking their bodies back and forth as if catatonic. The bleached and convoluted layers of their torsos moved like vanilla pudding in the chill, early morning sunlight. One microbiotically starved young fellow with clearly not enough energy for prancing or dancing was sitting lotus fashion among the entire pack, risking kicks to the head and dangerous collision from the more energetic participants. One couple left the main body and at a dead run headed straight for the edge of the woods, where they hurled themselves into the ceonosis brush, rebounding like handballs off the foliage and then jumping back again and again in some weird attempt to communicate with the trees.

When Jorgi and I were almost ready to get the engine running again the Sufis were still hard at it, although fatigue and minor wounds were taking their toll. Toward the end I felt a strange urge to join in, to leave off wiping and tracing the damp and greasy wires of the truck's ignition system that Jorgi and I had been laboring over while Janett and her friends worked out like rookies in a training camp for whirling dervishes.

"Jorgi," I said, "why aren't you in the Sufi school?"

He looked up from the oil filter to me over the engine block in a strange manner which slowly changed to the suggestion of a smile.

"I mean," I went on, "there they are running around, and they must really dig it because they have some sort of bright faith in what they are doing. We're banging our knuckles against this cold engine trying to haul a dead whale around to save the environment and make a few bucks—and it isn't straight in my mind about exactly how we're going to do it. Why don't we shuck our wrenches and screwdrivers and get it on with them?"

"Christ, Stanley, you think too much. It sounds like your brain's rotting away in your own thoughts. I have Sufi faith. Listen to them down there, in a minute they're going to rap about mingling themselves with the essences, getting themselves holy and high with the energy of being which washes across the universe like waves on the sea. I'm into that, Stanley. I believe. But I don't *need* to throw my ass into the bushes to dig the essence of nature. I don't *need* to screw myself away into a wild dance. What I *need* is some *cash*. And *that* need is loftier than you think, Stanley, for *cash* is how we measure out the essences—how the energy is divided up and distributed according to need. Let them dance their heads off, as for me, I'm reinvesting mine in our whale for the big payoff. I'll cash him in on money and power and come back to the woods to live happily ever after on my interest. We all dance to a silly tune, depending how you look at it, Stanley. Most of those down there frolicking do it off their own or the earned interest of others or the state. But whatever, when the time comes and we return to the trees we'll be rich and then watch me dance like hell."

How he had got to money from Sufi dancing or what I had meant by even asking I'll never know. It served me as a lesson about either the frailty of human communication or my own ambiguous views on life. I discontinued the conversation and went back to cleaning the ignition to the now-waning drumbeats, my faith in my own thought and abilities as wobbly as before, yet strangely attracted to Jorgi's tautological reasoning. A sinister chill flowed from my brain downward through my spine, matching the cold where my bent knees rested on the fender of the truck as a new thought occurred to me: that all thought and speculation beyond any immediate task were wasted and useless.

After tuning up the truck Jorgi figured that the whale needed some touch-up work, and we dabbed it here and there with more plastic paint. Tired and spent, Janett's Sufi school clustered around the inert beast and conducted some Temple Talk while we carried out our task, but much of it was as Jorgi said it was going to be. Several of the participants got up one at a time and spilled their guts about "essences." It was like Weight Watchers, except they tried to trim out what they thought were the essences of their souls instead of fat. Crazy Alan, the skinny kid who had sat lotus fashion throughout the dance, gave a nice talk about our whale. He had a cherub face with panlike, curly, dirty brown hair on top of his head and it was rumored by those who met him every two weeks at the Elk Free Medical Clinic, where he got sulfa and penicillin shots for a lingering case of minor pneumonia, that this hair on his head was his only home besides the deep woods through which he wandered in search of tranquility and a diet of miner's lettuce and manzanita berries. It was also rumored that his father was the biggest real estate dealer in Orange County. He went on about something like "the void loves those who avoid excess and this whale is a death dirge against those who devour whales . . . ", which completely escaped me but not the Sufi school, because they all chimed in with the little bells that fit over their fingers. I was convinced that California will be the place where twentieth-century urban life will end once and for all.

Later that afternoon when the school broke up into more of a social than a religious function, I showed Big Lorraine around the whale, telling her everything. She was very impressed with the job we had done on the dead mammal and could hardly believe that someone like me, hardly able to feed myself or her chickens, could participate in such a massive project.

"Stanley, baby," she said, "when you come back I'm gonna put on my best wig hat, bake you some soybean bread, and teach you El Moheudi."

She tinkled the little bells on her fingers suggestively in my face. Undoubtedly the promised success of our venture had put Lorraine in a forgiving mood. I really couldn't blame her. I had used her; why shouldn't she use me? A sad little personal commentary on myself spoken by myself flashed through my mind as Lorraine smiled at me. The highest emotion in any relationship in my life had always been reducible to use. Lorraine deserved something from me, but already a voice in the back of my skull told me my return would entail a quiet withdrawal from her life.

The stars were out when we were finally ready to get moving on our crusade. Janett had prepared a fat dinner for us and a few of her more intimate Sufi friends who had stayed on. We had fried farina mush with home-made blackberry syrup and sage-blossom honey for dessert—which, with liberal amounts of dope, was delicious. Lorraine sat next to me and was already spending my whale money on tools and needed repairs on her property. She kissed me goodbye and departed with the last guests. I stood out by the whale in the dark while Jorgi and Janett got some last-minute details together in the dome. The vast clear star-bedecked sky over my head shone down just enough light to subtly outline the whale as I approached. I detected to my stoned amazement that his plastic coat was mirroring the stars. The Milky Way itself was reflected from below his tall dorsal fin up past his front fluke to his head. Orion the Hunter, just rising in the east, was outlined on his lustrous skin. My stargazing was interrupted when Jorgi and Janett came out ready to go. We took off, slowly heading south out of the woods to the freeways, on our quest to save the whales . . . and ourselves.

9

WORKERS UNITE

The road to Cloverdale, where we would meet the freeway south to the great urban areas, twisted and turned and we made slow progress through the night. The only light came from isolated roadside farmhouses along the route. From behind in the dark we must have looked like a logging rig headed to a mill with the redwood bounty of Mendocino County, but three of the cars that attempted to pass us from the back swerved off the road right alongside us, their drivers' minds blown as their headlights illuminated our cargo.

Around midnight we reached the top of the last grade before Cloverdale and I could see a glow in the sky that marked the termination of our county and the vast suburbs of California that stretched south in a network of highways and shopping centers to Mexico. Jorgi was rapping on about hiding the money we were going to make. He was worried that our success would lead someone sooner or later to the temptation to rob us.

"This isn't gonna be no racist white whale or anything like that," he said as I tried to doze above the steady drone of the engine with my head against the cold window. "We are going into suburb and ghetto alike; black and white together can get behind saving the whales. That will be part of our message. This is going to be a 'right on,' 'like it is' whale, Big Brother and Soul Brother all together pasting on our bumper stickers to save something that belongs to all of them."

I mumbled something in response about a profitable whale, not a political one, which prompted Jorgi to continue.

"We'll even cut the price for the poor. Two stickers for the price of one or half price, any way they like it. Only sooner or later some fool idiot will try to take advantage of us so we'll hide the money in the whale."

"What do you mean *in* the whale?" I responded, completely awake now to Jorgi's weird suggestion.

"That's right, in the whale, in a coffee can with a wire loop on it so that we can push it in and out of the throat. It's foolproof, Stanley. We'll let the whale digest our cash until we get back to the woods."

I looked over at Jorgi across Janett. Both of them were illuminated by the light from the dashboard. Nothing but the glow of impending success shone on their faces, which didn't coincide with the gentle loop-the-loop my stomach had just taken, for although I couldn't put my finger on it, explaining it fully to my own brain, a subtle surge of premonition washed through my body. I longed suddenly and ever so slightly for my water tank, its comfort and ignorant tranquility. What carried me through the night across the land, companions to people driven to pragmatic extremes, towing a dead killer whale to insure the life of other whales and make a buck on saving the natural world from those who had already paved it over? My imagination, straining with doubt, sent a telegram to outer space telling anyone out there that a strange, illogical creature stalks this planet, one whose survival depends on schemes of acquisition and consumption, schemes that will undoubtedly find the last of us chewing on our own foot.

"Well, what do you think, Stanley?" Jorgi said back to me after savoring his stash idea a bit.

"It's a great idea," I answered, either too stupid to comment on the insanity of our plans or too afraid of boredom to quit the activity of life's main attraction.

The next morning our campaign to save the whales was launched. Late fall had already settled over the mid-California landscape. There was a fresh carpet of green grass sprouting up around the edges of orchards converted to mobile-home parks when we reached Santa Rosa and our first major shopping center. The early morning sun glistened off the chrome and glass as we moved slowly off the freeway down a cluttered avenue of Jack-in-the-Boxes, bubble-machine gas stations, and brightly painted but sleazy-looking furniture stores until we came to Codding Town, a typical working-class shopping complex. It was still early and the parking lot was empty except for the little blue patrol jeeps that guarded it. Two of them converged on us before we even finished parking our whale. The men who exited from the jeeps had on private police outfits with silver trim along the tops of their jackets and on the edge of their trousers, giving them the appearance of paper-doll cutouts. However, their manner was anything but childlike and friendly.

Our whale and truck were parked across ten or twelve white lines that denoted parking spaces. But if the guards were awed or overwhelmed by our whale they certainly weren't showing it, for they acted like they were used to finding all sorts of monsters parked in their lot every morning. They walked around our rig and whale; they made calls on their jeep radios; they wrote up tags and handed them all to Jorgi, who was trying to persuade them that as soon as he could speak with the manager of the shopping complex everything would be all right. But everything wasn't all right. A few minutes later a squad car came screeching across the pavement, adding to the din and confused explanations Jorgi was rapidly handing out all around.

I had alighted from the truck and stayed as far away as possible from their conversation, pretending to fuss with the ropes and cables that held the creature to the trailer. He was in good shape after the night's journey and looked unbelievably fresh and real in the early morning sun. The only thing that I could detect as wear and tear were his eyes, which had assumed a milky appearance under their coat of plastic. They were slowly decomposing. While the argument continued up front, I got the needle out and gave each orb a shot of formaldehyde and another dab of plastic paint.

Jorgi won out and we were allowed enough parking time to wait for the complex manager, who wouldn't be in until Sears, White Front, Penney's, and all the rest of the department stores across the lot from us in a solid fifty-foot-high front opened up. Jorgi used this time to dispatch Janett to the nearest lithographer for the bumper stickers and me to an Army-Navy surplus store we had spotted on the way in to purchase a bunch of used semaphore-signal pennants to drape around the base of the truck and the whale.

By the time I got back the first crowd had gathered around the whale and truck and Jorgi was just climbing up on the roof of the cab, where he started to give a talk on ecology and the need to save whales to mostly gawking housewives leaning out the driver's-side window of their cars, which were in a semicircle disarray of traffic around our rig. But the guards and police made him get down; speeches were against the law on private property, that is unless the manager said that was all right too.

"Christ," Jorgi confided to me, "we're here to save their asses and they're treating us like criminals."

That was only the beginning. Maybe it was because the shopping center we had happened into was one primarily used by the lower working class. Men in plaid wool zipper jackets and denim slacks, women wiggling their asses in shiny white and tight knee boots and flashy yellow and purple dresses topped off with blond wigs or those with diminished sex lives in dumpy tan coats and inverted bowls of short hair, waddling like penguins across the parking lot into the temples of bargain. What did they care about saving the environment?

And that was only part of the problem. The printer couldn't get the bumper stickers out in time, which left us without a product. So Janett and I just stood around the edge of the shifting onlookers with coffee cans in our hands while Jorgi alternately spoke to the people, exhorting them for donations, and carried on a continuing debate with various minor authorities. I got nothing in my can and Janett didn't do much better.

At lunchtime a construction crew working on a new gas station on the edge of the vast parking lot came over and checked out our whale. They were a motley gang, and as they approached swinging their lunchboxes and jostling one another, I had a déjà vu from childhood, walking home after school with the boys. But this pleasant feeling vanished as the crew drew up to us and I could see that they were anything but kids. There were big burly fellows in tan overalls and plastic and aluminum hard hats, fat guys with their stomachs spilling out of the front of their Frisco jeans under flannel shirts, little guys in immense engineers' footwear, the kind with the big brass buckles. Punks in seven-league boots. Several other nondescript working types sucked cigarettes in between bites of sandwiches. The workers surrounded our whale. At first, they seemed to like it.

The teeth were their favorite part and Jorgi had me go back and make sure they weren't getting pulled out for souvenirs, for the work crew was opening the whale's mouth as wide as it could go, exposing his ferocious conical curved teeth. They were really getting it on for the better-looking housewives in the crowd. One little worker, carried away with himself, even attempted to climb up onto the back of the beast, but the slick plastic surface couldn't be bested by his bulky boots and he came sliding down on his face with his yellow plastic hard hat banging on the pavement, accompanied by the laughter of his buddies and the crowd.

If only it could have continued at that level of merriment. Although we weren't making a dime off the whale, we were safe. But Jorgi chose that moment to harangue the crowd further about ecology. He started off diplomatically enough by standing up on the edge of the bed of the trailer next to the whale addressing the crowd as "Ladies and Sportsmen," which quieted everybody down and made the work crew hang back with attentive faces. But their attention hid a subtle hint of ridicule. And worse, as is the case with all workers who sense that they are about to have a novel and slightly deviating world view presented to them, I thought I detected the narrow gaze of trouble in their eyes.

"This unfortunate dead killer whale," Jorgi began in a not too forceful but loud manner, "this dead whale is our fault."

I quickly glanced over the staring eyes of the crowd. They were vapid and without a trace of guilt.

"The truth is, we will all be as dead as this poor creature unless we stop destroying our environment, choking it with cars and smog, paving it over. This animal is dead because of trigger-happy hunters, because we don't have sense to take care of our natural world."

The faces of the crowd for the most part remained blank. Already around the edges the women were turning back to their shopping tours. And the workers, seeing themselves deprived of the audience they had held only moments before with their buffoonery, stared more intently at Jorgi as he went on. Worse yet, they were starting to smile at him—the national prelude to attack. Before I knew it one of them was engaging him in an argument, an argument Jorgi was stupid enough to participate in.

He was a short and thin older worker with big ears sticking out under a blue hard hat. His coveralls had a loose appearance above his waist, suggesting a caved-in chest, as he sucked on a cigarette between sentences. His first words were somewhat subdued and senseless, something about registering guns, but as soon as he spoke he realized from the glances of his pals that he was spokesman and he was spurred on to confrontation.

"We're taking care of our environment," he said loudly. "We're working every day for a living, paying taxes for parks and freeways so as freaks like you can tow dead fish all around the state. That dead whale of yours never had to pay no welfare. People are part of your basic environment. I take care of my own and don't have no time to protect no whales."

The speaker sensed the attention of the crowd, which brought out the latent Will Rogers in him. "Hell, God gave me hands to make a living and a whale a tail to save his own ass."

Jesus, Jorgi cared as much about ecology as the man who was confronting him. He was no different from anyone else. All we were trying to do was parlay our investment of energy along with the whale as a hedge against standing in the food line every month. We really had no "cause" other than profit, but Jorgi's tenacity made it look otherwise. He got carried away with himself, gesticulating wildly on top of the trailer with the whale on one side and the angry and jeering group of workmen snapping away at his feet. The crowd around us swelled and Jorgi went on, motivated as near as I can guess by a sense of frustration at not having made any money, as he had wildly anticipated.

"Your own sewers will choke off, flooding the land with a sea of stench," he yelled at the crowd, too angry and into the confrontation as set up by the workman to change the subject. But he did have enough presence of mind and con to introduce religion. "We're all God's children, one big family—whatsoever we do to the biggest we end up doing to the littlest. It's in the Bible. Our families are in trouble. The buffalo, the Indians, now the whales are stinking up our beautiful beaches; what's next? Whatsoever we do unto the smallest and largest creature, we do unto ourselves. It's in the Bible."

It wasn't in the Bible, but for a second he had them going his way with his cultural-religious platitudes.

Jorgi threw me a quick, knowing look and I fully expected to be passing the coffee can around the crowd in the next few seconds. But the worker came back at him too fast. He had a note of violence in his voice; "What's next is hippies and shit disturbers, that's what. Take your family—your Manson family—your dead whale and let progress be. There's no way, we ain't gonna pay for no goddam dead whale. Our lives are full of big-enough monsters already."

He was yelling right up into Jorgi's face; he had stepped forward next to the trailer. The sun glistened off the top of his plastic helmet as vividly as it did off the body of our whale.

"Taxes, recessions, depressions, losing our jobs, welfare cheats, all that shit. Hell, we're being swallowed up by a whale of a mess, so there's no way we're ever going to pay for yours."

That did it. The crowd, reflective a second before, now had Jorgi's thought pattern derailed by a more emotive appeal. It's true Jorgi was responsible for stirring them up, what with his vague appeal for the crowd to somehow blame themselves for their own fears, but the worker seized the day by directing what inner pangs they felt to a readily identifiable source—outsiders. Us.

The first empty beer can hit Jorgi right on the ear, bouncing off his head, the whale, and finally the ground, where it came to rest with a melodic metallic ring fitting nicely into the vacuum of silence that occurred just after the worker who threw it stopped yelling. After that the crowd broke into mean laughs and pandemonium erupted as they split into two distinct groups: those who were trying to get out of the way of trouble yet wanted to remain close and drink of its excitement and those trying to push through them to make trouble.

There was a brief surge of random scuffling and shoving, but the mob soon organized itself in our direction and besieged the truck. Jorgi was pulled down by his legs and given several good clouts by the workers before Janett and I could make our way along the side of the whale on the trailer and pull him back up. We tried to scramble onto the whale's back to escape, but to no avail, and we had to endure several misdirected swings apiece before we gained the top of the truck cab, where we dodged missiles and stomped on fingers trying to reach us before the police arrived in force.

They threw us out of Santa Rosa that afternoon.

I drove the whale back up onto the freeway headed south, bracketed by a two-patrol-car escort. Jorgi sat sullenly near the passenger window while Janett from time to time nursed his wounds. There was a large, bluish bruise extending up the side of his left jaw, disappearing under his red hair below his ear. We had hardly reached the city limits when he started tearing up the several parking citations and disturbing-the-peace summonses they had laid on us before departing.

"Screw all those Nazi ditch-diggers," Jorgi said angrily as he let the pieces of paper slip in the stream of air out the window. My eyeballs searched the rear-view and side-view mirrors with fear, but our escort was gone and hopefully our chances for getting busted for littering also.

"Even if we had had the bumper stickers, nothing would have worked with those dolts—we've got to find us some shopping centers with class."

And so we drove the rest of the day and part of the night searching for a shopping center with "class." Several appeared outlined in neon before we hit the Golden Gate Bridge, but Jorgi kept us on the freeway because they were all located near too many mobile-home courts and garish strips of commerce.

"We've got to find where the rich and powerful live and shop," Jorgi said. "It takes an intelligent man to understand the plight of dead whales. Only through them can we succeed, Stanley. We've got to take this baby to the top."

And so we spent the night behind a truck stop somewhere south of San Francisco as inconspicuously parked off the freeway as you can be towing a thirty-foot whale. The night was foggy and cold, and while Jorgi and Janett slept in the cab I attempted to get some rest on my air mattress in my sleeping bag curled up on the trailer next to the whale's broad tail. But my sleep was broken as all through the night truck drivers came over with startled oaths and examined our creature. We still hadn't hit the promised land.

10

BOARDWALK AND PARK PLACE

But we did the next day. Palo Alto. Janett knew where it was, for near this residential city she had on occasion delivered some of the obscene driftwood sculptures she and Jorgi traded in. We headed farther south in the early morning sun rising amber through the light smog. Commuter traffic slowed in the opposite lanes as rubber-necks tried to catch a glimpse of our whale, but soon we turned off through a tree-lined street with homes spaced so far apart another home could easily have been built in between. The rich architecture of the inhabitants of Palo Alto slowly unfolded on either side of the street as we passed. There were the bold square and rectangular patterns of fake English manors with thatched roofs, California haciendas with red-tiled roofs and spacious well-tended walled patios next to three- and four-car garages, rambling ranch-style homes cleverly oozing over the property in ever-expanding boxes, and finally homes styled in what I would term "wedding cake": mini-mansions, either white or tan, with two or three stories piled on top of one another, trimmed with little fake columns and heavy ornate balustrades. One or two palm trees usually reigned supreme in front of this style, strange, tall freaks in the otherwise suburban forest of spruce, maple, and elm that lined the streets. Jorgi liked the looks of things, and I must say I did too. The environment was less hostile—the trees reminded me of Mendocino. There were even broad green stripes painted on the sides of the streets—bicycle lanes.

"This is it," Jorgi shouted. "The bike lanes prove it. They'd rather pedal than pollute. I'll bet they'll save whales too."

"Something better save our ass," Janett chided. "We're down to seventeen dollars, which isn't even enough for gas to get the truck back to the woods."

"This whale will be spouting in a sea of money before we know it," Jorgi said, ignoring Janett's somber pronouncement on our financial state of affairs; his enthusiasm seemed aimed at me. I glanced at him across Janett's glum face as he sat behind the steering wheel. For an instant I wasn't even sure if he was in the same cab. His face was wide with smile and anticipation; he raced the engine ahead as if driving for some unseen finish line.

The main shopping center in Palo Alto was hidden away in clusters of oak trees. It was still early morning when we arrived and two sweeper trucks were scouring the parking-lot asphalt like giant parameciums. We maneuvered our truck and whale into the periphery of the lot between a large well-preserved oak tree and a red-and-white Goodwill container overflowing with the generous leftovers of the community. A good sign. The stores and shops were practically camouflaged by the environment. Oak trees were growing right out of the tops of some of the stores, which were built in a low and rambling architectural style keyed to massive weathered redwood beams and barnwood. That portion of the roof visible through the trees was of early California red-adobe tiles. No Sears, Roebuck or J. C. Penney reigned here in massive used-car-lot opulence. Tucked away in this shopping center were precious import stores, bookstores dealing in hardbound copies only, toy stores for creative kids, and expensive boutiques. The big outfits were at the far end of the center, situated in such a way as to blend into the meadow and eucalyptus landscape that defined the property line of the city of Palo Alto's main reason for existence—Stanford University. Saks Fifth Avenue, Shreve & Company, Bloomingdale's—all looming up in tasteful adobe and antique brick fronts.

"Boardwalk and Park Place," Jorgi said as he alighted from the truck.

My stomach took a nervous jump as the two cleaner trucks converged on us in a whirl and four guys in light blue jumpsuits emblazoned with large red letters on their backs saying CITY AND COUNTRY surrounded us like pro football players. "Jesus," said their spokesman, a balding blond fellow, "the circus is in the next city."

But my fears of another riot were soon gone, for they were interested and understanding of our endeavor. Jorgi dealt with them. He turned on a virtual faucet of warm, jovial conversation spilling out the words "ecology," "conservation," and "cause" all over the place.

They were obviously well-paid maintenance men. They let us stay where we were without calling the cops, and the balding blond fellow invited Jorgi to hop into the cleaner to ride over to the manager's office. Janett got out the several hundred bumper stickers that we had picked up before fleeing Santa Rosa the day before and arranged them around the edge of the flatbed, although I cautioned her to wait for Jorgi's return. I walked over under an ivy-covered arcade and bought us two cups of coffee from a place called The English Tea Room. The Styrofoam cups warmed my fingers as I returned with them in the clear but chill morning.

Wreaths of real evergreen and cypress done up with red and silver bows were dispersed here and there about the shopping center in anticipation of the Christmas season, although the first day of winter had not yet arrived. Here and there, early morning joggers bounced healthfully along in solid bright colors trimmed with fashionable stripes. Several left the bike lanes and came our way, running in place as they gazed in wonderment at the whale. Their blood-flushed faces signaled true vigorous prosperity. Off in the distance past the eucalyptus-tree backdrop for the shopping center, a massive tower rose up in the early morning light, marking the epicenter of Stanford University. But farther off in the distance something more massive caught my eye. In the low foothills that rose up behind Palo Alto, amid distant oak and meadow, I noticed a strange device that interrupted the horizon like some giant spider web. I suspected what it was and later I found out for sure, that it was a giant antennae field, a great parabolic antenna with which Stanford searched the universe for other encampments of life. I went back to the truck and pointed it out to Janett, who was drinking the hot coffee in quick sips over her lips, chilled to a pale pink.

"That's far out, Stanley. Maybe somewhere out in the stars whales tow dead people around in trailers and piss away their lives living in the front seats of trucks."

Leaving the woods hadn't been too good for Janett. The on-the-road discomforts were much harder on her than on Jorgi or me. Besides, she was pregnant and undoubtedly experiencing some morning sickness although not complaining about it. She was trying to comb out her long brown hair in the rear-view mirror of the open cab door. A strange feeling of protectiveness came over me.

"Can I do anything for you?" I asked in perhaps too kind a tone.

"Yes, take a hike, Stanley. Find the bathrooms and see when they open, then bring me my breakfast of champagne and eggs Benedict."

I did what she told me as best I could, and while she was gone I arranged the bumper stickers with the simple outline image of our whale on the truck's running board. The great antenna was fully illuminated now by the sun's rays but I didn't give a damn about it. Our great monetary adventure was only beginning its second day and already showing signs of going belly-up. I shuffled the bumper stickers, living in hope but expecting to die in despair.

I have always been one who has cautioned himself to inner or outer optimistic outbursts about fate as it reveals itself like a pinball bouncing off knockers and flippers, springing between WIN and TILT in its steadily haphazard journey downhill. But that morning when I saw Jorgi returning across that parking lot with a smile on his face as broad as an Arab's scimitar, my heartbeat and my brain knew we had lit up the board.

Our immediate benefactor was Kingsford J. Champion, whom Jorgi had in tow as he came back to the whale. Kingsford was the shopping center's vice-president; his old lady, Blyth—young socialite, art patron, and mother of four—we learned later also happened to be the daughter of the late Mr. Louis Tillingworth, who with his brother had been the biggest owner of shopping centers in the state. Kingsford was short and heavy and was wearing stylish tweed slacks and a blue blazer with a gold emblem above his heart saying CITY AND COUNTRY. Essentially, in spite of a bronze tan, his face was that of a young weakling with rootless blue eyes that seemed to float in their sockets. I didn't know what kind of a trip Jorgi laid on him, but it worked, whatever it was. He was really pumping Kingsford up, running down to him the story about how the whale fell into our hands, even embellishing the account with an added touch of heroics—claiming that the whale, once wounded by the hunters, washed ashore alive and that we got a boat and tried to tow it back out to sea where the pack of cruising whales awaited their leader's return.

"But it couldn't be done," Jorgi fictionalized. "No matter how we revved the engine on that boat and churned the sea white, the whale wouldn't come loose. The whole time we were circled by the high cruising dorsal fins of the rest of the pack, but for some unknown reason they wouldn't attack us, somehow knowing we were trying to rescue one of their own kind. Finally it was hopeless and we returned to the beach. It died as we stood next to its head, laying wet sacks across its gigantic brow. Not once did it try to nip at our legs.

117

Strange wheezes and beeps came from his throat as he tried to answer the pack making the same kind of noises out beyond the surf. No one could help. He died staring at us almost as if he were asking 'Why?' just as the sun set."

Janett and I were stone-faced. Jorgi's head slowly shook with pity but Kingsford Champion ate it up. At the time I figured the fact that he was a landlord for a parking lot cut off from the real world of nature was the reason he believed Jorgi's lie, but later, I didn't know. Kingsford had a thing about nature. He had been involved in a TV adventure movie called *Dark Fathoms*, a filming expedition of the sunken atomic wrecks of Bikini Lagoon. He intimated to me later that he wasn't in any of the underwater shots but had participated in the land sequences on Bikini Atoll in search of radioactive paraplegic coconut crabs. During the rest of the day when things really got going and Janett and Jorgi were peeling off bumper stickers to the crowd at a buck apiece, Kingsford kept hanging around, talking about the plight of wild animals, backpacking, trips to the Grand Tetons, mountain-climbing trips to South America, the Brooks Range, and various other accounts of his and his wife's exploits. In spite of his falling for Jorgi's animal shell game, I believed him: he was too rich to lie.

But most of all I believed her. Blyth alighted from a black-and-tan station wagon almost the length of our whale, briskly parking next to the Goodwill bin and approaching us in a quick stride as if she were about to leap over a tennis net. She was thin, tall, her face angular and firm, the kind characteristic of female athletes or policewomen. Her hair was cut close and she

wore light-green plaid slacks with a tan vee-neck sweater exposing a plain white blouse. Except for a thin gold
watch, she was tastefully done up in absolutely no
jewelry or makeup. She looked delightfully fresh, as if
she had just taken a bath in cold milk, and her entire
being emanated "will" and "character." I tried to cau-
tion Jorgi before she reached us not to shoot off his
mouth too much, but his sense was undoubtedly as good
as and even better than mine. He let the fiction lie,
confident Kingsford would fill her in later. Jorgi simply
and humbly showed her the whale, telling her, "Somebody, Mrs. Champion, has got to announce to the world
the wanton destruction of the earth's last wild creatures.
If we don't save them, who will save us when we are
threatened with extinction?"

What Jorgi said was totally illogical, and later he
admitted to me candidly "Whales don't give a shit about
us." But Mrs. Champion was so busy filling herself in
for the "somebody" that she missed it. With both of
them biting, Jorgi set the hook and played them for
what they were worth.

Which was quite a bit. With Blyth Champion handling
the publicity and Kingsford roping off, on her directions,
at least twenty parking spaces, we were in business. By
the next morning, as housewives picked up the damp
throwaway *Palo Alto Shopping News*, everyone in
town with money to spend knew about the plight of our
whale. Blyth's uncle owned the paper and she and Jorgi
had spent the better part of the night setting up the
layout for the front page. It consisted of a facsimile of
our whale bumper sticker across the top half of the page
and a large picture of our truck with Jorgi, Janett, and

me standing alongside the Champions below the whale. In the background and off to the side, but still prominently in the picture, stood the City and Country shopping-center sign, discreetly carved into a giant redwood slab.

The response was immediate. Throngs of shoppers crowded around the rope barriers in an attempt to see the whale and buy a bumper sticker. Kingsford put four men on crowd control; Blyth helped Jorgi, Janett, and me sell the stickers from off the tops of two card tables donated by the Champions that we had set up next to the ropes. By noon there was hardly an automobile that cruised into that shopping center that didn't cruise out again without our blue-and-white bumper sticker.

"Business is beautiful," Jorgi said toward evening of our first day in business under the arc lights of the parking lot, still filled to capacity and requiring several traffic cops at the exits and entrances. A sea of headlights moved about us, illuminating the whale, Jorgi, Janett, and me in our flush feelings of success. City and Country wasn't doing so badly either. A small, thin wire finally made connection in my brain, but I kept to myself the suspicion that the whale was good for everybody's business.

Blyth and Kingsford had left early in the afternoon but returned again after dark dressed in evening clothes, he in a white dinner jacket and she in a long, slim, blue gown with a silver wrap of fur across her shoulders. They were on their way to the Fol de Rol but as they left Blyth promised Jorgi and us to continue to "help the cause." Kingsford had provided us with a rent-a-cop to guard the whale and we spent our first fat night in a motel, the kind with a sunlamp built into the ceiling of the bathroom and a vibrator built into the mattress. The plastic interior of the place sent Jorgi, Janett, and me, accustomed to the rude yet peaceful simplicities of the woods, into spasms of putdowns, but it was still the first bed I had crawled into in four nights. I vibrated off to sleep with a hummm and visions of whales spouting in a sea of money.

11

SERVING THOSE
WHO RULE

The next day was much like the first, only better. Business was brisk and we had to contact another lithographer to print three thousand more stickers. Blyth Champion had kept the rent-a-cops on for the day and they enforced the cordon around the whale as the crowd pressed in to see the beast. For the most part they shook their heads and observed the creature with comments of pity. Jorgi had pinned up near the bullet hole a little sign that read HUNTER's BULLET HOLE. He was also giving speeches on the necessity of saving whales the morning of the second day with a portable PA system set up by the Champions, but finally he gave up. Not because he lacked the oratorical skills necessary to hold the interest of the crowd. On the contrary, the rapt faces below hung on his every word as Jorgi skillfully unfolded his tale of the whale's demise. The eyes of schoolgirls were moist, the eyes of young doctors, lawyers, dentists, and mothers vindictive.

"Stanley," he confided to me, "the great asset of having a dead whale for your main attraction is that it does absolutely nothing. People see the whale and out of curiosity they push and shove their way in. If there's nothing happening they buy a sticker and split, but if I get up and soapbox, that keeps the crowd from circulating. It's best they be on their way and back to shopping as soon as possible."

The third day was better yet. Mrs. Champion had gotten some volunteers from Hillmount Girls' School, where she was a trustee, to man the sticker tables, which released Jorgi, Janett, and me from our labors. That night we were invited to a special symposium at the school on Environment. The Champions gave us one of their cars to use—a small economy station-wagon Ford. They arrived in their two-hundred-horse tastefully tan Mercedes sedan. Jorgi was the guest speaker in front of an audience of balding businessmen and professionals there with their wives. Their daughters were dressed in the uniform of this exclusive school—checkered jumpers and white blouses with pubescent buds sprouting beneath them.

Jorgi had spent the afternoon shopping for new togs and when introduced by Blyth Champion to come on stage he appeared as a sort of continental Kit Carson, for he had bought an expensive pale deerskin hunting jacket cut in the style of Stewart Granger on safari. He wore a broad green tie on a white ruffled shirt background. Beneath that he was wearing a pair of dark bell-bottoms out of which a new pair of shiny pointed cowboy boots protruded. I detected a slight undercurrent of snickers

123

from the flush daddies as Jorgi mounted the rostrum, but in a few brief moments he had them as enthralled as they would have been with the closing Dow Jones Industrials.

"Ladies, Gentlemen, Faculty, Students," he began, at first a bit nervous, signaled by the fact that his fingers played quickly like spiders along the edge of the speaker's lectern. But soon his first sentences and his own voice and fantasies gained control, and he went on in a confident tone. His fingers turned to soft hammers that forcefully concluded each sentence.

"Saving whales is not a question of eating up too little of a supply with too big a demand. The real problem is how we use it, a question of *style*. Our world is a full-course dinner; eaten too fast it produces indigestion. But savored slowly, the natural world is a cornucopia of delight. With moderation and restraint there is enough for all of us who can appreciate this fact." From there Jorgi continued for twenty minutes with further tautological metaphors, the gist of which was that Eskimos and other such primitive souls have the only real need to slay man's great coinhabitor of the earth—the whale. He concluded on a semimystical note to the effect that actually the whale was one of nature's and God's sacred mysteries, which had something to do with the fact that its brain was as big as or larger than that of man himself.

"Freedom, I tell you. Freedom to do exactly as you want. The great seas of the world know of no underwater government that hinders the whale's movements as he cruises the continental shores in search of his livelihood. He crosses no property line as he gulps down his fair share of the ecosystem. No fear of taxation haunts his underwater dreams; his movements are as incapable of nationalization or socialization as are the mysterious routes he follows. The very globe itself is his sphere of influence and he is our brother in God's great scheme of creation. But at this very hour on some windswept and gray sea he is hunted relentlessly by the Japanese and Soviet fleets. Harpooned with explosives and electricity, his flesh tears and burns as would ours if we left ourselves unprotected from our great global adversaries. The spent and lifeless bodies are hauled up ramps and the flesh is flayed to feed the gourmet tasts of the Orient, or reduced to a tasteless powdery protein supplement to maintain the impressed workers of Siberia. And beneath those torn and mutilated bodies what is revealed for this shameless profit? Nothing, I say, nothing that we ourselves wouldn't recognize. A heart larger than our own but of the same shape and color, one that is undoubtedly too big to strike back violently at the ships and men that torment it. Fingers? Yes, fingers and toes once the flesh is peeled back from their great flukes. Fingers that once went hand in hand with us through the evolutionary Garden of Eden. A brain? Yes, a brain the size no man has ever known. The largest in creation, reaching the weight of seventeen pounds in the great sperm whale. And it is a brain which is no mere reptilian message center but one as is ours, convoluted and grayish-white. There may be no higher reason on earth itself, and we alone—all of you who sit before me—are the only ones capable of saving it."

"Yuk," Janett said as we stood in the wings of the stage, gazing out at Jorgi's animated body. "Jesus, what a sermon. Is this the same man who I used to help skin muskrats to be made into dope pouches that we sold at street fairs and flea markets?"

But the student body and their parents didn't share Janett's doubts. I could hear young girls whimpering in the silent lull that Jorgi left them with before the end of his speech. Gazing from behind the curtains, I could see the faculty ladies in the front row turning with watery eyes toward their charges. Mothers and fathers were visibly concerned, but Jorgi's timing was perfect and he broke the silence with his conclusion.

"The rest of the world's problems are secondary to the saving of this great beast, for somehow, if we can find the way to communicate with them we will better communicate with ourselves and our fellow man. If we save the whale, we save ourselves."

They ate it up. The flush daddies and mommies broke forth with a lather of response, for Jorgi had condensed a world of worry into a cause. He could have spoken on the Plain of Jars or in the most dismal village of Bangladesh; it would have made no difference, the audience was still his. His whale had devoured their fears and guilt whole.

The well-to-do flocked around him, and Janett and I came forward at Blyth Champion's bidding as she gained the PA system, directing the crowd toward the front of the stage, where we handed down bumper stickers to waiting hands waving dollar bills.

Afterward there was a get-together at the Champions. We sat down to a table decorated with miniature plastic trees topped with little Swedish flags for God-knows-what reason and had a late-evening supper.

The place was crowded with many of the people who had attended the ecology symposium. There was a continuous buzz of conversation around Jorgi, for Blyth had attached herself Siamese fashion to his right arm and was leading him around introducing him to her various friends.

When we had arrived it was too dark to see the exterior of the Champions' house, but a long walk up a gray gravel driveway through shrubbery lined up like soldiers told me that the grounds were spacious. A large hallway with a cloak closet on one side and a wide white stairway looking like a frozen waterfall on the other greeted us as soon as we entered. On the walls leading to the living and drawing and dining rooms were framed photographs of personalities. In the press of people I was forced aside several times and came up against several of these glossy prints, all of which had familiar faces but no name to fit them in my brain until I scrutinized the swirling signatures. "To Till, love Phyllis," "Till, forever with warmth," and so on till I realized that they were all pictures of major and minor Hollywood TV personalities. The girl from the old *Lassie* show was there, one of the *77 Sunset Strip* guys; Jack Webb and Ben Alexander were the most recognizable. Dressed for golf, they stood with a large square-headed man between them; *Jack, Till, Ben—the gleesome three-some* was scrawled under the print down by a club cart. From the look of things, the pictures had something to do with Blyth's uncle and deceased father, Arden and Louis Tillingworth. Some gear intermeshed between their shopping centers and the California TV industry, but I had little time to figure it out while we were swirled into the living and drawing rooms.

Janett stayed close by my side and I pressed toward her; we knew no one except the Champions and no one knew us. The rooms were in the style of Louis XIV. All of the woodwork, the chairs, the tables, the window moldings were a bluish-gray, the color of bread mold. The wallpaper behind the gilded picture frames was faded white ferns that matched a heavy-piled pure-white carpet that spread from room to room like foam on a wave. The house, the rooms, the people, all of it was a bit too much for Janett. We tried to get as close to Jorgi as possible but were forced back to the outer edges of the crowd of young stockbrokers and older financiers encircling him.

"Roger Hancock, Mr. Jorgenson; Devco Oil and Energy Systems." Jorgi was beset on all sides, but he gave undivided attention to the older man graying at the temples and dressed in a subdued green plaid jacket and a five-hundred-dollar hairpiece who addressed him.

"That was a hell of an appeal you gave tonight. Damn few young men in our outfit can seize an important issue of our time like that and bring it to the public. I don't think my wife has been so emotional since the government got Patty back for Mrs. Hearst. But what I want to say is that Devco wants to help—Hell, I want to help out. We'll talk later, but what I see is a TV shot of your whales swimming undisturbed past some of our offshore rigs."

The rest of the conversation was lost to me as several more people crowded in front of us. Janett and I were further separated from Jorgi's group. The two of us were amazed by the Champions' surroundings and wealth. We attempted a little putdown conversation with snide remarks that ironically contrasted our dwellings back in the woods but got nowhere with it. We were fish out of water.

Just before we sat down, I got to Jorgi for a moment in the crowd and told him "This place is unreal," and he turned to me and said, unheard by anyone else around us, "Reality serves those who rule, Stanley. Relax."

Which is what I did. I nibbled at the cold glazed salmon between sips of chilled white wine so delicious that the only aftertaste it left in my mouth was that of my own sweet saliva yearning for more. There was marinated wild duck à l'orange, tricky little rolls of meats harpooned together with toothpicks, even abalone sliced tissue-thin and served in strips on little platters ringed with parsley and imported cheese. Jorgi's reassurance took effect. We had arrived at the pinnacle, propelled by our guardian angel—the whale. I went deeper in debt to the effect of the wine.

Unfortunately, Janett did too.

A distinct yet firm tinkling of a crystal wine glass brought me out of my gastronomical glaze. Roger Hancock, standing at the head of the table on Blyth's right, quickly brought the dispersed attention of the guests together like suppliants called forth by the temple bells of a high priest.

"Friends of Hillmount School, friends of the Champions, friends of whales." He tipped his glass toward Jorgi, seated between Blyth and her stout little husband. "Friends of the earth and friends of mine. It gives me great pleasure tonight to announce unofficially an impending official announcement of great importance to all of us here at this table. It is an announcement, in fact, of import to every person in this state. Blyth Champion— that is, 'Little Blythie' who at the age of seven turned the key and drove off alone in her father's and my golf cart before crashing it into a sand trap from which she alighted unscratched, although the overturned batteries ruined my balanced set of McDougal Gold clubs—'Little

Blythie' remains unforgiven for that, but she will have my complete support and best wishes when she shall soon announce her candidacy for the vacant state legislative seat from Hillsborough and southern San Mateo County."

Instantaneously there was a burst of applause and enthusiasm that broke through the polite laughter. The men rose, clapping, the women remained seated. The outpouring lapped tastefully over the delicate edge of restraint. A couple of Johnny Carson yells broke through from the younger professionals at the table.

Blyth's acknowledgment of Roger Hancock's remarks and her short speech afterward would have given her old speech teacher at Hillmount reason for pride. She made her words humble and to the point, ending with an upbeat of optimism and humor.

"If I go to the capital as your representative, not only will I attempt to do the work that all of you want done—preserving the environment for planned and intelligent use, seeing that the good life is extended to all of my constituency—but also I shall donate my first paycheck to Hillmount School for any girl best suited for a professional golfing career, and this shall be done in Roger Hancock's name, for I am sure Roger would agree with me that it would be much better for young ladies to be driving golf balls rather than wayward golf carts across the fairways of our land."

By midnight most of Roger Hancock's entourage had departed, but not before all of the distinguished men and women had gathered around Blyth with encouragement, congratulations, and fat promises of financial support. I mingled in the sea of well-wishers and was infected by the air of purpose.

Janett, however, became increasingly withdrawn. Every time we bumped into Jorgi he was moored fast to Blyth as the center of activity. I did try to ascertain what political party Blyth was running under, but after a few impolite responses I was properly put in my place and thereafter refrained from other questions of poor taste. Practically all of the constituency she would be representing lived in some of the highest per-capita suburbs in America. The question was moot. Blyth was running as an independent, committed to no commitment, to offend the least amount of people. Also, I found out later, it obviously wouldn't hurt her when she exchanged the Mercedes for the Pinto and campaigned in East Palo Alto, the only black area in her district.

After midnight the party took on a different look. A core group of two dozen couples remained on, younger people the Champions' age. The table and the rooms about me had a mild underwater look by then from the wine, but I still had things pretty much in control. I found myself socially accepted by those about me since I simply said yes to everything addressed to me. Janett became more and more sullen as the night wore on. She looked out of place in her plain, faded tan madras smock with the simple hip embroideries fringing all of the openings in contrast to the smartly dressed women who sparkled and dazzled in the deliberate understatement of their own private designers or seamstresses. Loose, see-through, flowing thin satins and silks. Delicious and succulent Sausalito velours made my mouth water, although my stomach was filled with glazed salmon swimming upstream in a river of Meursault Pouilly. Janett seemed to be staring fixedly at Jorgi over her wine glass, which she held close to her lips both to soak up more drink and to hold the conversation with those around her to a minimum. I looked over at Jorgi and saw that he and Blyth were really getting it on, wrapped up in intimate, aside conversation between loud pronouncements to the party members in general. As I watched, he and Blyth got on one side of a good-natured argument and discussion with a loud, young, creative toy-store owner at City and Country. Jorgi was raving about some kind of utopian scheme concerning organic condominiums in the Mendocino woods. "A self-sufficient community, with enough bread to make it work, with solar electric generators and deep-well drilling to thermal springs." But Jorgi's visionary fantasy, seconded by Blyth, was challenged rigorously by the young prig, who actually took Jorgi seriously. The whole issue was soon forgotten, however, for Jorgi whipped out some "good, organic dope"; Blyth manipulated a wall of stereo equipment, producing a pulsating Afro beat; and the last of the whale-lovers swung into convulsive tempos and lively merriment beneath the crystal chandeliers.

The wild beasts were romping and stomping. Well, perhaps not as forcefully or as insanely as Janett's Sufi school. Blyth's guests were much more subdued, but in their hearts I could sense they wanted to tear the place apart. They danced on and in between they talked and laughed, but I was pretty much out of it, for I had no point of reference in their world of money, tennis, and sex. Janett was taken up by a young attorney and I lost her as he whirled her away, ruggedly dancing to the beat of anticorporate idealism. For a moment I stumbled into and through a wall of stalwart jocks slapping the shit out of each other with one hand over the finer points of football while they balanced drinks in their fingers with the other hand and tried to keep their bleary eyes on their wives, who were getting it on with dexterous psychiatrists and doctors dancing their asses off.

Kingsford Champion's rotund body ironicly was at the center of this athletic group. He had turned himself into a mess and I wondered if it was to impress his hearty friends or forget his wife, who as the evening wore on was held fast by a taut line to Jorgi's enthusiastic ideas. Jorgi in turn was carried along by Blyth's ambition. Who had fired the first harpoon, I'll never know, but I do know that the people who crowded about them were stirred up into a frothy sea of ambition and drowned in their wake of energy. By then Kingsford was hanging over the back of a leather chair. His head and shoulders were stretched toward the white rug on the floor and his legs and feet were desperately spread against the inner arms of this expensive piece of furniture so that his ass and plump stomach wouldn't pull him over the top.

"A vertical twist from the inverted on a belay off a piton near the belly." His muffled mountaineer's voice came from inches off the floor. He was describing to his pals a maneuver he had filmed that summer with a telephoto lens on the Glacier Point wall in Yosemite. A hearty slap on the ass by one of his stalwarts sent him plunging through space, accompanied by macho laughs, to the floor below.

I danced away into the arms of a wiggling, nimble English teacher whose husband, she told me, was a business manager at Stanford University. He was one of Kingsford's pals. She introduced me with a gesture in between bumps and grinds as we shuffled along with the other dancers heavily into an old Otis Redding. My head was reeling from the wine and dope. Her firm little breasts shook under a tan satin blouse. Only the steady beat of the music kept me from grabing her twisting body and nipping her nipples with my lips. I tried to hold on to her as the music ended and another set began but I lost her and my bearings in the crowd. I was just able to navigate toward the wall at the far end of the room covered with hardbound books, out of which had opened a tricky little bar complete with a boyish-looking bartender who shoved another crystal glass into my hand.

"Hey, good buddy." An arm wrapped about my head and Jorgi's bleary yet still energetic red eyes peered into mine.

"We're moving in. How about it? *IN.* Blyth's putting all of us out back in the carriage house, starting as soon as we want to." Jorgi was exuberant, but it took me a second or two to get him in focus.

"We're part of her campaign. We'll hit every decent shopping center in the county and then the state. Beverly Hills, Newport Beach—we're on our goddamn way. Tomorrow we're rolling right up to Sacramento with the whale. She's going to announce her candidacy officially right in front of the capitol building with our whale backing her up—saving whales, saving the environment, saving our asses, the whole rundown until she gets in. After that, who knows?"

"But what about the woods?" I had enough clarity left to know what Jorgi was talking about.

"Shit, we're out of the woods, Stanley, we're in, we're over, we'll take our garden with us wherever we go from here. I'm talking about that good ol' organic power, pal—politics. Instead of standing in the food line we're gonna run it."

I couldn't believe what I was hearing, but I had seen that same wild look on Jorgi's face before. Normally I would have stepped right in line behind him, but some fuzz of apprehension bubbled up through the alcohol soaking my brain.

"What about Janett? What did she say when you told her about this? This road life is getting to her. Running around barnstorming with a baby in her belly isn't going to be easy, Jorgi."

"Hell, Stanley, we'll worry about the baggage later. After we get to where we're going, that's when we can all lay back. That's where you come in. You tell her, Stanley. Tell her where we're going and keep an eye on her for me, because right now I'm taking care of business."

And he did. As soon as I was filled in and left to my task taking care of Janett he waltzed back toward Blyth's group of controlled friends chatting in a corner away from the din. I searched the crowd for Janett as best I could, but she was nowhere to be seen.

"Christine Mulhern." A voice, a name was coming in the same ear Jorgi had just left, but it was all mixed up in my funk and the loud music in the room.

"I know who you are; you're with the whale. I'm Blyth's student. Social Problems Seminar at Hillmount; her very best student, her pet in fact."

I was being beset, that much I knew, by a heavy dose of instant familiarity and my first impulse was to evaporate into the general din as far from the deliberately sweet, almost consciously snobbish voice as possible, but I turned and saw standing next to me a total knockout. Long flowing silken blond hair fell around a gorgeous fair face onto an ample chest. The only thing wrong about her was that she had on one of those silly blue-and-white checkered jumpers that the simpering girls in the audience had been wearing earlier that evening, only somehow she had turned her little uniform into an asset. It gave her a deliberate simplicity in contrast to the rest of the voluptuous females in their best party clothes. A white blouse was open at her neck down to the top of her jumper. A choker with a small cameo of entwined cupids on it encircled her neck and was the only show of decoration on her young body. At once I was flooded with feelings of innocent desire and the fear of statutory rape.

"What are you doing here?" I know I sounded like a gruff drunk, but my conscience had no control over my voice.

"Well, I might ask the same of you and your phony friend over there."

She gestured toward Jorgi and Blyth and continued speaking.

"Blyth has singled me out because she thinks I'm smart and into the social and political problems of the world. I'm always invited to her house for these little parties. She thinks they expose me to interesting people, but all I encounter are a bunch of phonies. My father is the head of a corporate chain of newspapers, that's why I'm her precocious protegée. I've told her as much, but she knows where it's at. She's phony too."

"That seems to be your favorite word. Why the hell are you hanging around them?"

"Because it's better than smoking dope in the back

seat of a car with a pimple-faced surfer. Blyth just laughs at my frankness; she even confided to me that my father's papers *could* be useful to her aspirations. Besides, she says, 'In a world of phonies it's easier to get what you want because at least you know what you want and they don't.' She deliberately disarms me with her confidence."

"And what do you want, sweet Christine?" I tried to make my voice charming and adult. She had hit some nerve of hidden big brother or father in me.

"Well, for one thing, not to be patronized by a half-drunk con man."

"What?" I was either being confronted by a precocious brat or a superior intelligence.

"The whale, your whale. It's hollow. You and your friend are out to make money so you can end up in a house like this surrounded by your dancing dumb friends. I don't think you give a shit about whales."

She was wrong and yet she was right. I was vulnerable from the booze. Flashes of the innocent giants cavorting in their sea of freedom flashed through my mind. I loved them. The ice cubes in my drink became their backs as they cruised the wooded Mendocino coast. I took a big gulp of indignation and turned to attack this young women's audaciousness but was stopped by the honest sincerity in her eyes.

"Let's dance," I said, thinking that would scare her off, but to my amazement she took me up on it.

Her young body was a fluidity of life that flowed out of her into me and even spilled over to the deliberately gyrating dancers around us who gave us room. She was nimble and rhythmic as we switched gears from the Afro beat of one number to the rock-out abandon of another. For an instant a wave of child-stealing fear washed through my brain, but nobody around us cared. Shit, they were liberal too. Christine seemed to be part of the scene; nods of recognition and smiles of appreciation were the only stares she and I received. A slow number found her close and tight in my arms and for an instant I thought of whispering to her that she, her generation, was the only hope for the world, but my better sense muffled my dumb words and I gave in totally to the feel and movement of her body.

Her pointed breasts pressing into my slight chest squeezed the last bit of chronological superiority I felt toward her. In short, I was overcome with lust. Screw the world's proprieties; I wanted into her pants.

Later things disintegrated. Jorgi was gone, Janett was nowhere to be seen. Couples were paired up arm-in-arm on their way out. Three stoned pairs were in a corner in a mini-encounter group with their shoes off touching six pairs of toes. A man and woman were having a subdued fight by the front door. Kingsford was looking for Blyth and I led Christine by the hand out into the garden, lit only by the underwater light emanating from the swimming pool.

"I want to participate in the search for the great apes," Christine said. I think she was answering my question about what she wanted to do with her life, which had nothing to do with what I wanted to do with her as I stumbled and strolled through the aluminum poolside furniture attempting to guide her toward a plastic chaise lounge.

"I'm going to live alone in the wilds of Africa or Borneo with gorillas or orangutans, away from all these screwed-up people. The only way of understanding them or even beginning to help them is through the study of animals."

I clumsily put my arm around her wide thin shoulders and tried to kiss her on the mouth but missed and found my lips against her ear. A small earring pressed against my lower gums painfully.

"What an ass!"

I fully expected to feel her young strong tennis backhand following through against my teeth, but instead she helped me regain my balance and then confronted me directly with the soft light from the pool undulating across her face. Before I knew it her arms were around me and her lips were against mine in a moist and delicious kiss.

Was I an experiment? Another proven manifestation of the decadent adult world around her before she sailed off to the jungles? Unfortunately we weren't going to measure the true essence of each other that night. We were directing one another toward a reclining lounge half hidden by the poolside shrubbery, my hands fumbling with the zipper on the back of her checkered jumper, when the party was brought to a close for me by a serious misunderstanding.

Janett was lying on the half-hidden lounge that Christine and I stumbled toward. She and the small life within her were covered by a coat from the chill and her bummer social debut in Hillsborough. But it wasn't our approach that startled her.

A crash of splintering wood and a bellow from Kingsford Champion came from the foliage beside the garden path. Even the finest class of people have their bad moments. Kingsford's had arrived.

"Rape! My wife! He's got my wife!" he screamed.

Three of Kingsford's macho stalwarts came charging from the patio. I wanted to get the hell out of there, but I couldn't desert Janett.

She wheeled and dashed after them, hot on their trail of overturned deck chairs as they tracked off through the plants. Her reflex reaction instantly told me that Jorgi—right or wrong—was going to be on the receiving end of their charge. I ran after her. Christine followed.

We had hardly gone fifty or sixty feet through the trees when we found ourselves in front of a little gingerbread house with a flagstone front illuminated by hidden lights in flowerboxes around the base of its brick foundation. Kingsford had been bashing at the carved wooden door with the remains of a deck chair, but now he smashed the window next to the door and reached in to unlock it just as his buddies hurled themselves en masse against it. They tumbled pell-mell through the suddenly open doorway, Kingsford bellowing, "Get the bastard!" with Janett right on their heels. I followed, not for Jorgi's but for Janett's sake. Christine was right behind me.

Once into the interior of the place nothing seemed amiss. A wall of books to the right, pieces of French provincial, Turkish rugs on well-polished hardwood floors. A porcelain Artemis, banner-entwined spear held aloft and coursing hounds transfixed forever running at her striding feet, stood in the center of a glass-topped coffee table. To the left, the back of a gray couch on hardwood feet faced an expansive bayed, waffled window. The stalwarts and I were momentarily stopped in our tracks, wondering what all the commotion had been about in the first place.

But suddenly there was a scuffling behind the couch and Jorgi's naked back bobbed up and down as he tried to thrust his feet into the twisted legs of his pants. There was a flash of white as Blyth, elbows akimbo, struggled to fasten her bra.

"Get the hell out of here, Kingsford!" she yelled. But the cuckold adventurer was undaunted.

Kingsford and his pals sprawled over the coffee table, smashing Artemis into a hundred pieces before they landed solidly on the back of the couch with enough heft and leverage to turn the whole thing over. A pile of naked torsos, legs, and arms spilled out before us like freshly cooked spaghetti dished onto a plate. The floor was alive with bodies trying to separate themselves from one another.

"Get out, get out," Blyth was yelling—and that's what everyone was trying to do at that moment—especially Kingsford, who was receiving her best forearm directed against his hapless skull. Once Kingsford was clear of her rage I thought the night had seen its worst moment of mayhem. I was wrong.

Christine and I were headed toward the door behind Kingsford's friends. Christine was laughing: "Big deal! What children, what ridiculous children!" But before my brain could agree, something flashed across the room. Janett. I had forgotten about her. But she hadn't forgotten about Jorgi.

Blyth screamed wildly at Janett, who was holding the floor lamp in her hands like a Marine in bayonet practice. Janett lunged at Jorgi, who had pulled himself up and backed against a shelf of books and a marble bust of Goethe, but Kingsford surfaced at that moment and the lampshade crashed across his shoulders. Blyth jumped to her feet. Her nude, tan athletic body was inadequately protected by her outstretched arms.

I rushed back in to grab Janett to save her from a life in the women's reformatory, but she lashed out again with the lamp and several rows of books and nameless antiques came crashing to the floor before I could get hold of her. One of Kingsford's friends hit me while Janett's wild body was still twisting in my arms. Jorgi's naked body flashed by all of us, headed for the door, and escaped into the chill dark night.

Jorgi took the car and I was left with the furious Janett, whom I hustled out of the cottage and back toward the pool. Disgusted with what she had seen of her fellow man for one evening, Christine had split and was undoubtedly off seeking the company of orangu- tans. I discreetly hurried Janett past the remaining questioning guests in the house and onto the tree-lined early-morning streets of Hillsborough. The police arrived immediately, pulling up alongside us without sirens, lights, or fanfare. They instructed us politely yet firmly to get in, which we did. Had we wakened Willie Mays, who lived one estate down from the Champions, with our commotion at the cottage, or had some unseen silent alarm in the shrubbery been tripped? The patrol- men in the front seat gave us no indication either way. They chauffeured us to the city limits and several blocks beyond, to El Camino Real. They even gave us the time schedules of the early morning bus that would return us to our motel and the whale in Palo Alto. I suspected the subtle power of Blyth Champion behind the whole thing.

Dawn was only an hour or so away when we arrived

back at our motel down the street from City and Country. Janett took the bundle of Jorgi's clothes I had been carrying and moved in to a renewed attack. I went to my room but couldn't get to sleep even after my third quarter in the vibrator. My brain was still hang-gliding around my skull from the drink and Janett was really laying into Jorgi. Their raucous words and movements were seeping through the thin paneling between our rooms. Blyth's name was yelled several times in a shrill tone I had only heard Janett use once before—the day after she got out of jail. Several solid objects bounced off the other side of the wall. Finally, I was unable to endure two people I loved continuing to destroy each other. I was also certain that a second encounter with the police would not end up so easily once the management summoned them. I put my pants back on and retreated from the room back along the streets to the parking lot, where our great beast slept in peace.

Several stars shone above his head as the impending dawn spread slowly across the western continent. His massive head and face were slightly illuminated by the purplish-blue arc lights of the vast parking lot. I was awed and overcome after another confusing night on earth by his serene beauty and tranquility. Even in the half-light of the parking lot his huge body lashed to our trailer seemed alive. His spirit lingered about his great carcass and, although stilled, he seemed alive to me, swimming in the great oceans of memory. Alone and perfect as he glided effortlessly through and under the troubled waters of our planet. Before I knew what I was doing, a strange feeling overcame me and I knelt down on the damp pavement. His dim opaque eyes looked down on me and for a freaked-out instant I saw myself

---

143

as a little monkey lost and sinking in a timeless sea but at peace with my destruction and about to be devoured by this great uncaring animal, who opened his jaws wide to receive me and swim on into eternity.

The sound of the motorized sweepers starting in the far end of the parking lot as the sun came up brought me to my senses. I hurriedly rose lest someone see me and scurried off like a crab toward a doughnut shop just opening down the street. It had been a bad night; only the whale slept peacefully.

12

OFF TO SEE

THE WIZARD

It was a beautiful fall morning, a fact that didn't coincide with my head and stomach. Neither Jorgi nor Janett showed up at the shopping center, which left only me to man the whale table. A few station wagons pulled up to the Goodwill bin near our whale to deposit boxes of out-of-style clothes. As an afterthought, a hurried matron would buy a bumper sticker, but for the most part things were slow. It usually took until noon, anyhow, for the well-heeled housewives of the area to recover from the morning's rush of dashing their children off to various private schools and their husbands to the great technological, financial, and educational institutions of the area.

Just before lunch, however, a schoolbus pulled up next to the whale and a field trip of colorfully clad preschool toddlers alighted and scrambled wide-eyed about our great beast to the shrill tune of teacher's aides desperately trying to corral and hold them all in one place. Pennies and nickels clutched tightly in their little white-and-pink fingers dropped ceremoniously into the Save the Whale can that I extended down to them. I Jo-Jo-the-clowned it up as I pasted two bumper stickers onto the back of their bus. Had Jorgi been there, I'm sure he could have given a speech and converted them into a little troop of crusading whale-lovers, but I did the best I could. In fact, unable to endure the tearful response to the most-often-asked question by the little toddlers—"Is he dead?"—I fabricated a story: "No, he's just sleeping and resting before he goes home from this job and takes care of all his little whale babies in the sea." Not all of them bought it. As the bus pulled away in a cloud of blue exhaust I could see that everyone wasn't waving happily to the "big sleeping whale." Here and there little smudges of moisture betrayed the very unhappy face of a young, sensitive whale-lover.

Janett finally showed up after lunch to relieve me, alighting from a lithographer's truck with several fresh boxes of bumper stickers, which signaled that she was still with us. But my initial considerate questions asking after her state of mind and health were met only with a curt "Stanley, mind your own business and go eat. If it's Jorgi and me you're wondering about, don't. I'm sorry for the trouble I caused you last night; he's a bastard and I'm not sure I understand him any more. This whale is swimming off with his head."

"Then you're staying and not going back to the woods?" I said as I looked at her tired eyes.

"Stanley, me and my baby are going to get everything coming to us out of this goddam thing. Everything we deserve. Jorgi can screw whoever he wants, just as long as he doesn't screw me out of what's mine. If you have any brains, that should go for you too."

She was right. All through lunch my brain played attorney to my nervous system and I finished determined to talk to Jorgi as soon as I saw him about some kind of contract for the three of us. Up to now Janett and I had let Jorgi count the money and put it in the can before he stashed it inside the whale. He had given us pocket money, but what had he been taking out for himself? A verbal agreement wasn't worth the price of the paper it is written on. I walked back to the whale armed with mental notes, convinced that I should clear this whole thing up with him as soon as I could.

But when I saw him the circus was in town. He was back at the whale as if nothing had happened the night before. In fact, he had a renewed confidence about him; commingling with Blyth must have set in motion other lusts. He seemed driven and directed by a great sustaining energy. I began to suspect that that force was simply power itself.

He was yelling at several cameramen on top of a nearby van as he stood on the back of the truck next to the whale. A small crowd of curious onlookers stood around the whale. A couple of priggy-looking young men and a shapely young girl were decorating the bottom of our truck with red, white, and blue bunting. The suspicion that Blyth Champion was near focused in my head the same instant that I recognized the girl as Christine Mulhern, my lovely little animal-lover.

I elbowed my way through the crowd. The din of a microphone testing shrilled through my ears and recorded fanfare music with drums and trumpets went off and on from large speakers nailed to the back of our truck. Christine gave me an all-too-long and obviously pregnant smile as I struggled to climb up to Jorgi on the back of the vechicle. I'm afraid the best I could send back under the circumstances was a sheepish Stan Laurel grin.

"Stanley!" Jorgi yelled, although I was up and by his side, face to face. "You're just in time. The vibrations from the trip down here have already started the paint peeling off down near his belly. Go cop more plastic from Happy Home Hardware over there. Just look at these turkeys, will you? We're off, boy, on our way."

"But where?" I said.

"Off, to the source, off to see the wizard. It's starting right here and now. We're rolling for Sacramento tonight."

"Wait a minute, Jorgi," I said, trying to make my voice sound like I meant it. "There are some things we have to straighten out first. That was a bum trip you laid on Janett, last night, and—"

"Hey, Stanley, later, okay? I'll square with Janett as we go along. She'll see that everything I'm doing I'm doing for business. Man, this is it; get your ass in gear. We're making our move. Help me hold this seaburger together. Blyth needs him, I need him, we all need him."

"But what about the money? I—"

"Oh." Jorgi pulled a fifty-dollar bill from the pocket of his new bell-bottoms with one hand while with the other he waved and beckoned to the camera truck, trying to get it to drive forward into the crowd and closer to the whale. It took me a moment to realize that the bill was for the plastic paint.

"No," I said, raising my voice. "I mean the money in the whale. I think Janett and I and you should—"

Jorgi turned and looked directly into my face.

"Money! In the middle of a lake you don't ask for a drink of water. The desert's behind us, back in the woods—which we're out of, thanks to me. Stanley, please don't give me the same shit I've gotten from Janett. We're no longer into nickels and dimes for bumper stickers. Blyth's giving us a publicity contract. Five thousand dollars for one week's use of our whale, and that's just the start. That old fart wasn't kidding last night. Blyth told me just an hour ago that Devco Energy Systems is laying out a scenario right now for our whale shedding tears as it peers down from the San Bernardino Mountains over the smoked-in Los Angeles basin—you know, 'the company that cares' shit. Stanley, we won't have to talk about money ever again, we will *be* money."

He was like a frenzied piranha devouring the fat possibilities around him. But the five thousand sounded temptingly close and I decided to drop the contract stuff for the time being and bring it up again when we were on calmer seas. Besides, I wanted to get rich as quick as the next guy and then go back to the woods and be poor for the rest of my life. I took the bill and bought five more gallons of plastic paint, but there was no time to start the cosmetic touch-up, for when I returned, Blyth was alighting briskly from the back seat of her Mercedes, camera strobes from the *Palo Alto Times* and *Shopping News* flashing in her face. Several young girls in their Hillmount uniforms struck up a tasteful cheer. The fanfare from the speakers reverberated through the crowd drawn out of the City and Country stores by all the noise. Blyth slowly made her way through the throng, impeded by handshakes and outstretched arms. She was followed by a small entourage of nattily dressed PR men. She ascended a jerry-built stairway bedecked in bunting. It led up to the rear of our truck, where near the whale's head several standing microphones had been placed. There was very little room to stand and the PR men nervously tiptoed their way into secure positions around the edge of the whale, decked out like Uncle Sam in his new red, white, and blue bunting.

Blyth seemed undaunted by the precariousness of the position. She was dressed in a plaid woolen suit with lapels trimmed in flat velvet that set off a white turtleneck sweater. A thin gold chain hung across the sweater and was matched with small earrings that glittered beneath her short yet slightly upswept hair. Her face was radiant, tan, firm, and continuously beaming a lips-together smile that only momentarily flashed her brilliant white teeth. Her skirt was a tasteful three inches below her knees. A bare inch of flesh was revealed between the dress hem and the tops of her black Spanish boots.

I had been pushed to the back of the truck bed and was looking for a way off, but there was nowhere to go except across the heads of the pressing, milling crowd. Jorgi was as close to Blyth as space would permit. A chain I had never seen before also hung around his neck. It was silver and on it hung a beautifully carved ivory whale held by its tail that dangled down to the top of his stomach over his blue workman's shirt with the elaborately embroidered collars that Janett had done for him. He was beaming and obviously awaiting some prearranged cue. Jorgi had hurried words with the PR men every few seconds as they nervously looked at their watches, but the fears that plagued them disappeared as another large car came quickly up to the crowd and then slowly into it with much fanfare. Out of it alighted, with flashing strobes exploding in his face, a man in his mid-forties with the taut good-natured face of your favorite service-station manager. He had very short brown hair and wore a gray-blue suit with a striped tie. The crowd gave a cheer, and Congressman Mike Mc-Henry made his way quickly through it and up the stairs next to Blyth. He gave her a big hug before turning to the microphone.

The congressman's introduction to Blyth was brief and to the point. The crowd quieted as he raised his hands.

"Fellow whale-lovers and friends of the earth—" The sudden quiet was immediately broken by loud cheers and clapping. The congressman measured it with a smile and then went on.

"I spend a heck of a lot of time in Washington, D.C., fighting against the encroachments of big power into our lives and some might think that I have no business sticking my nose in a state legislative race. But I don't care, for: 'whatsoever they do to the smallest of you they shall yet do to the large.' If we are to protect our environment we must do it in the littlest of places as well as the large. We must see to the flowers of the fields as well as the whales in the sea." A fearful recognition flashed into my mind; the congressman's words were frighteningly like Jorgi's.

From there the congressman went on for several minutes about what he had been doing in Washington to put pressure on the great international whaling fleets of Japan and Russia to curtail the slaughter of whales.

For a second or two I began to think that he had forgotten momentarily just where he was in his busy schedule for this day, but in a flash he brought it all back to where we were.

"I live in the Fourteenth Assembly District—Blyth Champion's district. Had there been a proper mammal-protection law in this state or even an intelligent licensing of hunters, none of us today would be standing here before this wonderful creature that rests tragically in peace behind me. There's only one person who could insure that this will never happen again; the next assemblyperson from the Fourteenth District—Blyth Champion . . ."

The congressman turned away from the applause of the crowd. He and Blyth gave each other big hugs as the clapping continued. Blyth judged the response and just before it died held up her hands for quiet.

"Mike, thank you very much for the kind comments. With people like you in Washington, I think we can all say that the great whales of our world will sleep more peacefully tonight."

The crowd signaled its cheering endorsement, after which the congressman slowly edged his way to the rear of the platform, positioning himself for a speedy exit once the opportunity presented itself.

I'm sure Blyth's speech was of great interest to her assembled potential constituency, but my woodsy apoliticalness got the better of me and my mind wandered as her voice confidently beamed promises at the crowd. No more dead whales, zero population growth, no pistols for the misguided poor, a clean environment, and a host of other issues that moved the well-fed faces in front of me to enthusiastic response. I was looking for Christine

Mulhern's cute little body, but she was nowhere to be seen with my limited range of vision crammed back by the whale's tail. I did see Kingsford Champion—at least I thought I did, way off in the distance. His blue shopping-center blazer set him off as he stood at the rear of the North Face camping and mountaineering store, set back from the main body of the crowd. He apparently wasn't taking an active part in his wife's political venture. My mind wandered effortlessly, floating above the sounds of political promise, contemplating the money the whale was going to bring. Rescue enough, for me, from the cares of the world.

The rising pitch of Blyth's voice signaled that she was concluding her speech:

". . . if we can attempt to save them, these gentle, great creatures, then we can attempt to save ourselves . . ." Just then there was a loud metallic crack that I felt with the soles of my feet before I heard it. The rear of the flatbed pitched down to one side. Blyth desperately clutched at the microphones before her and would have pitched over the side of the truck if Jorgi hadn't grabbed and pulled her back toward the whale's high head. There were loud shrieks at the base of the trailer as it appeared for an instant that the beast would roll off into the crowd, crushing a host of people. As it was, it did slide toward one edge, but it only was a matter of inches—which was enough to send one PR man into a squatting jump into the shrieking faces. The congressman leaped halfway down the steps but regained his composure and made a gesture of rushing to Blyth's aid as soon as the truck bed once again settled.

When Blyth was secure and on her way down the steps, Jorgi jumped off the trailer shouting and motion-

153

ing for me to follow him. I jumped, landing on the pavement where the crowd had suddenly drawn back. The left rear spring on Race Hubbard's old truck had snapped from the weight of the whale and everyone else crowding his act on the back of the flatbed. The steel tongue of the spring looked like a freshly snapped twig. Its broken end stuck knifelike in the wooden underbelly of the trailer. Jorgi moved into action, directing me to the nearest gas station for the largest hydraulic jack I could find. In the meantime he reassured Blyth and the rest of her entourage that they could do a retake of the closing movements of her speech once we had jacked the rear of the trailer level again. Luckily, Blyth's organization was more resourceful in the immediate situation than Jorgi and I. Within minutes, while they waited for me to return with help, they had summoned MiMi Wetina, a folk singer of some renown who lived nearby. That at least held the crowd, although the congressman was long gone when I returned with a tow truck and driver I had to bribe with a twenty-dollar bill, for I had no Triple-A card, and until he saw it he thought a whale on a trailer was the craziest thing he had ever heard of. Jorgi and I hurriedly managed to jack the back of the trailer upright while MiMi sang "Where Have All the Flowers Gone" and "He Sank 'Em in the Lowland." After that there was a din of cheering, handshaking, and directions for signing up volunteer vote-getters. Blyth was on her way.

But we weren't, not until we "got our act together." That's exactly what Jorgi told me Blyth told him after he returned just before dark from Blyth's kick-off reception. Janett and I hadn't been invited.

"She was pissed and threatened to cut us loose if

anything like that ever happens again," Jorgi said with a worried look, but I knew it was simply a prelude to another burst of his resourcefulness.

We thought about transferring the whale to a newer flatbed, but after much discussion realized it was too risky and might severely damage the creature. The best we could do was bring in a welding truck for quick repairs and make sure that in the future if we put the added weight of people on display with the whale that we blocked the trailer bed up like the roof of a coal mine with stout strong pieces of wood.

We couldn't figure out a way to slide the whale's head back into the center of his resting place, for after a few pries with two-by-fours all we succeeded in doing was cracking off more plastic paint. We decided to leave him as he lay, with his head now cocked ever so slightly to one side. Jorgi thought it made him look more lifelike— as if he were contemplating his predicament stranded among alien creatures.

It took until midnight for Jorgi to round up the posts, which he told me he pulled out of new units of sewer pipe he had discovered somewhere in a secluded expanding section of Stanford University. I supervised the welding of the leaf springs, which we had reinforced with half-inch steel plate. The blue-white sparks flashed in the night under the whale, making him look like he was being fried in a short-circuited electric skillet.

By three in the morning I had pulled the last flag off the truck and stacked the wooden posts. We were rolling. According to Jorgi, it was imperative that we make the capital by the following afternoon to coincide with Blyth's next appearance.

"The Governor definitely wants it on the whale. It

could even go national, but if it doesn't, enough shit will filter down to saturate Blyth's district. Once she pulls this off Professor Billie Brown, that chocolate Democrat from East Palo Alto, will be down to the Unitarian sympathy vote. With the whale, she's got every liberal in this county swimming her way," Jorgi said.

By then, I was so tired from repairing the whale's rolling resting place that I didn't care. Jorgi made me go roust Janett out of her pregnant sleep back at the motel so that we could get under way. He dabbed more plastic paint around the whale's base while I was gone.

During the last statewide election I had to chop wood for Big Lorraine so Marvin Hall, our organic governor, was swept to victory without my help. Billie Brown (who I had forgotten was running against Blyth) was only a dim memory at that hour—a teacher who had tried to smear Stanford's genetic researcher and Nobel prize winner, William Shockley, by attempting to uncover an abnormal amount of congenital insanity in his family's history. As far as I was concerned, they both were from Egypt. I was exhausted and had had enough politics for one day.

Our whale was making a good 45 miles per hour as we rolled along Interstate 80 in the late morning past onion fields and rice paddies of the great Central Valley of California. Tall power-transmission towers, their heavy cables sagging, marched alongside the freeway, disappearing off into the direction of the Sierra Nevada in the distance.

"He loves it, Stanley." Jorgi was shouting above the drone of our monotonous engine. At dawn he had picked up some Dexedrine at a truck stop. His eyes were wide open and electric as he sat behind the wheel high-ballin' it to Sacramento.

"Who loves it?" I said. Like Janett between us, I had been dozing off in fits and starts as we rolled along the straight boring pavement crowded with trucks and speeding highway patrol cars.

"The whale. This valley was once a great inland sea. That's why it's so fertile now. The dirt is full of ancient fish and whale shit. We're driving through an underwater garden of time here. He senses it, I'm sure he does. His ancestors' bones were plowed right into all these bean fields. God, what a fucking paradise. A man could grow dope ten feet tall here."

For a second I suspected Jorgi had popped something more potent than the Dexedrine.

"I thought you didn't have time for philosophical speculation. Back in the woods you told me that Janett's Sufi school were all a bunch of jack-offs."

"That was in the woods, Stanley. The whale has presented me with the possibility of wealth. The possibility of idle time and idle thoughts for entertainment. In fact, a few minutes ago the thought occurred to me that once this whale campaign is over I might become a consultant."

"What?"

"An advisor, a consultant to people and companies, banks even, governments. You know, sell them my attitude, my ideas on how to get ahead, write a book."

"Your ideas are great most of the time, Jorgi, but it's how you dish out their consequences that I'm worried about," I said quickly, hoping I could shame him back into the direction of the contract I had mentioned the morning before. But either he didn't or pretended not to follow what I was getting at.

"That will be part of it, Stanley." He threw me a quick energized smile as he went on. "How to live with the consequence of my ideas. That will be an important core of the consulting. Once a person has their great idea I'll show them how to have the will to carry it out. In fact, I'll frighten them into acting. Talk about death, total termination, the absolute stopper, no more possibility of getting anything they want, and I'll season it with numbers, about three billions' worth of people so that they really understand what competition is all about. Then I'll top if all off with ice, show them how we're in an interglacial time, tell them that mankind is going back into the deep freeze so that they won't put too much stock in living out their lives dedicated to the march of man and all that genetic, immortality, family crap. Then they'll be ready."

"For what? Drugs?" I interrupted, no longer able to stand such crazed and muddled thinking.

Jorgi was silent for a moment, but a smile that only he seemed to understand spread across his face as he peered over the wheel down the road.

"Drugged, Stanley, is what practically all of mankind is about. From birth to death—one big nod-off of state, religion, family, tribe, art, you name it. The world will cram it down your gullet and nail your feet to the ground. Humanity is full of fat geese and ducks, full of fois gras just waiting to be plucked. I'll make money helping people get their feet off the ground and fly above everyone else. It will be bigger than Synanon and not full of mental crybabies unable to act. I'll show my people how to pick up their spears and once again hunt for their destiny."

"How about hunting for a place to eat?" Janett said, now fully awake, totally uninterested in what either of us had been talking about. I sat in silence fabricating arguments to refute Jorgi's thoughts and insane plans to become the guru of modern man's attempts to lead the fully advertised life. But I soon gave it up and contemplated whales swimming under and through the power lines if once again the fertile civilized valley through which we passed was covered with the sea. After a bit, we pulled over and had a late breakfast at a place called the Nut Tree. But just before we did, we were passed by several company-strength phalanxes of Hell's Angels in a deafening roar. Their dirty hair blew back in the wind and their shiny machines glistened in the morning sun. For a mile or two they pulled up alongside the whale, surrounding us and gunning their engines in wonderment. Our friendly waves intensified when we were relieved to see them pull off. A couple of signs across some handlebars told us that they too were on their way to Sacramento to make an impact on the government. Only their crusade was not having to wear safety helmets so they could retain the freedom to smash their brains off the highways and guard rails of California, a cause I wholeheartedly endorsed.

13

OUT OF THE

FRYING PAN

We were met by the patrol car just before we crossed the American River bridge on the outskirts of the capital. When the red light pulled us over we knew he had us, for neither Jorgi or I had gotten a road permit for hauling anything around the state, let alone a thirty-foot killer whale, but the officer was apologetic as he stood below the cab of our truck in his tight-fitting tan uniform and jackboots. We were greatly relieved to discover he was on our side. Marvin Hall had sent us an escort to negotiate the suburban streets leading up to the capitol building.

"That's organization," Jorgi said, beaming as he followed the blinking red and blue lights of the patrol car through the streets. I felt lightheaded with importance as we passed rows of dilapidated Victorian houses interspersed with newer stucco boxes. Although it was only two days away from winter in California, pepper and mimosa trees were still in full bloom, with green branches hanging down into the sidewalks and streets. We could have been entering Memphis or Baton Rouge in the spring. The patrolman directed us into a curbside area that bordered a lawn surrounding the gold-domed capitol building. As we pulled in there was already a small group of people waiting for us, including Blyth, who stood out from the rest of the crowd. As soon as he got the truck parked Jorgi jumped down and gave her a big hug; she gave him a pile of memo paper which listed our complete itinerary for this and several days to come. But I was distracted, for emerging behind Blyth was the nimble little body of Christine Mulhern.

I jumped out of the truck and called her name. At first she pretended to be caught up in a vital conversation with one of Blyth's young PR people, but she soon gave a self-conscious turn in my direction and slowly walked over to me. I wanted to get down and kiss her young footprints.

"Hello, Stanley. Still trying to squeeze a dollar out of this poor unfortunate creature?" She gestured contemptuously toward the whale, but I paid little attention to her remark. My eyes were all over her tight-fitting, properly faded Levi's and loose silky shirt with pastel print of galloping horses on it. I got her far enough away from the crowd to talk, offering her my apologies for the night at the party.

"What for?" she said. "You made your best move. It's too bad that your Captain Hustle there ruined it for you."

"And what about you?" I said, totally into her foxy game.

Christine gave me a stare with just the slightest hint of a smile that was almost lost in a quick upward movement of her head. Some with-it English teacher at Hillmount must have been showing the girls old Bette Davis movies that fall.

"Why are you here with Blyth—why aren't you back in school?" I said, but I knew it was dumb even before the words were out of my mouth. I was going to end up her big brother, not her lover.

"I'm here to get used by Blyth, just like you are. I'm part of her youth angle. In fact, I'm all of it. It's a hell of a lot better than field hockey games and debutante parties. Since I'm the most intelligent and rebellious student in her Social Problems Seminar I'm a natural. I'm on loan, happily, from Hillmount. Besides, she owes me."

"What do you mean?"

"She owes me for a bummer summer. I could have been in the South of France at my aunt's summer home, and although it's a bore at least there would have been sex and drugs with skinny French boys in the hidden coves east of Nice. I might even have chanced hitching to North Africa to study the rock baboons of Morocco, although my father would have sent in the Green Berets after me. Instead I got sixty days in the CYCC."

"Sounds Russian," I said, trying to cleverly regain her confidence.

"The California Youth Conservation Corps. Marvin Hall's organic peace corps. She insisted that I go. Telling me glowing stories about backpacking around the Sierra all summer, planting trees and fighting forest fires. My family was too rich for me to qualify but she insisted that living with 'less fortunate' youth would be invaluable to me later in my career. It's the latest thing for privileged youth to help offset and nip in the bud any latent dropout tendencies that might develop later on in the middle of a thirty-thousand-dollar college education.

"With a phone call to Marvin she set it up, but instead of hiking around saving the mountains I spent sixty days in a co-ed barracks right here in Sacramento getting the grounds ready for the State Fair. Raking beer cans out of the muck of lily ponds; shoveling manure out of the horse-racing stables; chipping gum off the underside of bleachers; brushing my teeth in a urine-smelling latrine and falling to sleep at night on my army cot to the strains of the 'Disco Duck' and Donny and Marie Osmond. It was gross. Pimple-faced girls on Coca-Cola diets talking about becoming nurses or Air Force pilots. Grab-assing boys just off skateboards, destined for police work and gas stations. The cream of the lower middle class. 'Good kids.' It was awful."

"Sounds grim, but if she screwed you up that much I still don't see why you hang around her."

"I'm a social pariah. That's why. The girls at Hillmount all come from wealthy families, but my father is Morgan Mulhern. His power and wealth make all the doctor and banker laddies insignificant by comparison. They all know it and I'm shunned. The token black girls at school are treated like princesses compared to me. By making me the handmaiden to her schemes of liberation, Blyth is keeping my father's money behind the school and his newspapers behind her all in one stroke, plus she has the added trip of molding a wayward hip little sister—which I admit is better than the Nazi discipline of a school in Switzerland. I really am hip. Being around her and her friends has convinced me that people are just a silly mixed-up bunch of monkeys."

I had no time to respond to Christine, even though a

strategy of frankness to confront her blunt manner was forming in my head in order that I might win her mind and body. The possibility of showing her what a crazy ape I could be was beginning to turn me on, but Jorgi butted in.

"Later for this, Stanley," he gestured toward Christine and me contemptuously, calling me back from the possibility of pleasure to the necessity of work.

"Things are tight here," Jorgi said.

I left Christine and went over to where he was conferring with Blyth's PR boys.

"The Governor's aides have moved us back to a four-to-four-thirty slot and we've got to move the whale around to the west side of the grounds to catch the afternoon sun for the cameras with the capitol building in the background. They're sticking some Indians in ahead of us. There's a bunch of faggots ahead of them. This is government by demonstration, Stanley. We've got to get busy cleaning up our act. Look at our goddam whale—the ride up here has given him a bad case of psoriasis. The plastic's cracking all over his skin and you're spending your time trying to get in that kid's pants."

He was right. The whale was turning into a giant prune. The Varathane was peeling off everywhere in yellowing flakes from the wind and vibrations of the ride. I got out the five gallons of plastic that I had stashed in the cab of the trailer. Jorgi gave Janett and me a brush and we set about covering the bad spots and retouching our creature's underwater luster. Jorgi took off with Blyth to set up the fine details of Marvin Hall's appearance with Blyth and the whale. After he was gone I got Christine to take over Janett's job—which was a delight to me and fortunate for Janett, for she was looking very tired—and she left for the Howard Johnson's where we were supposed to be staying for the night. Christine and I cavorted with our brushes over the whale's blue-and-white hide.

"Hey, man, you're shitting on God." Christine and I had just finished our Tom Sawyer and Becky Thatcher act and had driven the whale around to the other side of the capitol mall, close to its final staging area before it met the Governor. I looked down as I started to get out of the cab into a dark face with long black hair tied off with a red headband. At first I thought he was a young wino who had wandered up from Sacramento's nearby skid row. But he wasn't. He was an Indian.

"Hey, you know," he went on, "this is a great spirit to our brother Chinooks in Seattle."

He wasn't kidding. In a hurried aside, I told Christine to run and find Jorgi. I told her not a second too soon, for already from under several trees on the lawn more men and women with red headbands were headed in my direction.

"This animal is a great spirit of the sea. He guards the Chinooks' dead as their souls mingle with their ancestors in the ocean. The salmon will not come up the rivers unless he appears—what are you doing with him, 'face, dragging him around on the back of a truck?"

The rest of the band were around me and the truck, backing up my questioner with taunting comments. I was certain that I was being confronted by a third-world anthropology major, but I passed the buck.

"Hey, I just drive the truck," I said, hoping I could hold them off with a feeble excuse, but they continued to swarm around the whale. A couple of them were kicking and fooling around with the tires; two more were up next to the creature, poking at the wet paint. Their tribal costume, both male and female, seemed to be basic Levi's with a few fancy frills on their shirts. Red beads, turquoise, and abalone-shell necklaces. One or two had a couple of feathers in their headbands. Large hunting knives strapped to slender legs sent a tingle of terror down my back. I kept smiling like a movie darkie on a bad plantation.

"Drive, my ass? You've killed a great being and now seek to disgrace him." I was confronted by another Indian who stepped out of the group. He must have been their leader, for all the rest stopped bad-mouthing me and what I had done to the whale when he spoke. His eyes narrowed under an overhanging brow. His face was much paler than the rest, heavily pockmarked with tiny moonlike craters on his forehead and upper cheeks. In spite of this he was a very handsome and rugged man under his red headband. He wore a beautiful cape of pale gray feathers protruding out of a piece of black cloth crisscrossed with red and yellow designs. He kept staring me in the eyes honest Injun fashion, but the words seemed more aimed at his followers than at me.

"First, 'face, you have taken our sacred Cash Creek Mountain to destroy all its trees and then cover it with campgrounds full of insane nature-lovers who refuse to pay us a cent while they walk all over our holy place. Now you show up with our brothers' sacred god and demean him for base motives."

"Wait a minute. We're here to save whales. He was killed by a crazy white hunter. We're trying to stop it," I hurriedly interjected, but I hardly had a chance to finish when the rest of the tribe overcame my pleas with righteous and indignant complaints. One young brave started beating on the truck's hood.

"Your promises of saving him are all lies. Lies we have heard before. You have destroyed this great creature to further your own ends. Only the brothers and sisters of the sun have a right to a sacred being such as this. We're gonna take him to show the world how Indian gods have been defiled, then we'll return him to his rightful place."

"Wait a minute!" I shouted above the cheers of the group. "You can't take our whale."

The chief looked directly in my eyes and gestured significantly with a shrug of his shoulders to his group of yelling braves. "How would you keep him in the face of such blood power as this?"

Take the goddam whale. My brain was already signaling my tongue. I wasn't about to sacrifice myself to their sense of injustice. I didn't even feel part of it. My ancestors were getting rousted out of their potato patches by British soldiers when their ancestors were slicing off Custer's golden locks. But I didn't have a chance to surrender, for before I knew it Jorgi had arrived on the scene like the avenging cavalry. He came running across the mall to the truck.

"Wait, brothers; this whale belongs to every race," he said, leaping on the hood of the truck and shouting at the militant band. "There's enough to go around for all of us."

I couldn't believe what I was hearing. Jorgi would have given them Janett before letting go of his whale.

"This whale is here so that other whales of this earth,

other great free creatures, spirits, and people can be saved and allowed to roam free. Brothers, let us share this whale."

The Indians quieted momentarily, not because they believed anything Jorgi was saying to them but more because he had the balls to jump up in the face of their riotous, hostile numbers. I think they were seeing how crazy this white man was before they beat him to death.

The young chief with the feathered cape left me and pushed his way through his braves and looked up at Jorgi. He raised his hand and everyone was still.

"What do you mean 'share,' Red Hair?" the chief said. For the first time their anger was directed away from me. I thought I detected a slight theatrical note to the chief's voice, like Marlon Brando playing Tonto. But before I had a chance to verify my suspicions Jorgi blew my mind. He was trying to get us both killed with what he said next.

"I mean this, Chief," Jorgi paused and looked all around the capitol grounds as if searching for some enlightened inspiration. "Since we got him first we keep our whale and do what we have to do with him. But when we're done he's yours and you can shove him up your ass till the seagull feathers fly off your back."

Silence. The antiseptic silence of a trauma room before the victims arrive settled over the crowd of Indians as Jorgi grinned widely down the chief's face. That last little bit of shock effect, stunning the Indians into inaction for a moment, was what Jorgi was counting on. I used it while all hatred was directed toward him to duck down under the truck, and when I did I could see through the legs on the other side the charging capitol police coming on at a jogger's pace with white helmets and black clubs held stiffly across their bodies. The legs around me broke into a run as the Indians fled. I came up on the other side of the truck just in time to meet Jorgi jumping down off the hood. He was screaming at the police.

"Get the one with the feathers. He attacked the girl!"

Once the police reached the whale they came to a halt. The Indians ran off into the downtown streets and traffic. It would have been fruitless to pursue them.

Jorgi got to me before the young capitol police lieutenant did and I was left holding the bag for the whole thing.

"When you sent her to get me," Jorgi said in a hushed conspiratorial tone, "that was the first thing I told them. I knew they would get their ass in gear a lot faster if they were out to save white girls and Christine from attack rather than a whale. They'd believe attempted gang rape but never whale theft. Tell them they just roughed the both of you up a bit, ripping her blouse and stuff like that. I sent Christine on to Blyth and I'll see that she takes her over to the capitol infirmary. Maybe I can talk her into ripping up her shirt before she gets there." With that he was off again across the wide lawn back toward the capitol building while I reluctantly ad-libbed my way through the police report. I didn't like lying to the police, but knew it was better to let them hear what they wanted to hear once they had acted. They left four officers guarding the whale after the main force left, which was a great relief to me. The lieutenant informed me that he was going to check with the Governor's staff to pull the Indians' demonstration permit.

A few minutes later the Hell's Angels came roaring around the capitol mall, two or three hundred strong, led by several news vans with cameramen lying on their tops holding TV minicams. They assembled in the distance in front of the capitol steps and the roar from their exhausts was deafening until on signal they stopped. On a loudspeaker bits and pieces of Marvin Hall's voice drifted through the trees toward me and the whale. I could see newsmen jockeying for position all around him.

"Under this administration, I want you to understand that a man has the right so long as he doesn't hurt the environment to do what he thinks is right. That includes doing what he wants with his own head."

There were boisterous macho cheers and the rest of Marvin Hall's short address to the bikers was lost to me. Twenty minutes later another deafening roar filled the capitol plaza as the bikers, satisfied that they had accomplished what they came for, kicked off their motors in unison and peeled off into formation, once more circling the capitol before they disappeared into the freeways of California's bloodstream.

At three o'clock we weren't due to go on yet for another hour, depending on whether or not they would allow the crazy Indians still to precede us. Tweedle-dee and Tweedle-dum, two of Blyth's young PR men, came over to the whale and started pulling bunting and flags out of cardboard boxes, redecorating the whale and truck. I helped them a bit, but quit after they chewed me out for stringing a rope of flags over the whale's head.

"He's king of the seas, not queen of the May," one of them said curtly as he pulled the flags from my hand. At their questioning I assured them that the trailer bed was now reinforced to the point where it could support several whales, but I soon discovered that my work of the night before was to go for naught, for under no circumstances were they going to allow Blyth or the Governor get up close to the whale, let alone on the truck. I unloaded the posts Jorgi had stolen the night before and piled them neatly in the gutter. By then all the little nooks and crannies of the mountain of political problems they seemed so concerned with were lost in the clouds above my head.

Jorgi didn't return for a good half hour after the Indians ran off. He was arranging last-minute details with Blyth, but when he did return he told me "Get your ass and the whale in gear." I told them there was another demo ahead of us yet, but he knew all about it.

"Birdwatchers and tree-lovers, small potatoes compared to our number," and he had me maneuver our truck and whale out into the street while he blocked traffic and gave me hand signals. I jockeyed the whale into the yellow curb in front of the capitol steps and plaza, but that wasn't where he wanted it. I had to go forward and backward several times before the whale was backed into and up on the plaza itself, scaring me shitless several times with fear that I was going to run over one of the assembled crowd. But they gladly parted their ranks for the whale, welcoming him with smiles as part of the "good fight" too. A couple of cops tried to wave me off, but Jorgi waved permits back in their faces and I was in for a safe landing. The Governor was already talking to them when I arrived. The minor commotion of the whale's arrival didn't even cause him to break one sentence. He was obviously on a tight schedule. The people he was addressing and whom I had backed the whale into had already passed the whale minutes before while I had been misdirecting the flags over his head. Sierra Clubbers joining the crowd below the steps with neatly printed placards and a matched step, understatedly attired in the dull garb of school-teachers. Except for a flashy attorney or two with wide-lapeled open shirts and gold chains entangled in curly chest hair, they were an orderly lot. I think I recognized two or three people who had been at Blyth's party but I wasn't sure, for their faces were often obscured with signs that read NOT ANOTHER TREE, SAVE CASH CREEK MOUNTAIN, and TREES CAN FEEL PAIN. They looked in awe up at the whale as they passed, like soldiers being reviewed by a respected and inspiring general. My sympathies went out to them, for my home was in the woods scarred by the loggers' chain saws. I was pleased once I got the truck positioned and stopped to hear Marvin Hall tell them that my woods shouldn't be turned into newsprint and toilet paper. I knew our whale was swimming in safe waters.

Blyth's aides continued to fuss with flags and decorations while the Governor talked to the Sierra Clubbers. A short distance away on the capitol mall's lawn I anxiously watched with a mild touch of stage fright the next group that was to precede us in taking an important issue directly from the people to the head of our state. Gay-rights activists were milling around under the lush capitol trees. Their uniform of the day seemed to be working-man camp—tight jeans, colorful plaid flannel shirts much like fishermen and lumberjacks wear, and baseball caps of diverse design with tractor, truck, and oil-product trademarks emblazoning their skulls. A couple of young queens were swishing it up with too much sheen and sparkle but more respectable types in natty business suits were bringing them under control. I got down from the truck and mingled in the back fringes of the Sierra Club crowd. They gazed like intent parishioners up the crowded capitol steps at Marvin Hall, who seemed to be finishing up his address.

The Governor was a slight, thin man in his mid-thirties with a serious, slightly aesthetic face. The kind I would normally avoid in any bar. He had an air about him of concern and a deportment of purpose. He held a microphone in one hand in an impromptu fashion. His other hand was casually placed in his pants pocket. This, and the absence of wild emphatic gestures, helped enhance his image of naturalness and openness. It was rumored during his campaign that he was a strict vegetarian and, widely published pictures of him at flush Central Valley cattlemen's barbecues aside, he did look stylishly thin. His vest was loose and his body turned inside it and his executive garments, which seemed better suited to an older, fleshier man. His hair was slicked down, giving it the look above his youthful face of being shorter than it actually was. He spoke in short staccato phrases with an almost total lack of inflection. An unflowery delivery that seemed deliberately genuine. A host of young aides was behind him. Behind the aides and partially obscured by newsmen stood Blyth. She was with several of her followers, four or five steps higher up than the Governor.

"While I have been Governor," Marvin said, looking directly down at the crowd, "not one additional acre of state forest has fallen to the axe, and I intend to keep it that way. I intend to extend the environmental impact law into every inch of private and national forest in this state."

Marvin was obviously telling it the way they wanted

to hear it. Polite cheers interrupted the faces around me, punctuating his remarks. And although I tuned out what he was saying as I walked back to the whale to help Jorgi make the final checks before his appearance, I felt content. The righteousness of the crowd was reassuring. My forest was safe in their and Marvin's hands.

"Shit, Stanley, they need the woods for scenery while they drive from their city home to their country home." Even Jorgi's cynical remarks couldn't upset my contentment when I returned to the truck. I tidied up the flags around the whale's great body like a happy little altar boy. I even forgot about the crazy Indians and suicidal bikers.

But my peace of mind was short-lived. At first I thought it was just the uncomfortable memory of the bikers' din coming up for air in my brain, but as soon as I thought about it I realized that this was a new noise. The crowd, the officials, and news people also heard it as it grew in intensity. Marvin Hall interrupted his speech and turned around nervously to confer with his aides.

"Friends of the earth," Marvin turned back to the Sierra Clubbers, "a development that we feared as an outside possibility is . . ." His remarks were now drowned out by the unbearable din that was fast approaching. Capitol police looked nervously around for orders, but everyone in the crowd was as dismayed as the next person until we saw the first of them turn a corner and enter the streets that ran around the capitol.

Trucks. Dozen upon dozen of them. Huge logging trucks were creeping in low gear around the mall as the bikers had done previously. They soon encircled the entire capitol grounds while more streamed in until they occupied both wide lanes in a double circle of almost unbearable vibration and noise. Most of them had their trailers piggy-backed, but several were carrying long loads of redwood logs festooned with signs: SUPPORT YOUR LOCAL LOGGER, SIERRA CLUB TAKE A HIKE, KISS MY AXE, ENVIRONMENTALISTS POLLUTE THE ECONOMY, DO IT IN THE WOODS, PAVE CASH CREEK MOUNTAIN. Men in plaid shirts waved axes and axe handles from the cabs of the trucks and from their perches on top of the logs. Air horns turned the inside of my head to jelly and it was impossible to hear what pickup loads of wives and honky-tonk angels were yelling in support as they moved along, dispersed here and there between the logging rigs.

Marvin Hall had stopped speaking and was huddled with his associates. The newsmen crowded more closely about them, more out of a sense of protection than a desire to hear what they were saying. The Sierra Clubbers sheepishly turned en masse now and were slowly compressing farther and farther back away from the street toward the Governor and the capitol steps. A few of them had already dropped their signs and were pushing and shoving one another as they sought what they thought was safety on the steps. I wanted desperately to run away myself, but Jorgi told me to climb up on the whale, imploring me to help him protect it. What I saw when I did only served to unsettle me further, melting whatever courage he tried to instill into a puddle of fear at his feet.

Raw power was pouring in around the capitol grounds. All the trucks seemed to have stopped now in unison, clogging every foot of street about the capitol. Their movement was obviously coordinated by CB radio, for I could see many drivers in the cabs with microphones in their hands. Men were alighting from the trucks with athletic leaps and moving toward the whale and the crowd cowering on the steps. They seemed to come from everywhere at once, not only from the streets but from all around the capitol building, swarming across the lawns and through the trees. We were about to be surrounded by a sea of militant moving woodchoppers, many of them carrying axe handles with and without signs. What courage I had had was completely drained out of me. Weak with terror, I envisioned another St. Bartholomew's Day massacre. The TAC squad and what police were on hand were swarming down from the inside of the capitol building, trying to get to and at least surround the Governor and his staff, causing everyone on the steps to bottleneck with no place to go. To make things worse the gays were now shrieking in our direction, fleeing the onslaught of the loggers. At first they held their ground with what seemed like a thin wall of wisecracks. The loggers were parting and started to move around them as if they were a colony of lepers. But a contingent of logger ladies and Anita Bryant banshees moved in and the encounter turned violent. Several of the gays manning the barricade of wit went sprawling, knocked on their asses by loggers' punches protecting their women's right of persecution.

I bailed out. When I hit the ground coming off the back of the flatbed, I stumbled and fell in the abandoned Sierra Club signs that littered the plaza pavement. I kicked and stumbled to my feet, desperately trying to free myself from the sticks and placards lest the loggers axe me to death by association. I looked back expecting to see Jorgi and the whale being chain-sawed into little pieces; the whale remained a looming island of serenity in the chaotic capitol plaza. Jorgi was right behind me, running to save his ass too. We both hit the outer edge of the Sierra Club crowd on the steps at the same time. In their fear they parted like Jell-O for us as we sought safety inside their mass. Together we pushed ourselves farther up the steps through the tight press of bodies. Blyth was calling Jorgi's name from somewhere above us over the din. We got within two steps of her and her terrified group but it took at least two more minutes for Jorgi to push up to Blyth with me right behind him. I got solidly elbowed in the stomach once and kicked in the side of my leg by a guy in a tweed jacket. When we reached Blyth the TAC squad was only a step or two above. They had completely surrounded the Governor, his aides, and the media. The police pushed out with their shiny long clubs held in leather-covered hands to hold back the crowd who were desperately seeking the safety of their protection. But there was no way in, up, or out. Hysteria was surging through the crowd. The nature-lovers were obeying the deeper urgings of nature. It was every man for himself. Jorgi pushed people away from Blyth, calling for me to do the same. A respectable-looking young man in a crew-neck sweater shoved his way up and into us. I pushed him backward at the shoulders. He came up swinging wildly at my face. A stick with a sign torn off at SAVE that Jorgi had grabbed flashed by my face and crashed solidly into the young man's head. Blyth kicked at his stomach as he crumpled below us.

The whale was surrounded now by a sea of loggers massed before the steps. But they held up short of actually attacking the crowd. Some of them were ripping the flags off our whale and truck but an unseen direction put a stop to their vandalism. They crowded onto the flatbed around him. Several men were even standing on the roof and hood of the cab, but my fears of their dissecting him with chain saws didn't materialize. They seemed bent on a better view rather than carnage, and they bided their time with taunts and jeers at the crowd huddled in fear of them on the steps. An empty beer can flew now and then from their ranks like a colorful flitting sparrow, bouncing harmlessly off the shoulders, out-stretched arms, and heads of the compressed Sierra Club, gays, and government officials cut off from Marvin Hall's protective cordon of cops. That something they were waiting for wasn't long in coming. A tree, a green redwood at least forty feet tall, was slowly moving through their parting ranks from the direction of the massed trucks in the street. Fifty or sixty little Paul Bunyans were carrying a frame of two-by-fours nailed together like a giant Christmas-tree stand that held the tree upright. They were cheered on by the massed loggers parting for them as they strained their way into the plaza below the steps. When the tree was in the center of the plaza they stopped, slowly putting it down in front of our whale. Out of the crowd several loggers appeared as a unit. They were wearing logger's hard hats, shiny aluminum wide-brim pots that looked like pith helmets with the canvas stripped off. A stocky man with a red face and short fat arms came forward with a slight limp. He held a bullhorn in his hands. Rumor surged through our crowd and Jorgi yelled to me and Blyth that it was Mike "Choker" Gustuson, the leader of the wood-workers' union from our very own Mendocino County. Dim memories bubbled up in my brain, for he was part of that other culture in my neck of the woods that the people I hung out with had very little to do with. But I did remember seeing reports of his exploits in the *Mendocino Beacon* and *Fort Bragg Advocate* and once even in the *Grape Vine* when he bulldozed through a commune, taking out tepees and domes that were denying access to a virgin stand of woods. He had received the name Choker as a young man while setting choke chains. One of them entangled his leg, pulling him and a thirty-foot section of tree a quarter of a mile up a steep skid trail. As with other living legends in our county, most of the people I knew couldn't wait until he was dead.

"Hall, Governor Hall." Choker was blaring away with his bullhorn. The loggers quieted down and the Sierra Clubbers about me didn't make a peep, thankful for the moment that the loggers' attention wasn't fully focused on them. By now I thought that the Governor had probably been whisked by the police deep inside the safest fallout shelter far beneath the granite interior of the capitol building. But all heads were straining toward the top steps, where the police stood as firm as Samurai warriors. Marvin was in their center.

"Yes, Governor, you. We're talking to you; that's why we're here." Choker's tone was familiar and contemptuous. The loggers cheered.

"Environmental impact—toilet paper." There were more shouts and yells from the massed loggers. "That's what this is." Choker motioned to a piece of paper tacked like a *Wanted* poster to the tree the loggers had carried in. "It says that before we can cut down a tree we have to file an environmental report about birds, frogs, snakes, bugs, and probably now from the looks of it," he gestured menacingly toward our truck, "even whales. We can't cut nothin' before a bunch of college professors and bureaucratic punkin heads come out to the woods—paid by our tax dollars—to tell us just what we can and can't cut. An' that includes Cash Creek Mountain. Kiss my axe, Governor." The plaza exploded with cheers. "We got our own environment to make an impact on, like house mortgages and car payments and wives and kids and goddam doctors' bills. An' we're here to tell you that this piece of paper here don't mean a *damn* thing to us."

With that, a huge chain saw suddenly appeared at Choker's side, carried by a slight young man with a handlebar mustache. He pulled the saw to life in a cloud of smoke and noise. The loggers started yelling again, but Choker kept his harangue up and it sounded like he said "This is what we think of this environmental crap!" just before the man with the chain saw stepped up the redwood tree and let it rip through the center of the paper tacked to it bark. The blade whined into a high pitch as it bit into the wood.

"If those bastards put one scratch on our whale, I'll burn their fuckin' woods down," Jorgi said in a vicious tone next to me. His face was full of anger and his eyes had the peculiar intensity they had held when he had told me about our getting rich in abalone and when he first told me about the whale. He frightened me as much as the loggers did, for I think he meant it. Blyth was giving him a strange look too as I saw her face briefly. But we turned back to our raving loggers as everyone heard the crack of the tree.

It fell away from the whale and directly toward the

capitol steps. Instantly there was a surge through the crowd as those on the bottom of the steps parted with screams in an attempt to move out of the path of the falling tree. But the loggers knew what they were doing, and the top of the tree slammed into the pavement with a loud crash a few feet from the steps and the edge of the Sierra Clubbers. They had dropped the tree as deftly as a knife-thrower in a circus places a blade next to his lady's rib cage and heart. Many of the women in our crowd were crying now. Men clenched their fists and swore legal vengeance. Jorgi tried to talk me into pushing our way back to the whale and truck. "We've got to save our whale from those turkeys, Stanley," he said, "even if we have to run a few of them down to get him out of here." I pretended not to hear him. The loggers would have beat us up before we ever reached the whale and truck. They were mad with success. Several of them had appeared with more chain saws and they were slicing up the redwood tree in the plaza like a loaf of French bread. I feared the worst for the whale now and was already envisioning him as giant fillets next to the fallen tree. But before any of that happened Marvin Hall made his move.

At first the loggers continued their gleeful victory dance of destruction while Hall tried to make himself heard. His PA system was turned full blast and those of us at the top of the steps cowered beneath its screeching blast. Slowly the loggers realized they were being responded to by the government that they had come to petition or destroy in the process. Choker signaled for quiet. To many of us on the steps he might have been the crippled elf of destruction from the Black Forest, but he was smart enough to realize when he had won political center stage. The camera crews and newsmen above us were having a field day.

"I can appreciate where you're coming from, men." The Governor's voice was breaking in above the slowly subsiding noise of the loggers. Marvin's first words were met with boos. "My grandfather was a lumberman and . . ." There was an isolated chorus of Rebel yells from the loggers coming from around our whale, but Choker's lieutenants soon quieted them down. "He knew, my own family knows what it was like to make a living from a hard environment. To fight fire, flood, and mud so that the people of this great state can have a roof over their heads."

I knew enough about Marvin Hall to realize that he wasn't quite telling the truth. His grandfather had been a lumberman, but he didn't chop trees. He owned the largest mill in Humboldt County around the turn of the century and had made a killing in redwood railroad ties shipped to Mexico and South America. It was this money that had springboarded Marvin's father into the governorship during the late forties and early fifties and set up the political dynasty that Marvin inherited. But any port in a storm. Marvin had at least gotten their attention away from their destructive frenzy.

"Now I know that there is hardly one of you out there who would wantonly destroy a tree that wouldn't get put to some useful purpose. Everyone's eyes on the steps looked nervously at the sliced-up redwood on the plaza. The nervousness turned to just a hint of suspicion as they gazed up toward the Governor.

"I've seen the reforestation and demonstration forests most of the companies you work for have provided, and as long as these programs continue, your jobs will be safe for your sons and daughters."

Another dim memory flashed into my brain. One day during the summer when I was rummaging through Big Lorraine's bookshelf of Far-Eastern lore, I came across "Memories of the Past," a pamphlet put out by the Mendocino Historical Society. In "The Nine Lives of Squealing Charlie," I remembered reading that his last life was snuffed out by a strike-breaker's bullet during the great McKinleyville lumber-mill strike of 1929. It had been Hubert McKenzie Hall's—Marvin's granddaddy's—mill. But I was sure I was unfairly suspecting Marvin for whatever his father's father had to do to survive. Wasn't he casting bread upon the waters of angry loggers to save my ass? They were listening attentively to him now and he told them that the environmental impact statements that they had come to protest weren't his idea but rather the requirement of the federal government. "These unfair impact statements are an imposed stipulation forced upon you in order that your companies can keep their timber depreciation allowance. Forced by the administration in Washington to help keep redwood off the walls of American homes and pine from South Carolina and Georgia on it."

The Sierra Clubbers had visibly winced at Marvin's words, but there was nothing they could do. Their seething doubts had to be contained as the loggers now whooped it up outside and all around us. Unfortunately, Marvin's efforts at quieting the streets of the capitol went in vain.

God knows why they did it. Were they still after our whale? Did they want to keep the loggers off Cash Creek Mountain that badly? Or were they just pissed off that they weren't allowed on stage that afternoon? Whatever their problem, they certainly weren't playing by the touch-and-go rules of peaceable assembly. Marvin Hall was still speaking when the first firebomb went off. It wasn't a loud noise. It was more like a huge swoosh of air, but as I looked over our whale and across the street in front of the plaza crammed with parked trucks the fireball came up into the air like a sudden sun before it disappeared into a black cloud. People all around me were yelling and screaming again. Loggers were jumping off trucks and running away from the billowing cloud, but they were crashing into other loggers running toward the billowing smoke.

Then I saw one. He was running through the parked trucks like a dodging toreador holding a smoking bottle over his head. He'd disappear and reappear around the fronts and backs of the rigs as he went. Two more daring young Indians ran behind him with unlit bottles. The first Indian was into the middle of the logging trucks when he threw his lighted bottle at the cab of a truck. It bounced off, back toward him like a tennis ball, failed to explode, and rolled unseen under another trailer. His two companions caught up with him and one of them went round the front of a truck, emerging on the edge of the plaza. The other two were lost to sight behind a pile of logs on a vehicle, but in a second or two another billowing ball of fire signaled their success. This time an entire logging truck erupted in flames, along with its piggy-backed trailer.

"Jesus, he's gonna cook the whale!" Jorgi screamed above the pandemonium all about us.

The lone Indian on the edge of the plaza, who looked more like a South American revolutionary to me, was

184

holding his Molotov cocktail at arm's length while he snapped a cigarette lighter under it. Three loggers started to rush him, but when they saw the neck of the bottle puff into a small flame they turned and ran the other way. Several cops were beating their way down through the crowd in an attempt to reach the plaza, but the young man with the red headband was already arching his arm to fling the deadly missile.

Jorgi was pulling me down through the crowd. I looked up to see the flaming arc flying through the air at our whale. The bottle hit the top of the cab squarely but skidded and spun off, landing in the near side of the plaza, where it exploded into a ball of flame that totally engulfed the fallen redwood tree, stand and all.

The heat was searing but Jorgi ran toward the truck and whale. Like a madman I followed. The fireball had singed the plastic on one side of the whale and it was smoldering on the beast's body. Jorgi jumped up on the flatbed. Smoke billowed from the burning tree and incinerated redwood needles fell back to earth all about us.

"Drive, Stanley, drive!" Jorgi said above the crackling flames. He was beating at the whale's smoldering side with his shirt. My body quickly climbed into the cab while my brain still resisted, wondering about the temperature of the gas tank on the fire side of the truck. The front seat was filled with empty beer cans deposited by the boisterous loggers. I shoved them out of the way and started the truck, hardly letting the motor come to full rpm's before I shoved it in gear and we lurched away from the burning tree.

The hood in front of me was aimed at the mall and lawn, but it was filled with curious and fearful bodies running around under large trees, so I aimed the truck down the sidewalk. There was no way to get back to the street jammed with trucks. Nearby, the Indian who had thrown the bomb was being beaten into the ground by the loggers who, in turn, were set upon by the club-wielding cops. But it was only a passing flash and one of many as I gunned the truck and roared down the sidewalk as fast as I dared through bodies that jumped away and ran before me. Several trashcans ground under the wheels and two hundred feet of parking meters cracked on the edge of the flatbed before I brought the truck to a stop far away from the still-raging fire. I jumped out of the cab but Jorgi had the whale under control. I climbed up and helped him throw off the few smoldering flags that were left on the flatbed. The whale's plastic covering was peeling off like large pieces of ugly sunburned skin where the fire had singed him. His real body beneath was still intact. Suddenly I thought of his eyes, fearing that they might have been cooked out of their sockets, but a quick check of his face relieved my fears. They were intact but thickly glazed and milky. I think the poor bastard had seen enough of the world of politics that we had sailed him into.

14

BALLS!

But Jorgi wasn't finished with the world of power. It took several hours for the police to clear the people and trucks from the capitol grounds. Marvin Hall was now running the government from an emergency National Guard trailer instead of the capitol steps. It really wasn't necessary, for by the time the first jeeps arrived the streets around the capitol building had been swept clean by the police. Giant tow trucks hauled off the destroyed logging trucks. The presence of the Guard, though, helped Marvin dispel the notion of some in the state that he was soft on law and order.

Jorgi and I drove the whale around Sacramento until it was dark, making sure we weren't followed by any Indians. Then we headed for Blyth's headquarters in a Howard Johnson's on the outskirts of town near the airport. The manager refused to let us park the whale in front, so I drove it around back and parked it in a freshly harvested onion field. Jorgi was in a hurry to confer with Blyth, who—along with the whale—had missed her political début. Janett was already in her room, and the one next door was mine. He left me to stay with the whale in case the Indians showed up. He also told me to repair the singed side of the whale. As soon as Jorgi was around the corner and into the Inn I decided that I was in no state of mind for cosmetic work, or a last stand. I headed for a shower and some much-needed food. It was already our sixth day out of the woods and I doubted that I could endure any longer at this pace. Even Big Lorraine was a fond memory now.

The manager gave me my key and room number, but I never made it to peace and quiet. As I was heading to the second level of orange doors, I ran into Christine Mulhern hurrying toward me with one of Blyth's aides. My libido took a soar and then an abrupt dive.

"You bastard, Stanley."

"What?" Before I could say the next word her lithe body sprang forward and she hit me square in the side of the jaw.

"The whole goddam thing's your fault. No Indian ever touched me, you racist creep!"

"You're responsible for the riot." The PR guy chimed in with a vicious smile on his face. Christine turned her back on me and the two of them disappeared into a nearby door. I followed, demanding an explanation, but before I knew it my sense of injustice was overwhelmed by turmoil. It was Blyth's suite. She was standing and gesturing emphatically at the TV set, which was doing the reruns of our big day in Sacramento. Jorgi was sitting on the end of the bed with other members of

Blyth's party. Two men I had not seen before were standing on one side of the room in front of an iridescent seascape on the wall. They seemed professionally apprehensive and I immediately smelled cop, but it turned out they were two of Marvin Hall's aides. One of them had a clipboard.

As soon as Blyth saw me enter behind Christine she threw up her arms and yelled, "Why bring him in here? Get rid of him. He's done enough damage."

"No, wait," one of the Governor's aides said. "Let's get it straight, that's the only way we can keep it locked up. Is this the guy, Christine, that told the cops you were being raped by the Indians?"

His partner moved menacingly toward the door to cut off my escape, but my whole body by now was flushed with an anger I had never felt before. Jorgi's eyes wouldn't meet mine. I was getting ready to leap at his throat even though he was smiling at me and making funny little gestures with his hands to keep quiet.

"Yes," Christine said, "Blyth was going to have me sent to a hospital before I had a chance to tell her that no Indian had done anything to me." She pointed to me with an accusing finger. "He told me to run and get the police and his buddy there when the Indians tried to take the whale away from them, but he must have run after me with his lies."

"Christine, that's not true," I pleaded, but before I could continue Blyth broke in.

"Christ, I was big with Indians." Blyth was concerned more with her political plight than with truth. "The whole peninsula is big on Indians. Stanford even changed the name of its football team for Indians. If the media ever finds out that someone from my campaign incited those Indians to violence I'll lose every liberal vote in my district. I could have gotten that chief to the shopping center."

"Blyth, the whale's the thing," Jorgi interrupted. "He's worth a thousand Indians, according to these guys." He gestured toward Marvin Hall's aides. "Only the police are checking out the Indians' claim that they were falsely accused of attacking Christine. If she takes a hike there's nothing for the media to follow up on."

"But I want the truth to come out," Christine blurted, giving Jorgi a hate-filled look. "I love Indians. They're close to nature, they only want what . . ."

"What they can take, that's what they want. They wanted my whale for a barbecue, a free ride. Half of them are greasers and wouldn't know which way to piss out of a tepee," Jorgi said, getting to his feet, confronting Christine.

Christine stared at Jorgi, trembling with fury, but Blyth intervened before she had a chance to explode.

"Yes, that's the thing. Will the whale still carry me?" She turned questioningly toward her aides and Marvin's men. "There's more than one tribe of Indians. Maybe my uncle could get Marlon Brando. Christine could go away for a while until the smoke clears."

"I think that's a concept we could go with," one of Marvin's aides chimed in. Christine's rage turned to a look of incredulity at Blyth. "The Governor would still like the whale exposure," Hall's aide continued. "Now more than ever, to balance out his hard-line approach this afternoon. It's just a question of where—Sacramento's out. It's too close to the people."

"How about Pebble Beach?" Blyth said, her voice rising with a renewed sense of optimism. "My uncle is on the board of directors of the Sinatra golf tournament, and even though tomorrow's the final round I'm sure it could be arranged. Marvin could get his exposure with my whale and I can still get mine with him. The whole place is fenced off for seventeen miles. No one gets in or out unless they belong."

"Blyth, that's great!" Jorgi was positively fawning. "We could even sell golf balls for Save-the-Whale donations. I can see it now, the ocean in the background, the very best sporting crowd in the country."

I suddenly had a very real sense that they were all crazy. Christine and I were totally forgotten now as everyone in the room besides us went into a flurry of planning and phone calls. I had to get out of there and left right behind Christine, who stormed out. I never got a chance to explain to her, for one of Blyth's aides hustled her away. I never saw her again. Blyth had obviously ordained that social problems and politics weren't her bag. They flew her out of Sacramento that night for Southern California and one of Blyth's connections at Marine World. The last I heard of her she was happily into the problems of fish and a star attraction with her lovely body, cavorting and putting dolphins through their paces for the tourists and the rest of mankind peering through the portholes.

My plan was to clear out as soon as I got my share of the money—and I wasn't the only one. Janett was waiting for me in my room.

She was lying on the bed. The colored glow from the soundless TV bathed her in its dull flickering light. Her pregnant stomach in its first noticeable swelling looked like a low hill on her otherwise thin body. She looked very tired. "I heard and saw it all on the news, Stanley.

What Jorgi told me about you and the girl was a lie, wasn't it?"

My heart reached out for the lifeline of understanding she threw to me.

"Yes, and I'm clearing out," I said. "I'm getting what money's mine from the whale and heading back to the woods."

"Get mine too. I've already asked him twice tonight, but he keeps putting me off for her and her political circus. Take it. It's hidden in a can inside the whale's mouth just like he said he'd hide it. We'll rent a car and go home."

It was all I needed to know. My body was halfway back to Mendocino when I left the room, headed for the whale.

The air outside had turned cold and a slight wind blew from the direction of the airport with the faint odor of burning kerosene in the air. The whale rested peacefully on the truck. He was slightly illuminated by the hundreds of bathroom lights shining out through frosted windows on the rear of the Howard Johnson's. A green-and-white light revolved in the distance from the airport tower. A jet gunned its engines. I approached the brute's head resting above the taillights of the trailer and stared up into his massive face. There was no doubt about it, I felt sorry for myself. Cheated. Betrayed. The commitment that the whale had inspired in me for the first time in my life was about to be over. Again I was quitting, running away. A life of perpetual leaving and drifting, of aimlessness and insignificant pleasure and pain was all I could see ahead of me. I stood before the great whale feeling like an insect—imperfect, misdirected, forever responding to forces beyond me before the

big shoe of death stamped me out. I decided to take all
the money for Janett and me. But my sniveling reverie
and plot was interrupted. I saw Jorgi come around the
edge of the motel just as I was climbing up on the trailer.

"Stanley, ol' buddy, I'm glad you're here." His voice
was hurried and I waited until his face was level with the
back of the trailer. That's when I was going to kick him
in the teeth.

"Don't 'ol' buddy' me, Jorgi. I've had enough of your
shit for one night."

"What the hell are you talking about, Stanley? What I
had to say was for business, for all of us. I'm the only
link between the whale and Blyth. I've got to be above
suspicion around her, or she'll cut us off cold."

I missed the chance to catch him in the face and he
climbed up next to me and the whale's head and went on
bullshitting.

"We're close, Stanley, close. If we can just pull this
Governor thing off for Blyth, then all of us will be
swimming in the big-time sea of ecology and money.
Which reminds me. Help me get this baby to cough up
some loot right now."

"Whatever money comes out of his mouth, Jorgi, I'm
taking for Janett and me and we're heading back north,"
I said as firmly as I could, ready to hit him if I had to.

"You're crazy, Stanley. This close and you go belly-up
on me. No way, boy, no way. The money that's left
inside this sucker is needed right now."

I could make out the dim features of his face as we
stood in the dark on either side of the whale's head and I
sensed his ever-present smile. My stomach knotted with
apprehension.

"What do you mean 'left,' Jorgi?"

"Just—left. What's there after the rest is gone. I had to send Race Hubbard several big bills to cover the cost of the truck or else the whale would be laying on the street and our bodies beaten to pulp by chains next to it after he sicked his biker buddies on our asses. And don't think that all this motel life and eatin' out and supplies for the whale and new clothes and stuff was free. We've been getting *fat* off this whale, Stanley."

"But we must have taken in close to three thousand dollars for bumper stickers during those two days in the shopping center. And what about the five thousand from Blyth?" I said, angry and weak at the same time.

"We don't see a nickel from her until our week's up and the publicity with the Governor's finished. These rich people aren't into cash, and when you do get what's coming you'd better believe that you've done everything they want right down to the fine print. Until then, she's got us and the whale by the short hairs. I don't know what kind of crap Janett has been feeding you, or you her, but you both better get it together. If you run out on the whale now you're both sunk. It's going to be a hard winter in the trees up to your asses in mud and rain standing in the commodities line."

"So what's left?" I asked nervously, knowing full well that it had been he who was living high, not Janett or me.

"Just enough for about three thousand golf balls. In a few minutes I'll roust Janett and we'll be on our way to Pebble Beach. It's on. Blyth's uncle pulled it off. Frank Sinatra, Bob Hope, Gerald Ford, lots of big-time entertainment, network TV, and all of the most important people in California, not to mention half the country. It wasn't easy, 'cause they're already into the last round—

they're parking us away from the main clubhouse, afraid that the whale might steal too much of the show. But the Governor will set down nearby in his helicopter, do a set with Blyth in front of the whale for the cameras, and then do what he has to do with the bigger fish in the clubhouse. By then we'll be shittin' in tall cotton, Stanley. This last eight hundred dollars will cover the expense of the balls."

"What balls?" I asked incredulously.

"I figured we'd sell them on the side of Blyth's main event. Save-the-Whale souvenir golf balls. By morning we should be trucking through Sunnyvale halfway to Carmel. I've got an old abalone-diver buddy there and he runs Pearl Divers, a golf-ball salvage operation with major contracts with every golf club in northern California. They dive in water traps and lakes on golf courses for lost balls, then sell them back to the clubs. It's a harder racket than you think, because children are their major competition. My buddy has to drive steel rods into the bottom of the lakes to keep kids from pulling basket and buckets across that scoop up all the balls. They place jagged pieces of metal too in water traps so the kids can't wade around in the shallows. Between here and there all we have to do is figure out some way to stamp the balls with a little blue whale. In that crowd they ought to be worth at least five dollars a donation."

"It's crazy! You're nuts," I said disgustedly.

"No, I'm not, Stanley. You're the fool. Maybe you and Janett *deserve* to go back to the woods and live on roasted soybeans for the rest of your lives. I'm staying on the outside with the whale and filet mignon. Help me get this stash out if you're still in. If you do, both of you will be wearing diamonds by Christmas."

What could I do? Without money, I knew, the country could be as cruel as any city street. I made another deal with my conscience and resolved to paddle along with him until Blyth paid us off. I mumbled a dejected "okay" and stooped to help him open the jaws.

I slid my fingers into and over the gums of the whale's mouth, getting a grip alongside his large teeth. Jorgi did the same and we lifted up in unison, but the jaws seemed to be frozen shut.

"They weren't this tight last night," Jorgi said. He got a crowbar out of the cab of the truck and we pried the mouth open with just enough room for him to reach in with his arm. I strained to hold the jaws open as he reached into the whale's mouth, and in a second or two he was pulling on something. But in that same second as I lifted hard on the upper jaw a powerful odor rose and filled my nostrils.

"That's it; I got it," Jorgi said, as he pulled a thin wire with a coffee can attached to it from the whale's throat.

"Jorgi," I said, "do you smell that?" He obviously didn't at first, for he answered, "Yeah, sweet money," as he hurriedly removed the lid off the can.

"There's something rotten inside our whale," I said, but he paid no attention, stuffing the bills into his pocket.

"Jorgi," I told him in a hushed voice in case anyone might be listening to us through one of the windows in the back of the motel. "We screwed up when we embalmed this whale—it stinks."

"You're putting me on, Stanley," he said. But I wasn't, and I invited him to squat down by the whale's mouth—which I continued to hold open, pulling it even wider as he did.

"Jesus," he said as the first whiff caught him square in the face, "shut the damn thing down."

That one whiff was all that was needed to convince him, but it certainly didn't plunge him into the despair I was now feeling. His brain simply flushed the bad news and spread action throughout his body. He gave me strict instructions to let no one get near the trailer, especially anyone working for Blyth.

"Be ready to roll as soon as I come back." He jumped down off the trailer and ran around the back of the motel. I pushed down on the whale's upper jaws in an attempt to stem his unbearable halitosis from spreading on the wind into the motel.

He returned in about an hour with Janett in Blyth's station wagon, blasting right through the onion field and stopping alongside the whale. He switched off the headlights immediately. I could hear Janett arguing and swearing at him even before the motor died, but Jorgi seemed to be paying her little attention. He called to me to help him and started unloading the back of the wagon. I passed Janett as she sat sulking in the front seat and tried to explain by saying "I'm sorry, the money is . . . ," but she interrupted me with an abrupt "Yes, I know, Stanley. It's not your fault," and I hurried over to help Jorgi. We carried several cases from the back of the wagon to the back of the trailer, and the only explanation he gave me at first was "We'll fight fire with fire, Stanley." It didn't take long to find out what he meant.

Mothballs, millions of them. He had Janett hold a flashlight on the whale's mouth and while she did Jorgi and I opened package after package. He explained he was damned lucky to find them at a open-late Payless supermarket drugstore. We pried open the mouth again, overwhelmed at first by the stench, and left it propped wide with the crowbar. We stuffed mothballs into his mouth and down his throat as far as we could with a long-handled dustpan Jorgi had stolen from the motel. The inner tissues of the whale's throat were soft and mushy. The more we piled mothballs in and pushed, the worse the odor became. The poor creature's tongue had become soft to the touch and mothballs went right into it like jellybeans into Jell-O. It was a hideous job; my skin tightened while my stomach revolted. Several teeth fell loose from his gums, releasing an even worse stench, but we did root-canal work with more mothballs and put the teeth gently back in place. Janett started vomiting and I reached down for the flashlight before she sought the clean open air of the plowed onion field. We filled his mouth and throat with so many mothballs that I was high from their medicinal odor. When we finally closed the jaws again, hundreds of them were rolling out over his gums like white marbles onto the back of the trailer and ground below. Jorgi kicked the rest of them over the side.

"There," he said, "that should cover the odor just long enough for us to make a killing. If we keep people at a distance no one will know the difference. If they get close just say it's the enbalming fluid they smell, explaining it cost us thousands to have him preserved. Then hit 'em up for a donation."

The three of us piled into the cab and drove off with our festering whale into the night back across California toward the sea and the promise of Pebble Beach.

By dawn we were slowly cruising through the early morning freeway traffic near Sunnyvale. As usual, the whale didn't contribute to the orderly flow. Gawkers slowed and stared, even in the opposite lanes, straining their necks to get a look at our strange cargo. There was a noticeable lack of traffic, however, directly behind our truck. In the side-view mirror, I could see cars veering out of our lane several hundred feet behind us to avoid the pungent slipstream. By the time we hit the off ramp at Sunnyvale to pick up the golfballs there was a highway patrol officer on a motorcycle tailing us. He pulled us over and advanced with his hand over his face and nose, but Jorgi got us off the hook by telling him we had gotten lost on our way from Marine World to a dog-food factory with a dead killer whale that had pined its life away after being captured and separated from its mate. Janett, who sat between us and had said nothing as we crossed the state during the night, stared at me in disbelief. When the cop left and Jorgi had us rolling again she turned to him, sarcastically asking how he intended to keep the odor of the whale from the crowds at Pebble Beach.

"Because stink rises straight to heaven. We stay downwind from any crowd, maybe even scattering a few crushed mothballs under the trailer; then the only smell we'll have to worry about will be that of money as it piles up in front of our noses."

Janett said nothing. I kept my mouth shut too until we reached the house of Jorgi's old diving buddy. It was a vintage tract home that looked to me in need of recycling by a bulldozer. The stucco was broken off all over its exterior, revealing chicken-wire sores. There were a couple of broken-down trucks and hundreds of peach baskets littered all over the driveway, the porch, and front of the house. A partially inflated yellow life raft was lying in the small square area that doubtless used to be a lawn but was now just adobe dirt and dust. The rest of the street didn't look much better. It was obviously an old development where the lower classes were either moving into or out of suburban life. Jorgi went into the house while Janett and I waited with the whale; he soon emerged again through an opening garage door with a fat balding man, barefoot and wearing Levi's and a tee shirt. Jorgi yelled at us to come help him. Janett stayed in the truck. I couldn't blame her for her uncooperativeness. But, like me, her soul was stuck to the whale until we could liberate ourselves with some cash and flee back to the woods.

"Reef Rat Ronnie," Jorgi said, introducing me to his friend, who still seemed half asleep. The interior of the garage was filled with cardboard boxes and baskets, most of them filled to the top with dirty golf-balls. There were ropes, compressors, steel rods, and lots of nondescript hardware scattered in among the boxes and bushels. Three massive diving suits hung from the low rafters like victims on a gallows, and the bad memories of our night in the abalone business returned with an unpleasant rush. Jorgi had me carry the containers of balls out to our truck, where I placed them all around the whale where there was room on the flatbed. He and Ronnie were still dickering over the price while I was portering the fourth load out. After that Jorgi gave me a hand, gleeful over the fact that he got the balls three for a dollar instead of Ronnie's regular seventy-five cents apiece to the clubs. Ours, of course, were unwashed, direct from their rescue in mud and duck shit, but Jorgi said a bucket of soapy water and rolls of paper towels would take care of that. He borrowed a small square of spongelike Neoprene from one of Ronnie's old diving suits and with scissors cut out the miniature outline of a whale. Then he pasted the whale to a small block of wood and got Ronnie to get a bottle of ink out of his house. On the first few balls Jorgi pressed, the ink was too thick. The image of the whale ran down in a blue stain onto his fingers, but with a bit of practice and a light touch it would be possible with his impromptu rubber stamp to place a little whale on each golfball once they were cleaned. As soon as I learned how to do it Jorgi was in a great hurry to leave. We secured the containers of golfballs to the truck with some rope Ronnie lent us. Jorgi speculated out loud that over two thousand whale balls, as he called them, at five dollars a donation would be worth over ten thousand dollars.

"Jesus, Stanley! The sooner we get there the better. There's bound to be thirty to forty thousand people for the last day of the tournament, and two thousand balls will just take care of the hard-core whale-lovers."

"What about Blyth?" I interrupted as we secured the ropes. "Pebble Beach is a class area with seventeen miles of chain-link fence to keep out the solicitors and peddlers."

"Screw her. What we pick up on the side after she's done her thing with the whale is our business. For the rich the appearance of charity is an almost sacred pursuit. The whale balls will help her as much as the whale."

It took us an hour and a half to grind up the Santa Cruz grade with the engine whining for all it was worth, hauling the whale over the low coastal mountains. As he drove Jorgi started speculating on all the marvelous things he was going to do as soon as the whale made us rich, including a Japanese hot-bath business that served gourmet desserts on floating trays. This precipitated an argument between him and Janett. She broke her silent mood from the night before and forcefully insisted she just wanted enough money to get back to Mendocino to make it through the winter and her pregnancy. I tried to tune them out by immersing my brain and eyes in the passing scenery. We passed a place on the side of the road painted a brilliant red called Santa's Village. Children and parents alighted from cars and rushed toward the Xmas Tree Corral. I was reminded that the end of the year was less than two weeks away and that not everyone in California led a screwball life with a dead and rotting whale tied about their necks as their only hope of salvation. In another hour we were rolling through misty flatlands covered with legions of artichoke plants before hitting the congested outskirts of Monterey with its hundreds of motel signs flashing No VACANCY. Janett and I made loud protestations of hunger but Jorgi was high and without the need of food, totally into an early arrival at the golf tournament in order to get set up for our latest killing. We went up another grade through pine and coastal cypress, then turned off at the Pebble Beach exit to the Seventeen-Mile Drive.

The guard at the gate stared at our whale in disbelief and wouldn't let us into the exclusive residential area. Jorgi got out and made a phone call to tournament headquarters. Blyth's assistants were on the ball and the guard reluctantly passed our dilapidated truck through, but not before we were met by Blyth's station wagon and the tired-looking PR prig who had only arrived an hour or so before himself from Sacramento. Blyth had flown to Monterey during the night in a plane her uncle had sent up for her. We followed the station wagon through a lovely road lined with trees and elegant homes with spacious well-kept grounds until we came around a low granite wall lining the roadway and the ocean spread before our eyes in all its vastness. Below us lay the famous Pebble Beach Golf Course. Although it was still only ten, the early morning rounds were already under way. Thousands of people moved between the well-cordoned greens in orderly processions as the nation's best golfers stroked their way to riches. There were several high towers on top of which TV crews stood. A Goodyear blimp circled lazily like an airborne leviathan high in the air.

"A gigantic balloon shaped like a whale; that's what we need to fly ahead of us and announce our coming," Jorgi said as soon as he saw the airship.

"The coming of what?" I replied, tired and hungry and not in the mood for a breakfast of Jorgi's schemes. "Ten tons of rotting blubber?"

"Stanley, I've been giving that some thought during the night, and I don't think we're in that bad a shape. Basically, I think we did a great job on his outer hide. In fact, the whale is a fucking cosmetic masterpiece. It's his heart and guts that're going to hell. If we can keep him together for just two or three days more, then we'll have the cash to operate."

"Operate?" Janett said, interrupting with disbelief. It was the first thing she had said since their argument coming up the grade.

"Right. Operate. We haul him to a boatyard and have a mobile sailboat lift back right over his ass. They work the straps under his body and haul him up in the air a few feet so we can get a clean cut at his stomach. Then we cut him open with a chain saw from his chin to his asshole and dump out everything that's rotten. The rest's easy. We wash the hollow cavity with more formaldehyde, pump his empty belly full of Styrofoam, sew him up, and he's as good as new."

Janett and I looked at each other and said nothing.

We kept following the station wagon into a service road that skirted above the main clubhouse, heavily congested with limousines and stylish sportsmen and their ladies entering and exiting the building, which resembled a large Spanish hacienda with a blood-red tile roof, ornate wrought-iron-covered windows, and a circular fountain in front replete with nymphs spouting water out of the tops of their bronze heads.

"That's where we should park the whale," Jorgi insisted as soon as we stopped, but Blyth's PR man bitchily informed Jorgi that we'd stay exactly where he put us. We were a good fifty yards from the clubhouse, directly across the main road and overlooking the eighteenth tee, already filling with people in the roped-off gallery areas. From where we stopped I could look down at the verandas adjoining the clubhouse's south side. It opened into a vast patio which fronted the eighteenth green. It was evidently an area reserved for the chosen few. The smart set and tournament officials in dazzling red blazers and blue slacks mingled in a compact crowd. Everyone on the patio was wearing a small gold badge with a white ribbon over his heart in contrast to nothing but gaping envious stares from those packed in the nearby galleries. For a moment I thought I saw Paul Newman and Clint Eastwood standing together like Mutt and Jeff before television interviewers, but they were soon lost to my sight in the crowd of tight-pressed dignitaries. There was little time, however, to spy upon the hoity-toity. The task at hand was the whale.

We were parked in a small lot that was a staging area for television crews. Large white and gray vans with network symbols emblazoned on their sides purred importantly with the sounds of their own generating equipment. Camera crews were atop the vans making last-minute adjustments as they aimed their cameras like machine guns down toward the clubhouse and green. A host of black cables like tentacles ran from the vans under a culvert in the road toward the clubhouse. Upslope from us, at the edge of the lot, there was a small, immaculate practice putting green; it was here, the prig informed us, that the Governor's helicopter would land. The script called for Blyth to greet him at the copter as soon as they landed. Then they would both make a short appearance in front of the whale before they went down to the clubhouse to mingle with the rich and famous. The PR man was striking large Xs on the pavement near the whale where the two of them would stand so that the tournament and the Pacific Ocean would fill the background.

"What's that foul smell?" he said as he scurried about with the chalk and his schedules in his hand. Jorgi hurriedly embraced him with an arm around his shoulders and maneuvered him to the other side of the whale with a host of questions, but the PR man broke loose from his grasp as soon as he saw Janett and me unloading the golf balls.

"Blyth said nothing about a carnival concession," he said to Jorgi in an overwrought tone but Jorgi calmed him down again by promising that we'd do the flag work on the truck, giving him a much-needed rest plus one hundred dollars commission off the whale balls. The ploy worked and the little whelp was soon gone. Janett and I strung flags on the truck, keeping up a good front in spite of what our noses and stomachs told us. We unloaded balls and I cleaned them while she started stamping some of them with the little blue whale. Jorgi rolled green litter cans from their locations around the parking lot and placed them strategically in a barrier in the front and rear of our whale to keep people from wandering around to his upwind side. A slight breeze blew from the west off Monterey Bay. A gray wall of fog loomed in the distance far out to sea. From time to time as I looked up from my work I could see foamy white breakers colliding with the rocks that lined the golf links below us, but the sound was lost to the occasional roars and applause of the crowds and the blare of loudspeakers coming from the clubhouse announcing the latest scores of the players. The seas looked much as it had that day I glimpsed my first migrating whales with Big Lorraine and I secretly yearned for the great grays to surface, beckoning me to depart this festering scheme I was committed to. But it was only a momentary lapse and I turned back to the task at hand. From what I could hear, the pro game sounded close. Jack Nicklaus, Gary Player, and Tom Wieskopf were all only two or three strokes apart finishing the front nine.

A trickle of people was leaving the gallery now and walking up the hill to our whale, and more followed when several TV crews with minicams came over and taped us while Jorgi bullshitted away about the sanctity of seagoing mammalian life. Jorgi kept them well in front of the creature while he gave the pitch, directing the crowd to the golf balls that Janett and I were preparing. We sold at least two hundred dollars' worth in the first few minutes, before Jorgi was called down to the clubhouse by one of Blyth's assistants. Jorgi tried to talk Janett into giving the sales pitch while he was gone, but she wanted no part of it. She looked disheveled from the past forty-eight hours of bouncing back and forth across the state. The lovely sharp features of her face that I remembered from the woods seemed dulled now by a sort of puffiness I attributed to her pregnancy and fatigue. She wore Jorgi's flannel-lined jean jacket buttoned tight against the chill breeze from the sea. A long, wide, and wrinkled cotton skirt with zigzag patterns draped below the bulky jacket. Janett looked more like a peasant refugee from the Ukraine than the lithe and nimble Sufi dancer I once knew. Jorgi's conversation with her was brief. He looked around nervously, and I got the distinct impression he didn't want to be seen with her.

He had me take over the spiel and pulled a brand-new patent-leather suitcase out from behind the truck seat, one that neither Janett nor I had seen before. Then he hurried down to the clubhouse with Blyth's assistant. Janett and I watched him disappear into the ornate hardwood-and-glass entrance while we toiled on like a couple of hippie serfs.

Business was good for another hour as the two of us cleaned, stamped, and handed out more whale balls for another three hundred dollars. Tweedle-dum showed up again with a large neatly painted SAVE THE WHALE sign which he wanted to hang over the slightly burned area on the beast's hide left over from Sacramento. I practically had to grab it out of his hands, insisting I would put it up for him, lest his sensitive little turned-up nose discover the whale's internal flaw. He was considerate enough, though, to send up doughnuts and coffee to the two of us. A young man in a white serving jacket whisked them over in an electric golf cart with a great steaming stainless-steel coffeepot on the back after first servicing the TV crews with the vans on the other side of the lot. After that, though, business fell off as the great tournament started down to the wire. Instead of coming up to our whale the crowds were now filtering in from all areas of the course to pack the galleries around the eighteenth green. Janett and I munched on stale doughnuts as the announcer's voice reached us over the PA system. It was loud but his tone was hushed to the point of sounding religious. From the other end of the eighteenth green the crowd roared in the distance as Wieskopf and Tom Watson fired off, followed by the amateurs in their group. The crowd's controlled yet exuberant response to Wieskopf's play moved closer and closer to the eighteenth green, and soon I saw a golf ball bounce onto it across from us. The gallery roared. Three more balls soon followed and there was more applause for the players themselves as they strode onto the green, seconded by their faithful caddies. Wieskopf putted from a far corner of the green and the whole gallery sucked air into their lungs as the ball slowly lost speed, rolling up to the hole where in slow motion it rimmed halfway around the edge before falling in. There were boisterous cheers from the gallery followed by pleas from the announcer for quiet as he announced Wieskopf's final two-under-par 71 score. He was definitely the tournament leader, although Nicklaus and Player were tied

208

coming into the eighteenth. I was engrossed in the game. Happy to let my mind wander away from the cares of our festering whale business and Jorgi and Janett's growing animosity.

Nicklaus and Player both had to shoot a one under par three to catch and tie Wieskopf. Watson putted in and the crowd politely applauded. He was out of it. So was Janett. She sat dejectedly on the running board of the truck, unable to at least escape our problems as I was, digging this great sport of the merchant class. I heard the distant roars again. Nicklaus and Player were making their charge, but my attention was diverted from the game as I saw Jorgi returning.

At first I couldn't believe it was him. Only his rosy face and smile were identifiable as he strolled up from the clubhouse with Blyth and her entourage. He was wearing a whole new outfit—and it wasn't the one he wore that night at Hillmount School. Yellowish-tan slacks blended loosely over a shiny pair of expensive-looking leather shoes. A stunning blue blazer covered a vest that matched his slacks, and out of the vest flared a light-blue wide-lapel shirt. Around his neck he wore the chain with attached whale that I first saw the day of Blyth's kickoff at City and Country. He was fingering it and talking to Blyth as he approached. My mind quickly registered "sucker." It looked like Jorgi hadn't been entirely straight with me the night before when we pulled the stash out of the whale. But I had no time to vent my anger, for they were quickly upon me. The PR men nervously informed me that the Governor would be dropping in at any moment, timing his arrival with the jubilant culmination of the tournament. Jorgi pointed out our whale-ball concession to Blyth. He told her the proceeds would be used for life-saving devices for baby whales—some kind of huge inflatable playpen.

"With this money, we can fly them anywhere to the shores of America if one of the little creatures loses his way and becomes stranded," Jorgi said to her and she turned unexpectedly toward me.

"Yes, your whale-ball idea is great, Stanley. Jorgi told me a bit about it in the clubhouse," Blyth said, with a note of forgiveness in her voice, as if I was now being let off the hook for the Indian riot. I stared back at her silently and incredulously as she stood there in sporty Scottish-plaid suit with matching beret. The white ribbons on her and Jorgi's clubhouse passes fluttered in the breeze. A few cameramen got in position in the parking lot. The gallery cheered again in the background.

Blyth turned away from me hurriedly. I had no chance to tell her the truth. Jorgi would not meet my eyes as I gazed at him with vindictiveness. But before Blyth left us next to the whale for her assistants off by the helicopter pad, who were now energetically motioning for her, she paused briefly in front of Janett, who continued to sulk on the running board of the truck. Blyth then made one of the major errors of her life.

"And, of course, this is your little earth mother, Jorgi," she said, glancing down to Janett. Jorgi took Blyth's shoulder, gently motioning her away, but it was too late.

I remember hearing the sound of the helicopter in the distance and then the roar of the gallery close by as Nicklaus also stroked mightily for the green on his second shot. The next ball hit Blyth in the back of her beret as she was turning away from Janett. Staggered, she fell forward to her knees and Janett fired two more that just missed the top of her head. As Jorgi pulled Blyth up and away, two more barely missed his face. An aide reached her and he and Jorgi started to retreat toward the clubhouse, supporting her by the shoulders. A trickle of blood appeared out of the tightly trussed-up hair on the back of her neck. I lunged for Janett but fell into the bucket of soapy water and balls. The sky spun above me. Janett was grabbing handful after handful of unmarked whale balls, throwing them madly at anyone who tried to approach. She dragged a peach basket full of them out into the road, attempting to keep Jorgi and Blyth in range as they headed for sanctuary. They beat it into the clubhouse and Janett insanely threw the rest of the balls over into the pavement, kicking like a crazy women at the little rolling orbs. They quickly rolled across the road and into the low stone wall that bordered the edge of the embankment where one edge of the green rough ended. They bounced back from the wall, ricocheting into a paved culvert, and accelerated rapidly along the edge of the road to a bend, where one after another they disappeared with metallic noises into a drainpipe. It was a well-designed drainage system. The drainpipe from the road was aimed at another underground drainpipe that absorbed the runnoff from the eighteenth green. But the pipe that ran beneath the green to the sea was covered by a metal grid to prevent the loss of golf balls. None of them was missing when the crowd suddenly heralded their arrival. I could see the balls fanning out onto the green as they were fired out of the pipe and off the grid. Nicklaus's ball was unfortunately arriving at the same time and Gary Player's sat alone fifteen feet from the flag. Several fleet-of-foot spectators broke through the ropes and attempted to intercept the fast-rolling balls and a caddy dashed forward to throw his body over Player's ball, but he was too late. It was hit in the wave of crazy rolling whale balls like a pebble in the surf. Nicklaus's ball was hit too and shot off at a neat right angle. The players were wild with anger and protest and the crowd surged out to engulf them. The PA system pleaded for order. Several heavy bettors were already taking swings at one another while their well-dressed wives screamed on the sidelines. The police were struggling with members of the crowd who were yelling that the balls they were throwing off the green were the ones that didn't belong there. Suddenly, police and a group of angry gallery members were streaming up the embankment and over the wall after us and I screamed at Janett that we should run for our lives. We ran back across the parking lot just as the Governor's helicopter was settling; he energetically exited the door with a smile in a swirl of noise and air just in time to see the angry public bearing down on him.

15

TURMOIL IN THE

MARKETPLACE

It was probably better that they beat up me instead of Janett. Some of the blows and kicks administered to my body would have aborted her baby.

Janett and I were discreetly bailed out at three the next morning. We were hurried out of the Carmel jail into a waiting squad car that hustled us off into the night unseen by any newsmen. When I picked up my things at the booking desk one of Blyth's bleary-eyed assistants warned me in a vicious tone that under no circumstances were Jorgi, Janett, or I to tell any member of the media that we were in any way connected to Blyth Champion or her campaign. If we did, the long influential arm of Blyth's uncle was going to reach out and snatch us into an eternity of incarceration for attempted murder, assault, inciting to riot, trespassing, and peddling without a license. Mental anguish added to the physical pain my body was already feeling.

"Take that rotten whale and dump him," he said as the police moved me out smartly. His parting suggestions were my sentiments exactly. But they weren't Jorgi's.

Janett sat silently and so did I, nursing my wounds, as we were driven in the back seat of the patrol car to a secluded road somewhere outside Castroville, The Artichoke Capital of the World. There we were reunited with Jorgi, the truck, and the whale bracketed by two police cars along the side of a field in the early morning darkness. The instructions from the police were simple as they let us out of the car: "*Go!*" We climbed into the truck and left.

Jorgi started in on Janett as soon as we started rolling. "Five thousand fucking dollars thrown away in a crazed fit of female temper." I told him to shut up or I'd jump across the cab and choke him to death. Janett was zombielike throughout the encounter. I sensed that all she wanted out of life at that moment was a truck ride home.

She wasn't about to get it. We rolled up Coast Highway 1 with the whale in tow, but instead of continuing on across the Golden Gate Bridge and north to Mendocino Jorgi took a right at Half Moon Bay, heading back toward Palo Alto.

"What? Are you crazy." I protested when Jorgi told me we were going back to City and Country. "It's insane. Blyth and her uncle will have us all put back in jail."

"No she won't," Jorgi replied forcefully. "They flew her out of the state last night incognito. She's taking an official break in her 'hectic' campaign in an isolated ski lodge complete with no phone above Vail, Colorado. As far as her uncle is concerned, he's up to his ears in the biggest golfing snafu in the history of the PGA. They'll be sorting out protests, court cases, bad press, the rage of the sporting public, and the balls well into the new year. That should give us just enough time to slip back to City and Country quietly for whatever cash we can salvage out of this baby."

His voice sounded committed although a bit desperate. I hit him with the *big* problem, sure that it would dissuade him from continued insanity.

"The whale's rotting all to hell, Jorgi."

"I got that covered. Go back to the woods and the commodity line if you want. Take her with you," he said, gesturing with contempt toward Janett. She didn't respond. "Live off acorn mush. I don't care. Not when there's still a chance to pull this whale out of the fire and make it."

I looked at Janett and touched her arm gently for support. She turned, meeting my gaze with a look that only served to mirror my fears of impending and total poverty. I shut up and the two of us were carried on by our crazed captain of con.

We pulled back into our old spot at City and Country in the early afternoon. Everything looked the same in this citadel of upper-class commerce except that there seemed to be more Christmas decorations strung everywhere. As soon as we stopped I fully expected the police to swarm down on us like the flies that hovered around the whale. But it didn't happen. Jorgi was a frayed wire of energy as he set about obtaining several boxes of bumper stickers we had left behind at the lithographers.

Janett seemed as resigned as I was to whatever fate befell us.

After Jorgi conferred with the parking-lot police he hurried over gleefully and informed us that Kingsford Champion was still off in the Brooks Range of northern Alaska, where he had been ever since Blyth had launched her campaign for the assembly. It looked like Kingsford found it easier to endure the deadly Alaskan winter rather than his wife's ambitions.

"Keep the crowds away until I return with the solution for the stink," Jorgi told Janett and me confidently. Bankrupt of any other possibilities, we did as he said. I was filled with an inner sense of dread as I smiled to the women and youngsters as we cordoned off the whale with ropes. They were clamoring to come forward to him and lay their money down to save the cetaceans of the world. But behind me I knew some dreadful eruption was festering in the bowels of our creature. A process that within time would build its own internal pressure and release its message to the well-intentioned crowd.

Jorgi's solution showed up just before dinner. Hip candlemakers. There was a heavily bearded young fellow with his hair pulled back into a tight knot behind his head and a straight-looking girlfriend in a double-knit Alvin Duskin jumpsuit. They had a sleek little VW station wagon filled with cardboard cartons, which Jorgi had them hurriedly unload. I lent a hand, and as I picked up a heavy box I was immediately overwhelmed by the scent of lilac, rose, sandalwood, even clove, all mixed together. "We'll douche the crowd's noses with pleasant odors before they get a chance to smell the bad ones," Jorgi told me. He grabbed a carton of the candles and placed the contents around the bumper-sticker tables that Janett and I had set up again in front of the whale on the side of the trailer. The candlemaker couple kept thanking Jorgi for the business opportunity.

"This is really far out of you, brother," they said, completely unaware of Jorgi's real intent. Jorgi conversed with them for several minutes, showing them a drawing of a candle he wanted them to create. It was a whale candle. A humpy headlike mound of wax with a wick sticking out for a spout and a little tail to the rear.

"Give it a sea or seaweed odor if you can," he told them before they hurried away to complete the order, assured by Jorgi that they'd get seventy-five percent of the profit off all the candles.

Jorgi and I climbed back up on the trailer, stepping delicately over the candles, again testing the air near the whale's head. We could detect nothing but the ersatz scent of flowers, spices, and fruit. Jorgi beamed with delight. It smelled like we were on a float dedicated to a Hindu god.

As soon as the sun went down we lit the candles around the edge of the whale, both to release more scent into the air and also as an added attraction to the crowd who, from a distance, may have thought they were approaching a beautiful Nativity scene instead of a chapel dedicated to the prevention of the rape of nature for a slight profit.

Everything might have worked out fine. We could have concealed the odor with candles through enough of an indefinite period to insure a halfway happy winter in the woods. The whole thing would have gone smoothly if it hadn't been for the competition. The success of our smokescreen candle operation ended up exposing the rottenness of our main business. The marketplace is not only an arena dedicated to the contest of profit and loss, it is also a stage for certain deep-seated human emotions: greed and jealousy.

The next day the candlemakers returned before the shopping center opened with boxes full of whale candles, just as Jorgi had ordered. Several shopowners also showed up: the creative-toystore owner we had met at the Champions, The Continental Experience store manager, and the Basket Heaven storeowner. All of them were angry and they took Jorgi aside near the tail of the whale for a quick conference, the gist of which I overheard.

"Jorgenson," the toy fellow said, "we don't care if you save whales, but when you cut into our business we've got to save ourselves. This year all three of our shops have got the market here on Mexican and Italian candles. By the end of the Christmas season it adds up; in fact, it covers the lease money for December. Since you've brought in those street merchants, we haven't moved a single candle. They've got to go."

Jorgi took the whole thing pleasantly, smiling at the little delegation the whole time. When they were finished he shook their hands sincerely and said they had nothing to worry about. To my astonishment he told them that the candles would be gone. The disposition of the little shopowners seemed much more relaxed after that. They were all smiles. They made comments on ecology, the good work Jorgi was doing with the whales; they even checked out the candles, especially the little whale ones, asking Jorgi to send the candlemakers over to them after he told them to pack up. When they went back to their shops I approached Jorgi.

"You can't take the perfumed candles away—our cover will be blown."

"Don't worry," Jorgi answered, the smile suddenly gone from his face, "that was just business, just smoke to get some time."

Which he didn't waste. He took off hurriedly and returned later with a little sign which he affixed to the bottom portion of the big SAVE THE WHALE sign. It read: *Candle Sales Benefit Organic Life Church Reseeding and Reforestation Project, Mendocino County.*

The shopowners made their second move that evening. They returned to protest, their faces lit by the hundreds of candles aglow around the whale. Jorgi's charitable explanations fell on angry ears, but the candles stayed.

Their third move was to bring in a city fire marshal, who wrote us up, citing us with "burning without a permit in a public place."

Their fourth move, just minutes later, was the arrival of the assistant manager, a nice-looking young man with the worried scowl of first enforcement of responsibility on his face. He looked a bit like Clyde back at the loan office and was obviously distraught and wondering if he was overstepping the wishes of the Champions, out of touch in the icy heights of North America. Had he known their true feelings about us by that time he surely would have had us arrested immediately and his salary doubled by Christmas morning. Jorgi stood on the end of the trailer near the whale's massive head, staring defiantly down at the manager. A row of scented candles burning at his feet made him look like he was on a nineteenth-century stage. I'm sure it was this obnoxious stare that sent the young fellow over the brink, into the heady exercise of authority.

"Out! The candles are out. Either they go or you *all* go, including the whale," the assistant manager said to Jorgi in a tone that was obviously backed up by the rent-a-cops behind him. I stood with Janett behind the donation tables. Neither of us said a thing.

"Wait a minute," Jorgi shouted back. "What about Blyth? Your ass will be hanging on her Christmas tree if you kick the whale out of here. He's ten times more vital to her interests than any amount of shaky shopkeepers." Jorgi had gambled on the Champions' isolation and Blyth's uncle's power with the press and police. It seemed to work. The front page of the morning's *Chronicle* blamed the disruption of the Pebble Beach tournament on terrorists. Two local Bay Area groups had already left notes in telephone booths claiming responsibility. The whale was off the hook for the time being. The encounter with the manager was a stand-off. He walked off briskly with the guards, undoubtedly on his way to another round of transcontinental calls. Luckily for us, it was also closing time. The reprive didn't matter anyhow; disaster was poised to strike.

Jorgi, Janett, and I blew out the candles around the edge of the whale and put them back in their boxes. The parking lot cleared of the last late shoppers and we were left with our rotting whale once the smoke cleared. A new and deeply fetid odor seeped down off the beast. It was acutely painful.

We worked through the night trying to save the whale, at first rushing around town in the VW borrowed from the candlemakers buying several gallons of Lysol disinfectant, which we poured into the whale's mouth only to find that most of it ran out over the edge of the truck in a vomit of mothballs. Since the Lysol containers were made out of plastic, we tried to push the jugs through the throat and into the bowels of the whale and then puncture them with a nail on the end of a stick. It only made things worse. The rotting process had begun eating away the throat, and pushing the bottles through only enlarged the opening, letting more and more of the internal odor out. We worked like pearl divers, holding our breath.

Next we tried plugging him up. We drove around town looking for potato sacks which we hoped to find in the garbage behind supermarkets. It was past midnight before we could find enough. We even bought out a Seven-Eleven of all its baking soda and went racing back to the whale, where we tried to seal up his mouth and throat with the sacks soaked in the Lysol and covered with the baking soda. It didn't work. The whale's mouth, filled with sacks, was open grotesquely in the dark. It made the creature look like it had bitten off more than it could chew. Worse, all the stuffing and pushing had loosened things even more, and by now a steady trickle of venomous liquid was seeping out over the top of the teeth on his lower jaw.

Janett couldn't stand it any longer and had to move back from the task at hand. I was practically fainting in between breaths myself, but Jorgi drove me on relentlessly stuffing sacks in a desperate attempt to stay the flow of juices and the overpowering odor of our decaying scheme. Toward morning the smell had gotten worse, and in a last-ditch effort Jorgi attempted a diversionary movement calculated only to get us through one more day if we were lucky. I pleaded with him that two wrongs don't make a right and that we should tow the whale the hell out of there to the nearest dump before it was too late, but he was determined to try and save it. He was going to blame the stench on a plugged sewer line.

"Jorgi," I pleaded, "so far only the whale is diseased. You can't infect the whole city just to save a rotting whale."

"Stanley," he answered, "another day, another thousand dollars. We've got over nine hundred in the cans since morning. Either we blame this stench on something else or we're finished. We have to protect his reputation. There are other shopping centers if we can haul him to the boatyard in time to do the foam job.

He started searching the streets around the shopping center until he found a manhole cover. It was almost 4 A.M. There was no traffic at all except milkmen going to work. With a crowbar from the truck we tilted the cast-iron disk off its opening and quickly threw all the remaining sacks we had down the hole, along with all the sticks and pieces of shrubbery we could rip up, plus the contents of the Goodwill container next to our whale. By the time we slid the lid back on, the sewage was already rising and backing up under the earth toward the shopping center.

By dawn the stench was appalling, from both our whale and the sewage backing up through the pipes in all the bathrooms that were located in the City and Country shopping center. Water damage was already occurring in the backs of some of the small shops as toilets bubbled up like springs. Apparently the sewer junction that Jorgi and I had plugged handled waste from the surrounding neighborhood as well, and the rush of early morning activity unleashed by the white-collar workers and commuters filled the system to a rapid state of overflow. Little streams and trickles of water began to appear from under the back doors of the shops and stores. We had overdone it.

"Christ, Jorgi, let's get out of here," I implored. "If they find out we did this we're going to jail to stay this time. But it was no use. As soon as the maintenance men arrived Jorgi was the first to run over and warn against the watery pestilence. When plumbing trucks got there he directed them to the worst spots, and when none of that worked he helped fill sandbags in the flooded shops to protect floor merchandise. It was already too late for some stores. Pressing my face to a huge plate-glass window, I could see the thick-piled carpet with its hard-edge geometric designs in the Scandinavian Country Store floating in two inches of water. A polar-bear rug, its eyes and mouth beseeching-ly open, turned in an eddy of liquid between two aisles of Danish-modern tables tiptoeing on their slender legs. It was in that instant I realized all was lost and that Jorgi was guilty of overkill. No one, unless he wore a rubber suit with an oxygen tank strapped to his back, was going to shop at City and Country on either that day or many more to come. All he had expected was a little sewage bubbling up on the street near our whale just to carry us over through the rush of Christmas shoppers, but in-stead we had succeeded in wiping out for the season one of the loveliest merchandising centers in northern Cali-fornia.

I knew the time to flee was at hand, in the thick of the battle against the sewage spreading its watery tentacles through the parking lot. Once things were under control and the investigation began they would easily trace the sacks back to us. That morning was but the dawn of a whole age of litigation that would hang over that shopping center for years to come. The shop and store-owners, the Champions, the city, an army of attorneys, all of them were in for years of maneuvers and lawsuits designed to assess each grievance and attach the blame. The sooner the real cause split the better, both for our own good and freedom and theirs. The satisfaction they would all seek would never be forthcoming from us with our limited means. All we had was our rapidly deteriorating whale. They would want our ass.

Jorgi already had the engine of the truck idling when I got back to the whale. He was up alongside him on the trailer, pleading for Janett to help him secure the whale for moving with ropes, but she turned away, got in the cab, and sat there resignedly in a sea of turmoil and sewage.

"Stanley, what are you waiting for?" he said. "Get your ass in gear and let's get our investment out of here before that shit reaches us."

It seemed hopeless but I responded, helping him secure the ropes before I policed up the remaining sacks of evidence we had left lying around near the truck.

As we drove out of the parking lot our truck and whale had to cruise through several inches of stinking water and we encountered the young assistant manager desperately trying to give commands from his shopping-center patrol jeep, cruising like a boat through the shallow flood. He was issuing a stern command to one of his maintenance men to get moving through a particularly deep place to rescue a mailbox set in what had once been a shallow bed of flowers near the entrance of the center. When he saw us his stern face assumed a bleak and hollow look. Jorgi cruised over alongside him. A spray of putrid water flew up from our tires. Before he had a chance to speak, Jorgi yelled down to him from the driver's side of the truck.

"Hey, pal, we came to fight pollution, not live in it." Jorgi shifted into low, returning our rotting whale to the open road.

16

WHALE HELL

I yearned for only one thing: to return to the woods. To once again sequester myself away under nature's lush blanket, letting crusade and profit pass me by. But Jorgi insisted otherwise, even though Janett felt as I did. We had over fourteen hundred dollars among us, five hundred left from the tournament and nine from City and Country. A small fortune by Mendocino standards.

We lumbered onto the freeway headed north. Cars passed us, blowing their horns, while passengers held their noses in our direction. There wasn't a vehicle behind us for a mile in the rear-view mirrors.

"Jorgi," I said, "is this the shortest way back to the country? Let's dump this whale, return the truck, and cool it for the rest of the winter."

"Country? Are you crazy, Stanley?" Jorgi replied,

turning his head away from the wheel. "We can double our money today here in this vast city. There's a million dogs and cats here and they've got to be fed."

He was hauling our whale to the pet-food factory. I wanted no part in this last desperate venture and insisted with Janett that he drop us off anywhere along the freeway. We'd hitchhike home. Jorgi wouldn't stop to let us out, insisting that he wasn't going to give us our share of the cash unless we came along. I had no choice. Janett sat in silence. Hatred was smoldering behind her eyes. The truck droned on toward the pet-food factory. Jorgi already had it circled on the road map. Point Richmond. Janett and I spread the map across our laps and with resignation called the proper turns at all the freeway interchanges as we sailed on with our catch.

The factory was located near the water on the north end of San Francisco Bay, although we never saw the water until we walked into the pet-food center. The shore was lined with abandoned factories, shipyards, trucking facilities, and a naval base. The place had actually been a former whaling station before government antiwhaling laws had closed it down. There was a high wooden fence outside and next to that a large building topped with a billboard reading DR. ERIK'S DOG AND CAT FOOD—THE BEST FOR MAN'S BEST FRIENDS.

It looked like everything was shut down early for the holidays, but a double-windowed office building next to the high fence flowed with a twinkling Christmas wreath and office lights behind that. Jorgi went over to check it out and then returned, telling me to drive the truck through some big gates that soon opened. The foreman of the station was a leathery-faced man in a

khaki shirt. He was there along with several slaughter-
ers waiting for the last truck of mustangs to come in
from Phoenix.

I rolled the truck in and my first impression was that
of the upper reaches of hell. A Hieronymus Bosch
painting for horse-lovers greeted my eyes. Next to the
truck, on a wide cement ramp that stretched down to the
water's edge, lit by big floodlights, was an absolute
spectacle of carnage. There were huge red and yellow
chunks of horses, disemboweled horses, heads of horses, tails of horses, and guts of horses lying all over the
ramp amid cables and machinery used to render the
beasts into chunks small enough for the factory to
handle. A sprinkler system sprayed down over the slain
animals continuously from overhead to wash the blood
away. The smell made my mouth dry and my throat felt
like I had swallowed acid. Janett looked as if she was
going to puke. She got out of the truck and left the yard,
content to wait for us on the outside.

Three men approached, one of whom was the foreman.

"Let me handle this," Jorgi said. "They're supposed
to only buy horses, but we'll take half the money for
whale meat if I can persuade the man in charge to mark
it up as one truckload of plugs and pocket the rest of the
money for himself." Jorgi talked vigorously, telling the
foreman how we had found the whale only yesterday on
a beach up in Mendocino County. The other two men
looked like longshoremen. They both wore little white
stevedore Stetson caps on their heads above broad
flannel shirts and black Frisco jeans.

All I can say is that it was a nice try.

In fact, we were lucky to get out of there with our own bodies intact.

The foreman and his assistants seemed to pay little attention to what Jorgi was telling them about how fresh our catch was. They quickly jumped on top of the trailer and examined the whale. The first thing that they noticed funny was all the wax around the edge of the whale where we had burned the candles. The second thing was, of course, the sacks stuffed in the mouth. The aroma of our creature didn't seem to bother them too much, for it was lost in the general stench of the factory. The third thing they noticed, and that really queered the deal, was the formaldehyde. One of the men made an incision along the side of the whale with a hunting knife. All three of them at once were able to distinguish the chemical smell from the surrounding odor of rotting flesh and exposed bowels.

"Listen, Jack," one of them called down to Jorgi and me, "we use this stuff to feed dogs, not to poison them."

Jorgi shrugged and tried to lay a story on them about how he had washed down the skin of the whale with formaldehyde to keep the flies off, but they didn't fall for it and told us that they definitely couldn't take our whale. Jorgi's insistence, making up lies as he went, almost cost us a severe beating, for one of the men lingered on as if some wheels were slowly turning in his head. He kept asking Jorgi about the wax around the edge of the whale, half-joking about did we "try to cook the sonofabitch with candles?"

Jorgi was in the midst of making up some jive about attempting to cover the whale with wax to prevent decomposition when the worker's face flashed with recognition. He called the other two men back in an instant, yelling to them, "These here are the turds who want to put animal-killers out of business. It was right here in the paper about putting people who kill whales and horses and all other sorts of wild things in jail."

The other two came walking toward us through the carnage while the yelling man backed Jorgi up against the truck. He had seen our whale in the newspapers, thanks to Christine's daddy.

I hopped into the driver's seat of the truck and fired up the engine. Jorgi tried to climb up into the cab on the passenger side but the worker pressed him too close as he yelled for his partners to join him in "getting these sons-of-bitches." As they crossed in front of the truck I gunned the engine and moved ahead with the vehicle to keep them from ganging up on Jorgi, who was by then hanging on to the half-open door on the other side. The lunge of the truck almost shook Jorgi off, but he held on and scrambled up high enough to kick the attacking hulk right in the head with his new boots. I rammed the truck in reverse, headed straight back for the open gates behind us, but didn't quite make it; I tore down a good five feet of fence going out backward slightly askew through the opening. However, once clear of the jangled and jammed wood, we had enough time for Janett to jump on board in front of Jorgi, who slammed the door shut as we drove off back toward the freeway. The goddam whale was turning out to be a dead albatross tightening its hold around our necks, and there was no way to shake it.

I drove the first stretch. Midway through the night Jorgi took over. He was silent for a long time. Janett slept between us. I dozed on and off, but the vibrations of the slowly moving truck would only let me slip off into that halfway land between sleeping and waking. A dream seemed to appear and disappear along with headlights and passing neon. I was drowning. I struggled to the surface of the water. My head popped out. I gulped fresh air until my eyes began to make out a scene, then I would plunge downward, returning again and again until a brief second of sleep revealed the surface images. My head had surfaced in a green sea. Jorgi drove by, circling me on our whale, his back resting against its huge dorsal fin. A steering wheel protruded from its blowhole. He kept circling on the whale, and their wake was creating a vortex that I knew was going to suck me down once and for all.

I awoke to Jorgi's voice speaking for the first time since we left the pet-food factory.

"Stanley, I've got it. We dump the whale in the woods way down in the bottom of some deep gorge. Winter passes, then spring. Its insides finally rot away and we're left with its well-preserved hide and outer flesh, held up by its own skeleton. It's a natural. We charge tourists a buck to lead them down to him. 'The strange case of the land-locked whale.'"

"Are you crazy?"

"Don't you see, man?" he said, completely disregarding my comment and sounding more and more enthused as his imagination began to grasp its latest scheme.

"For the straights it will be an evolutionary mystery, for the freak angle we play the area up as some kind of ancient Indian medicine place. You know, we pile strange rocks all around, fix up some kind of cave where Big Foot reportedly lived, point out as many weird mushrooms as we can. You know, a holy place where the Indians tripped out and hallucinated the whale right into the woods. We might have to cover the tracks real good from getting the whale in there, but after that it's a seasonal occupation. Can't you see it, Stanley?"

Unfortunately, I could. At least in the context of Jorgi's world view. An endless chain of money-making schemes seemed to link his brain, shackling it to one continuous endeavor: parlay this into that and that into something more, continuing on in an insane singularity of purpose and action.

"Jesus, Jorgi," I blurted, "isn't there anything more to your life than telling lies and making money?"

He turned away from the wheel briefly again and gave me a quick look that was framed on the bottom with a slight smile lit up from the glowing green instruments on the dashboard.

"Stanley, either you're too dumb to see or else you miss your old job of playing hermit and serf. I'm not making money, I'm making life. That's right, life. Action, movement, like taking something dead and useless, like this rotting whale, and changing it into something functional. There's your use. That's what I make."

"But what about love?" I said. "What about ideas that give life meaning."

"Love, meaning," he said, practically laughing out loud in my face. "Don't you know where that's at yet, Stanley?" Janett was wide awake now.

"Stanley," Jorgi went on. "Stanley, everything gets back to function and usefulness. Would you love an ugly woman? Can you eat your ideas? You see, Stanley, most people like you go through life with visors of ideas and love blinding them from the truth, which is—all is function. No matter how you slice it, Stanley, that's it. And either you make it work yourself or you leech off someone or something else that does. Like you do, man. I'm making it. You've gone along for the ride and made it too. You want to hide your eyes from that, from the fact we've taken something dead and useless, something nobody wanted, and made out on it. What I've done, Stanley, is cheated death out of its own. Death—and I'll be functioning just as long as I can at its expense. There's no lie to my life, Stanley. The world is a garden of decay and degeneration. All I've done is let people hear the reality they needed to fit their best expectations so that they can tend their own gardens. I fertilize their souls, man."

He was beginning to sound like some wind-up horror toy. When greed fixes its mind upon a definite object it ceases to be a vice. Its excesses become offerings; a great and garish altar is erected in the mind dedicated to the cause of completion, no matter how vile the purpose. I had a bad feeling that I would never see the money that was rightfully mine.

"Gardens," I laughed, grasping the dashboard and turning toward him. "Since we've been in business towing this rotting whale around we've left nothing but sorrow and destruction in our wake. When are you going to open your eyes to that?"

He was quiet for a second and I sensed that for the briefest of moments I had made some impression on him, but it blew away in a flash, for his self-confident, slightly humorous voice flooded my ears above the drone of the engine.

"How can I help it if people really don't know what

they want? The garden I'm telling you about is full of farmers no smarter than their own vegetables. I've given them exactly what they wanted. If they can't tell fertilizer from insecticide, that's their ass. I've left nothing behind us that wasn't there before I came. It's a world of weeds, man. People are weeds covering the face of the planet and they're all going around trying to become the flowers they ain't."

"That's crap, Jorgi," Janett said. "You're making life out to be no more than an accumulation of money and crap. Other stuff can emerge. Even the people, or weeds as you call them, who you've run over with this whale at least can get up again and have a chance to love and hope. It even makes no difference if their hopes and loves are wrong; at least there's something there, something more than a fast-buck mechanic like you who turns everything around and inside out. Yours is a wheels-and-pulley world, Jorgi, devoid of meaning."

"And your's is a Disneyland of delusion," Jorgi snapped back. "If you live in hope you'll die in despair."

I hated their fighting and myself even more for precipatating what was going down between them. I wanted to dive head-first out the door onto the fast-moving pavement.

"Screw you, Janett," Jorgi went on maliciously. "When the bucks were rolling in both you and Stanley never blew the whistle on any finer sensibilities. Neither of you minded it when my ideas, good or bad, helped you stash the bucks away. If I hadn't *killed* the whale, then we'd all be back in the boonies eating our government starchies and counting the raindrops hitting the roof."

"What do you mean, killed the whale?" I gasped.

Jorgi was silent for a moment, intent on the road ahead. Janett was staring at him.

"That's right." His tone was calmer now, but his confession had a hushed note of malevolent triumph. He turned slowly and looked us both in the eyes, then turned back to the road.

"Yes, killed him. There were no hunters in a camper. The whole idea was mine from beginning to end. I used Nog's rifle just like I did before when we needed a few bucks. I'd shoot a sea lion, let him wash ashore, hide the rifle and then get the burning fee for disposing of him from the county beach and park warden. Only that morning it was different. When I saw the great beast in among the seals I knew he was mine and I zapped him."

Except for the groan of the engine that strained to pull the whale, there was nothing but silence in the cab. I knew Janett felt as numb and hollow as I did as our brains convulsed, trying to digest what Jorgi had just told us. There was nothing more to say. It was pointless to continue. Jorgi had twisted everything to his own advantage, including me and Janett, who I now sensed felt as revulsed as I was at being implicated in the great creature's actual death. Our assistance had led Jorgi on in his cruel enterprise. No definite thought would materialize; my brain was continually bouncing back to Jorgi's ramshackle logic and labyrinth of pragmatic thought. It seemed to me as the night wore on that unless I found a way to lead him out, I was condemned within the maze myself. I rode on, in my bitterness hoping Janett would offer a magic elixir of hope and love to save me, but she also was despondently quiet.

The morning found us back on the winding roads of Mendocino County. The sky was a sharp blue, the air chill, but the winter sun shone brilliantly down on us and our cargo. We ate breakfast in Yorktown with none of us saying anything at all and continued on through hillsides already delicately green with the first inch of next year's spring grass, yet still softly brown from the decaying weeds of last summer. The skeletons of bare oak branches stood out against the sky. We passed through vineyards, the grapevines trimmed and bare of leaves in freshly plowed earth looking like gnarled hands reaching from the grave. It was Christmas Eve; the passing fields and the deep, dark wooded valleys were still undrained of their morning layer of tulle fog as we cruised on. I felt the unresolved issues of the night before among Jorgi, Janett, and me entrench themselves in my nervous system and reflect themselves in the passing stark landscape. I had been made a partner in murder to something I loved dearly.

17

DUMPING GARBAGE

Merry Christmas. Our truck pulled up to Jorgi's dome late in the afternoon. It was one of those deceptively bright and sunny California winter days.

The vast interior of the dome was damp from Jorgi and Janett's absence. I built a fire in the drum fireplace while Janett fed the chickens, cats, and goats. They looked like they were tearing her to pieces as she threw them the food. She cursed Lorraine, who was supposed to come by and feed them regularly. Jorgi more or less walked in circles, as if he had nothing to do while he had everything to do. I went back into the dome to warm my body from the chill I found between them.

Later when I went back outside I found the two of them together upwind from the whale. They were at each other's throats again. I wanted desperately to split and seek the refuge of my tank, but without wheels it was impossible. Besides, from the sounds of the argument it sounded as if Janett were about to become the sole owner of the festering whale which dominated the yard under a cloud of noisy flies and yellow jackets.

"Take off, go back to that rich bitch. Just leave me what money's left and the dome for the kid," Janett screamed.

"If I could think of a way I would," Jorgi shot back. "You ruined me with your insane golf-ball attack. Poor Blyth will be lucky if she even remembers her own name after that."

"Right. And the next thing she'll remember is how your whale and schemes screwed up her campaign and destroyed the shopping center."

Jorgi stared at her hatefully for a moment.

"Without my idea and action there wouldn't be any money at all. You'll get exactly what I give you—and that will be exactly zero, the exact total of your existence."

Seemingly defeated, Janett turned and walked back to the dome, completely oblivious to my presence. Her face was contorted. Jorgi gave me a beseeching and then blank stare when he saw the hatred in my eyes. Whatever turn his brain had now taken, I wanted to know about it immediately. He was holding the coffee can with the fourteen hundred dollars tucked casually under one arm. It wasn't only Janett's money, but mine too. A contagious rage from their argument filled my whole being.

"Listen Jorgi," I said, controlling myself as much as possible.

"Listen? That's all I've been doing around here since I got back. I've had to listen to that woman's moans and groans about what went down with the whale and Blyth. Hell, you were there, Stanley! Put yourself in my place. I was just trying to make out for all of us. Now it's give me the money, fix the fence, find the missing chickens, cut some wood, get the rotting whale out of here, don't forget I'm pregnant—shit, that woman's getting heavy. She's an anchor around my neck. I've got better things to do with my life."

"One thing you'd better do is give me my share in that can," I said as calmly and firmly as I could in the face of his tirade.

Jorgi stared at me. A fly from the whale was crawling across his forehead.

"Look, you're a man, you should be hip to these things."

"What things?" A feeble courage surged through me although I was light-headed with anger.

"If a man can't make his own opportunities then he has to take the one handed to him or he'll forever wipe his ass with his own regrets. I've got to try while its still there."

"What are you talking about?" I said, distracted from my own purpose by the direction his brain was now going.

"Blyth. She's still going places. That bump on her head won't last forever. Wasn't it me who saved her life—or at least her face from major plastic surgery? Christ, where she's starting from is further than any us can ever hope to go. I'm sure I can work my way back into her body and campaign. Pebble Beach was Janett's fault, City and Country could be made to seem . . ."

"My fault, Jorgi?" I said, anticipating his cheap thought process as fast as the quick glance he had thrown me in midsentence. But before he could wiggle out of it our conversation was abruptly interrupted.

The shot didn't sound like much. Kind of a puff and a ping together. It was a full second before my gut feeling matched the look of shock on Jorgi's face. It was real. I turned around just in time to see Janett charging out of the dome with Jorgi's varmint gun, waving it like a stick.

"Get out of the way, Stanley," was all I heard from her. I was already running for the truck, diving under it. Jorgi was hauling ass toward the pickup. The second shot sucked wind high in the air. The can of money spun wildly on the ground like a giant dradle. Jorgi raced the engine down the road while Janett fell to her knees in despair. The gun was thrown out before her on the dirt. Her sobs were mingled with the sound of the screaming engine and disappearing truck. I crawled out from behind a tire.

Early that evening after I had calmed Janett down I had to run over to the nearest neighbors and borrow their beat-up old Volkswagen. The hip mama owner came along with me and helped put Janett into the car to drive her to the Elk Free Medical Clinic. Janett was having very painful cramps and bleeding where it shouldn't have been.

After they left I banked the fire and walked outside into the night to clear my depressed head. The sky was clear and the air nippy. There was no wind at all. I'm not a religious man but I thought briefly about Christmas, surveying the heavens and remembering that cock-and-bull story of long ago—the moving star, the ancient kings following. A chill thought matched the air that enveloped my body: all that which remains in our memory is a hype that robs us of the present. What ancient confidence man set the world on its ear with virgin births and men walking on water? But these ridiculous thoughts vanished as my nostrils were overcome with the stench of our own whale.

It had assumed ghastly proportions. Even Jorgi's animals had cleared off back into the woods to get some distance from the smell. Traveling along the freeways and roads the smell had slipped unnoticed behind us into the towns and communities we passed, but now at rest, it was unbearable. I walked over as near to it as I could without gagging and saw that it looked as nearly intact as when we had first left Jorgi's over a week ago. The huge dorsal fin still stood erect, outlined against the night sky and stars. The massive head rested sedately on the trailer. On close examination, only the telltale drops of putrid liquid coming off the back of the trailer were any indication of the terrible internal decomposition that must have been continuing inside him.

I found the can of money illuminated by a rising half moon. My Christmas present, but was it any compensation for the rot and deterioration around me? I was a lonely carny man with a can of money whose schemes lay dead in the night before him. If there were wise men looking for stars, I yearned for them to ride my way. I walked back into the dome, headed for Janett's stash of cooking spirits.

Hours later, after a pint of sherry and several shots of bourbon, my slow melting before the fire was interrupted by the sound of an approaching car. My heart took an upbeat. It was Big Lorraine, come at last to feed the animals. Alerted by the fire and light, she cautiously called out Jorgi's and Janett's names before entering the dome. I sat there quietly making myself into a surprise, but the welcome Lorraine gave me was anything but pleasant.

"What a stink! We could smell it a mile down the road . . . Oh, it's you, Stanley. I might have known that you'd be behind something as foul as that."

Someone was with her, another woman dressed like Lorraine in a long, flowing Mother Hubbard skirt, only she seemed much younger. I didn't feel like running down the whole story to Lorraine, but I sketched the outlines of the situation, and she didn't seem to need more.

"Another backstabbing man," Lorraine commented with a conspiratorial glance at her friend. "I always wondered why you chased that creep around, but I should have known."

Lorraine had definitely not come bearing gifts.

"And while we're on the subject, Stanley, since you last bugged out on me a lot has happened in my life. I have been born anew. I have accepted Jesus and he has taken me in."

"Amen, sister," the girl added righteously.

I was either too drunk or too overwhelmed by events to be startled. Concern was at the bottom of a hole and I was reaching for it with a short stick. "That's nice, Lorraine. God bless you," was all I could muster from my funky state.

"It's you who will be needing the blessing of the Lord, Stanley. You won't be leeching off *this* woman ever again. You're a castout. I've moved Cludia into your water tank." She gestured toward the young woman beside her. "Your crap is in cardboard boxes and they're already spongy from the first rain. The sooner you come get them the better."

She was beating a whipped dog. I told her that the animals were already fed and slumped back into my chair as Lorraine and Cludia departed for Christmas night festivities at a nearby Jesus commune. She didn't even say goodby, but, then, neither did I.

I didn't get up until the middle of the next day, but I awoke to a suffocating feeling and it wasn't until I was fully awake that I realized it was the smell of the whale I was gagging on. I got dressed and went outside for some fresh air but ran into a wall of worse stench. The whale sat as placidly as ever on the trailer, undisturbed except for the loud infernal buzzing of flies and yellow jackets that swarmed about his huge head. I grabbed a hose and tried to water him down, thinking that it would some-how dilute and wash away his putridness, but it was to no avail. All I did was stir up the flies and make the yellow jackets angry; several buzzed around my head and one stung me on the ear before I retreated to the safety of the dome.

Janett came back that afternoon. It was a false alarm. She was all right and as far as the clinic was concerned; so was the baby. I tried to help her out of the car but she brushed me off, telling me that she was okay. The fact that we still had the money cheered her up a bit, but as soon as she started walking toward the dome the whale overwhelmed her.

"Stanley, this thing has got to go before it kills us all."

I agreed but for the life of me had no idea how to dump ten tons of rotting whale, or even where.

We resolved the issue by seeking refuge in the dome and lighting all the sticks of incense Janett owned. It felt like my lungs were being washed down with a sickening sweet soap, but it was easier to endure than the putrid stench of the whale. We thought of getting Nog to come over with his tractor and dig a gigantic pit in which to bury the creature but decided against it when we both realized that the cost of such an operation would take just about all the money we had made. We could have soaked him in diesel oil and burned him, but we had no idea how to get him off the truck and no money to pay for it if we burned it as part of the whale's funeral pyre. As much as I had grown to hate it, we could have used Jorgi's pragmatic, scheming brain at that increasingly sickening moment.

He came back after dark. Janett recognized the sound of the truck first as it drove up the road. I saw her body tense and I kept one eye on the rifle next to the door, but she made no move for it.

"Tell him to keep his ass out of this place, Stanley. We're through." Her speech was venomous and peeled any thoughts I had of them reconciling right off the inner walls of my brain. A secret satisfaction flushed through my body, for in spite of the stink I was already starting to feel quite cozy with Janett. I went outside with a flashlight to put Jorgi off.

For a few minutes he stayed behind the wheel of the truck with the motor running so as to illuminate the whale in his headlights. I walked up beside the cab and was going to tell him what Janett had told me to say, but he hardly recognized my presence even though I flashed the light in his eyes. He was staring straight ahead at the whale; his mind seemed to be synchronized with the idling of the truck engine. Jorgi remained in that position for several minutes. Only then did he take notice of me standing there. I felt stupid and wanted to go back to the dome, but I didn't want to fail Janett.

"They dumped me."

I didn't know what he was talking about.

"They threw my ass out for a goddam foreigner. Jean-Paul Merdieu, underwater frog of the seven seas, currently filming subsurface effects of sewer outfalls in San Francisco Bay on crabs and shrimp. I couldn't get past the front door, but I knew she had returned from Colorado, trying to get her campaign back on its feet. Instead of slamming the door in my face, that simple-minded servant should have known I was there to help. When I went over the fence I found Blyth taking lessons in the heated pool with that bony frog in a jockstrap bathing suit. She screamed so loud when she saw me that she fell over backwards in the wading end of the pool. The heavy diving tanks held her under, but he pulled her up by her bathing cap. I don't know. Maybe her head was still hurting. The cap came loose in the Frenchman's hands while he was pissing all over him-self to get her up again. Her bandages came loose and started unwinding like a goddam turban. The silent alarms already had the cops rolling, and when they burst in she was still hysterical. I was cornered between some garden furniture and they hauled my ass away for trespassing and resisting arrest. I had just enough money left in my shoe to bail before a horde of attorneys came down on my ass for the City and Country thing and I've got a court appearance in two weeks, but they'll never see me or my whale agian. I've got better plans for it. Fuck politics! I'll make him a basic mystery of life."

I backed off toward the dome but Jorgi got out of the truck and followed me, and in as friendly a tone as on the first day I met him he said, "How's about giving me a hand dumping the whale before we all get hepatitis of the lungs? The sooner he's down in the woods the sooner I can fix him up for tourists, We'll shoot for early spring, Stanley."

"Look, Jorgi," I said, trying to remain calm in the face of his insanity, knowing full well that his ideas could be as infectious as the bacteria that were now devouring the inside of the whale. "I'll help you dump the whale for Janett's sake, and to get this monster the hell out of my life. But that's it. After that you can do whatever the hell you want to do with it. Janett wants you out of her life. Your wheels just don't stop spinning."

"Well, it's like in the song, Stanley. Those not being busy born are busy dying." My flashlight lit up the constant and obnoxious smile on his face, a smile that had no right to be there. I said nothing, but had a horrible feeling he was taking over again. "We'll talk about Janett, you, and me later, but right now we've got to dump this garbage. Get her out here, Stanley, we need three people to send this whale on its way."

I went back inside the dome and told Janett what Jorgi had said, but in the same breath I told her she should consider her condition and forget what Jorgi wanted her to do. But she insisted she was all right.

"I'll do anything to rid this property of that stench." With that she dressed warmly and followed me outside. She didn't say a word to Jorgi, nor did he to her.

Jorgi got three old hydraulic jacks he had used for moving the timbers for the dome and several long, thick fir planks which he hurriedly stashed on the side of the trailer. Both of us then piled into the truck and drove the whale away from the yard onto the main road that wound farther back into the woods. Janett followed in the pickup. Jorgi said we would need its headlights to illuminate what we were doing.

"Long Walker Gulch should do it," he said with a tone of anxious anticipation in his voice. I knew he was already counting the dollars he was going to make off the tourist trade next summer as he led the tender and seeking down to the beast's last resting place. I also knew that he was probably insane.

We drove on for a good half hour, with the headlights floodlighting the legs of the forest giants and the stumps of those that had fallen. Soon we turned off the main road and continued on a dirt logging road, going up a ways until we stopped on a curve on the edge of Long Walker Gulch. Long Walker was a logger of some seventy years ago whose Mendocino legend had it that he chopped and sawed the trunks of trees all week long faster than any other man, letting not a branch fall until Sunday, when he went forth into the woods and took the last few whacks on the last tree. Then whammo, the giant redwood domino effect. The first tree fell into the second and that into the third and so on till a vast swath of downed trees ran off a mile or more through the woods. There are several Long Walker gulches in the county in memory of the little giant of yesterday.

At any rate, there we were above this Long Walker Gulch. We stopped the truck, got out, and Jorgi and I went to the gulch side of the road and peered into the darkness below. I could tell that it was a very steep place in spite of the darkness, for a slight breeze blew up from a dark canyon below, possibly from the sea. Trees and branches creaked disconcertingly below my feet. We were on the edge of a deep precipice. The wind chilled my face. Jorgi started prying a piece of log left behind on the side of the road by loggers as a guard rail and called me over to assist him. Janett parked the pickup so that it would light up the truck, trailer, and whale, but the light shone on nothing but mist-laden empty space over the gulch.

"Let's test it," Jorgi said, and we rolled the log a foot or so before it swung over the edge, hurtling faster and faster into the void with a crashing sound that went on for nearly a minute.

"Nobody will ever find this whale ever again unless I take them there for money." Jorgi was still looking upon our task as simply another business venture.

His plan to dump the whale was to work the planks slowly under his belly and then gradually jack their ends up so that little by little we could tilt and tip the creature off the edge of the trailer into the abyss. He got into the truck and jockeyed it back and forth until it was maneuvered as close to the edge of the gulch as we dared go. We then set about the grisly task, for it was unbearable working up next to the stench. I thought I was going to pass out several times from the smell and we had a hell of a time jamming the huge planks under the belly. We had to beat each one through with a sledgehammer, gaining only a couple of inches with each blow, then we had to jack it up in order to beat another alongside just a few inches more. So it went for a good two hours until we reached the point where we had succeeded in inserting three big planks with jacks under the ends. The belly of the whale looked as if some horrible three-fingered monster had seized it around the midsection. Poison was seeping out along the planks and covering my hands. Jorgi had brought along a Coleman lantern, which he placed on the top of the truck cab. The hissing of the burning mantles lent a hellish light to the scene. Janett raced the engine of the pickup for more light and from time to time ran over to help us on a jack when Jorgi and I had to exert all our strength pounding and inserting a plank.

Overwhelmed by stench and cold, it seemed like forever before we were ready to begin tipping. Jorgi and I were going to work the jacks under the planks on the trailer bed and Janett was going to stand back at a safe distance behind the trailer and shout out the progress of the tilt in the eyes of the pickup.

"Scream if one end slips more than the other," Jorgi yelled at Janett shivering in the cold. "It's got to go all at once, not head or tail first. It's got to go all the way to the bottom in one straight roll."

We got into position and Jorgi gave me a signal. We started pumping up each jack just a little bit at a time. The whale moved slightly to the precipice side of the trailer. We jacked some more and it tilted further; then we jacked more.

"Nothing that time," I called to Jorgi.

"Shit, it must be hung up on the outer edge of the trailer," he shouted back. "Get Janett over here on my jack and I'll get a short plank and pry up along the outer edge where he's stuck. If it starts to go I'll duck under the trailer out of his way."

The whole thing seemed shaky to me but I did as he said, convinced that he knew what he was doing. I helped Janett up onto the side of the trailer and she positioned herself at Jorgi's jack. The stink was killing us, for with the whale now tilted crazily on its side all sorts of things had shaken loose inside. Jorgi was soon in position, prying up and away, and he yelled for us to start again. Janett and I looked at each other in the pulsating light of the Coleman, and as she began slowly moving the lever of the jack up and down I tried to copy her every move with two arms to make the tilting uniform. Again nothing happened. The whale was already halfway over on his side and still he stuck to the trailer.

"Hold it!" Jorgi screamed. But before he shouted, Janett and I froze as we felt it. The rear wheel of the truck gave a sickening quick lurch.

Jorgi came scampering on all fours out from under the truck on our side of the trailer beneath us. "The ground is soft and giving way under the rear wheel back there," he reported nervously.

"Maybe Janett should get off, Jorgi!" I said, but he paid no attention.

"I'll drive the truck ahead a couple feet," he said. "This stinking whale is going down tonight."

He ran forward, climbed into the cab, and started the engine. I could see him behind the wheel through the rear window. He eased the truck into gear and moved ahead slightly at a snail's pace over the loud roar of the engine, slipping the clutch slowly as if he were maneuvering through a roadway of eggs. The vehicle inched forward and for a brief instant it felt like the trailer had moved onto more solid ground. Jorgi's smiling and satisfied face looked back through the window as Janett and I crouched in terror near our jacks, fear coiling inside us and ready to spring in an instant to the roadway below. Jorgi was laughing at our nervousness.

Then the universe turned upside down. A terrible twisting noise filled my ears. The cab and trailer of the truck started tilting sideways. One of the boards I had been jacking flashed upward by my head like a mighty baseball bat. Out of the corner of my eye I saw Janett fly off the bed of the trailer; in an instant I was flying through space after her. When I hit the ground the truck was already going over the edge before my eyes. The whole bank under it had collapsed and its wheels and axles were already exposed. The door on the passenger side of the cab burst open straight up and a head, arm, and shoulders flashed in the opening like a jack-in-the-box. Jorgi was trying desperately to jump free of the cab, but in that same instant the weight of the whale pulled the truck completely over and I never saw Jorgi in life again.

The rest was illuminated emptiness and the roar and the snapping of trees and the wrenching of metal as Jorgi, the truck, and the whale accelerated into the wooded depths. When the noise stopped there was nothing but the gentle breeze still whispering through the dark trees and Janett crying in the road.

EULOGY

There was nothing more we could do that night. I drove Janett back to the dome in the pickup and wrapped the swollen ankle she had gotten jumping from the truck. I called the sheriff from the neighbors' and was back in Long Walker Gulch just as the sun burst through the trees. It was almost two hours before the sheriff's patrol arrived from Ukiah, but in the meantime two pig hunters came along in a jeep and assisted me in a descent to the wreck. A huge scar on the earth reached down from the embankment, lined with broken trees and branches. We found Jorgi's body a hundred feet or so above the wreckage of the truck that hadn't reached the bottom of the deep gulch. The trailer and whale had rolled over him and disappeared below. The deputies wouldn't believe the part about the whale and didn't hike down to the bottom to check it out when they arrived. Jorgi's mangled body and I were under suspicion of truck theft for several hours until they cleared it up with Race Hubbard. Race came barreling out with a tow truck a half hour later, mad that his truck was beyond salvage and even more enraged as he informed me as angrily as he could with the deputies looking on that Jorgi had never paid him a cent for the rental after the initial deposit.

I wish I could say Jorgi met his end in some significant, symbolic gesture, crushed to death in his great, rotting scheme. But he was not cut down in a final moral act like an Ahab driving himself on and beckoning all to follow to their doom. Jorgi was only serving the vitality of his method when death found him.

Accident. He was cut down in midflight by accident, like the quail I had seen fly into the wire fence that morning early in Indian summer. Accident, that unknown factor that slithers unseen through our lives like a hidden snake in the tall grass, its presence only subtly revealed through the slightest movements of the tallest stalks. Accident, common accident passed his way. He was killed dumping his garbage.

Janett's Sufi friends wanted to make a big production of Jorgi's funeral. They took his ashes out to Ten Mile Beach and commenced a dirgeful dance and songfest as they waded barefoot in the surf. The idea was to scatter his ashes on the edge of the sea and let the tide carry him into eternity, but they miscalculated the prevailing afternoon breeze. Jorgi blew back into their faces, still spinning his wheels, until he settled finally in the sand. I searched the horizon in vain for a glimpse of a passing whale, looking for a sign of just commentary on the proceedings, but they were all out of sight, lapping up the sun in their southern vacationland while we mourned our dead in chilly winter latitudes.

I stayed with Janett because there was nowhere else for me to go. I tended the animals, repaired the dome, and picked up the commodities at the distribution center once a month. We spoke only of the most perfunctory of life's tasks in the beginning, avoiding our common memory of the whale and Jorgi's death.

Winter wore on, and with it came the first snows Mendocino County had seen in fifteen years. Four or five inches lingered on the ground and clung to the trees for several days. At first I danced exuberantly in it alone, tasting it off the twigs it clung to, but after a while the coldness got to me—and Janett too—as we remained confined in the dome. I was cold and, worse, bored with my existence. Janett only reminded me of other times, but deeper feelings and urgings also swam through the depths of my soul. One night late in winter the incessant beating of the rain on the roof panels drove me to confess my love for Janett, who sat nonchalantly sewing patchwork baby clothes before the fire while she sipped herb tea. Her reply was orderly and affectionate. She stared at me for a long time in the flickering light, then gave me a steaming bay-leaf rubdown. Later her moist eyes met mine in the dwindling firelight. I promised gentleness and kissed her swollen stomach.

Spring found the bracken ferns spreading in broad green tongues about the dome. Wild iris, lush mattings of clover, and thick new moss spread over and around the rotting stumps. The first black-and-white swallow-tail butterflies appeared, soaring in vertical climbs and dashing in sweeping falls between the tall redwoods, yet my soul was still strangely dormant. I no longer cared about expanding my awareness, my main concern in life was to be useful. Janett's well-being and impending delivery occupied most of my time and I pondered and worried about our future when what little money we had ran out.

One morning I was suddenly seized with a whim, a compulsion, to see what had become of our whale after the terrible crash of Christmas.

I took the pickup and drove out to Long Walker Gulch. Behind me I had passed logging crews freshly at work ripping into last winter's growth, but Long Walker Gulch was vacant of workers—as it will be forever because of the steep terrain. The scars of the wreck were hardly visible under the new growth of ferns and I slowly made my way around and down into the gorge. The twisted and torn wreck of the truck was still there, although by now it was slowly being covered by the long tentacles of blackberry and wild raspberry vines. I continued down toward the bottom. The going got thick. The side of the gulch was honeycombed with springs hidden in willow trees and giant fern clusters. The springs were gushing forth with visible trickles and small streams of water and I was soaked to the waist before I reached the bottom, which was a tangle of ancient downed timber decorated with white brackens leering at me like open mouths. There were large salmonberry bushes and a maze of roots and vines. Little sunlight penetrated there even though it was midday. I stumbled on, separating the foliage as I went with a stick.

I wasn't lost, but I was rapidly making up my mind not to go any farther when I came upon our whale set on a shelf of land almost at the bottom in a place where several springs converged. The huge dorsal fin was still intact; it caught my eye first. The beast itself was on a blanket of ferns that surrounded his body like parsley on a giant dish of trout. He had come to rest on his belly and the stench was gone. It was unbelievable but he was totally intact, much as Jorgi supposed he would be. His thick hide and outer tissues were mummified by the formaldehyde and were as tight as a drumhead over his intact internal bone structure. Except in three or four places, where there were tears in the skin from the fall and the man in the dog-food factory, he looked almost as good as the day Jorgi had shot him. The jaw hung open at a grotesque angle, the only major damage that had occurred in the long tumble down through the woods. I peered into his mouth. The teeth still shone in their awful ivory brilliance, but back behind them in the interior where the throat and heart had once been I made out in the dim light the beginnings of the beasts's internal skeleton. His rotted insides were gone, eaten away by bacteria and insects, yet he rested as quietly as if he were asleep on the bottom of the sea.

I sat back and watched him quietly for a long time.

It's summer again. A strange energy finally fills my veins. The woods are dusty and hot along the roads. Only the deeper redwoods promise coolness and the whales have spouted back along our shore to their Arctic smorgasbord. The tourists, straight and hip, are once again seeking the promise of solitude and naturalness in our county. I feel much better. My blood and thought flows industriously and Janett has consented, when she isn't occupied with little Jonah, to make the signs and collect the money from the people I will lead into the woods.